Callie
The Women of Valley View

SHARON SROCK

THE WOMEN OF VALLEY VIEW SERIES

Callie
Terri
Pam
Samantha
Kate (coming fall 2015)
Karla (coming 2016)

DEDICATION

To my heavenly Father. This is my Samuel. Use it for Your glory.

ACKNOWLEDGMENTS

The publication of this book is the fulfillment of my dream. My dream, but not a solitary journey.

Jo Smith, you took the time to listen when God whispered in your ear. Thanks for not being too timid to share what you heard.

Everyone needs a chief cheerleader, Kaye Whiteman is mine. She held my hand, sent me Scripture, encouraged me, prayed for me, and believed in me on days when I didn't believe in myself. There are no adequate thanks.

Robin Patchen, you are simply the best critique partner in the world. The chance to work with you has been a gift from God.

Sandy Patten, Wanda Peters, Anne Lee, Lynn Beck, Carol Vansickle, Emily Whiteman, and Teresa Talbott. I'm sure you had better things to do than read this story five times, but you did it without a single complaint. Thanks for all the prayers, support, and honest input.

My gratitude to each and every member of the Oklahoma Christian Fiction Writers. You took a rookie who didn't have a clue and molded a writer.

A special thanks to fellow writers Linda Goodnight and Janice Thompson, your input on this project in the early stages was invaluable.

Last but never least, my husband Larry, and my two daughters Amber and Tammi. You didn't always understand what I was trying to do, but you never failed to listen to the dream.

CHAPTER ONE

Callie Stillman dabbed raindrops from her face with a linen napkin as Benton dodged a server with a loaded tray and took his place across from her. She smiled into her husband's blue eyes and reached across to wipe water from his beard. "We'll both have pneumonia if we don't dry off soon."

Benton took the napkin and finished the job. He sent a wink across the table. "I've been told the food is very good. A few sniffles should be worth it."

Callie's gaze roamed the room. "The décor is lovely. It's..." Recognition slammed into her chest, forcing the air from her lungs. The man crossing the room behind her husband nodded and continued to his table. Was that the bailiff? *Do you swear to tell the truth...* She gulped for breath and fought the familiar darkness that crowded the edges of her vision.

Callie ran a finger around her collar, tugging the neck of the blouse away from skin suddenly dewed with a fine film of sweat. *Too hot.* She took a sip of water, dismayed at the tremor in her hand as she lifted the glass to her lips. *I won't give in to this. Not here, not tonight.* Callie closed her eyes and practiced the breathing techniques she'd learned over the last six months. In through her nose, hold for a few seconds, and out through her mouth. Concentrate only on the current step in the process, the next breath. The tightness in her chest began to fade. *Thank you, Jesus.* She raised her water again and held the cold glass to her flushed cheek.

"Callie?"

Callie met Benton's eyes across the table. The concern etched on her husband's face threatened to break her heart. Benton had been so supportive during the last few months, so protective while she tried to heal. She would beat this. For him, she would move on.

"You OK?"

Callie smiled. "I'm fine. It's just a little warm in here all of a sudden."

Benton cocked his head to the side. "You sure? You look like you've seen a ghost.

A ghost? She closed her eyes, the images unbidden but ever present. Sawyer's pale, lifeless face. Callie's hand reaching out to stroke baby-fine hair, bruises the mortician's makeup couldn't hide. That tiny coffin lowered into the ground. Callie could have lived with a ghost, but her haunted memories and the never-ending *what ifs* that traveled with them would drive her crazy.

Two more breaths, another swallow of cold water. Callie straightened in her seat and smiled at her husband. "This was a nice surprise. Thanks for thinking of it."

Benton took her hand. "Anything for the woman I

love. Have you decided what you'd like for dinner?"

"I—" A vicious bolt of lightning lit the dark Oklahoma sky outside the windows of the restaurant. Thunder rattled the building. The lights flickered and went off, plunging the room into sudden darkness. Across the room a frightened child began to wail.

Callie jumped to her feet. Her chair tipped sideways onto the carpeted floor. *Oh Jesus, please make the crying stop.* A harsh voice cut across the child's frantic cries. "Andy, sit down and stop that noise. It's just thunder."

The lights came back up and Callie's awareness narrowed to the cries of the child. *Is that how Sawyer sounded?* Frightened howls as his eighteen months of life surrendered to the beating his father dealt him. *Oh Jesus, I'm so sorry. So sorry I let Janette deceive me. So sorry I didn't ask you before I testified. I know you've forgiven me. Please help me forgive myself.* She couldn't breathe, couldn't think. Callie bolted from the restaurant.

"Callie!" Benton called.

She was letting him down. Still she ran for the door.

When Benton found her several minutes later, she stood by the car. Rain cascaded over her, mixing with her tears. Benton pulled her into his arms, wet and all. He held her close, his bearded chin rested on her head. "Shh, baby, it's OK. I'm sorry. This was a bad idea."

Callie clung to him like the lifeline between sanity and madness he was. "Benton, no. It was a great idea. I know you were trying to distract me. Trying to make me forget Sawyer's birthday. I thought I could." She allowed Benton to help her into the car, only to bend double in the seat as the panicked adrenalin gave way to nausea. "How could I have been so stupid?"

Benton started the car and turned the heater up to

high. "Callie, you weren't stupid. You thought you were doing the right thing."

Callie shook her head. "I just wanted to help. I knew Janette wasn't abusing her children. She didn't deserve to lose them. Testifying to that...being at the hearing to support her...celebrating when it was over. I just wanted to help," she repeated.

Her husband navigated the rain-washed streets while Callie huddled in the seat, head down, arms wrapped around her middle. The images in her mind took on a life of their own. Janette, sitting in her office, tearful over charges of alleged child abuse, frantic because her babies had been taken from her. Callie's unhesitating agreement to appear in court as a character witness. The custody hearing, her nervous testimony, the endless waiting for the judge to make a decision, the joy of seeing those two babies reunited with their mother. *And Sawyer dead a short time later because of my interference. Jesus, give me strength. Give me the wisdom I need to never put myself in that situation again.*

Lightning flashed in the sky like the old strobe light in the skating rink back home. The thunder that followed rattled the windows in the two-room apartment. Eleven-year-old Iris Evans huddled in bed, drew a blanket over her head, and snuggled next to her four-month-old niece, asleep by her side.

The bedside lamp flickered and went out, turning the room into a dark cave until the storm produced the next explosion of light and sound. Iris cringed and grabbed her cell phone from the table next to the bed. She thumbed the switch, but the dim glow from the screen did little to illuminate the darkness. Eleven thirty. Sam would be home soon. *Please, be home soon.*

Iris slid out of bed and felt her way to the door. There were matches in the kitchen. She fumbled in the drawer, using the reflection from the cell phone to guide her search. Matches in hand, she turned to the table and the candle that sat in its center.

Mom's candle, one of the few physical reminders of her that she and her sister had left. Sam would probably be angry, but Iris couldn't stand the dark. The stubby wick flickered to life. Shadows danced on the walls, almost in time to the strobe of the lightening. It should have been spooky. Instead, she found it oddly reassuring. The lavender scent coming from the candle brought her mother's memory closer.

Iris carried the candle to the bedroom, juggling the cell phone, doing her best to shield the tiny flame with her hand as she walked. She placed the candle carefully on the bedside table and climbed back in next to the sleeping baby.

The infant stirred and whimpered at the disturbance. Iris patted her tummy, watching the baby drift back to sleep, her small mouth moving in unconscious sucking motions. "It's OK, Bobbie," she whispered. "Your mommy will be home in a little while. Don't be afraid. She'll be fine...she'll be fine." The baby grew silent. She probably didn't need the words of comfort, but Iris needed to hear the assurance spoken out loud. She couldn't help it. She hated thunderstorms.

It had been storming, just like this, the day the cops came to the house. The afternoon everything changed. Iris closed her eyes against the visions of men in blue uniforms, rain dripping from the brims of their plastic covered hats, their shadowed faces, and their crushing message. She searched her heart in vain for something to block out the painful memory of words she'd never forget. *There's been an accident.*

The thunder crashed again and jerked Iris back to the present. With her eyes closed tight she said the first prayer of her young life. *God, if you're really up there like Miss Callie says, could You please help us?*

Unsure about how prayer worked, she lay there waiting for some sort of response. Miss Callie talked a lot about faith in their Sunday school class. Faith sounded a lot like hope. Iris hoped God sent an answer to her prayer soon.

Surrounded by the comforting scent of her mother's candle, Iris's eyelids drifted closed.

Steve Evans slid his keycard into the slot. Bone weary, he was not looking forward to another night in a strange city. He'd boarded a plane in Chicago at 7 AM to begin three weeks of book signings. Illinois this morning, San Diego tonight, Dallas on Monday. No need to consider the hectic schedule beyond that.

The solitude and luxury of a pricy hotel room brought him no comfort. He never rested well on these trips—the strange mattresses always too hard or too soft. Even if the bed exceeded his expectations, and he slept well, he wouldn't spend enough time in the room to enjoy it. *At least tomorrow is Sunday.* Maybe he could find a nice church to visit and take a breather before getting on a Texas-bound plane Monday morning and kicking this tour into high gear.

A helpless sigh escaped into the empty room. He'd given his testimony to a packed shelter tonight, his heart broken by the sea of haggard faces. *There but for the grace of God...*

Steve scrubbed at his face in disappointment, brushing collar length black hair from his forehead. When he toured, he made it a point to visit homeless shelters and missions. He took every opportunity God gave him to share his story with men that might be helped by seeing what God had done in his life.

Not a single person had responded to his testimony this evening. When Chaplain Harris issued an invitation at the end of the service, the men had staggered away one by one. Most of them returned to street corners, stomachs full from the dinner Steve had helped serve, their souls just as empty as when they walked through the doors. Why couldn't they see?

He wanted to reach just one person, save someone from making the same mistakes he'd made. Steve bowed his head and worked to put those thoughts aside. The dead ends and wrong turns of his previous life would overwhelm him if he allowed it.

He dug through his suitcase, looking for the toothbrush he'd tossed in this morning. His 5 AM shower seemed more like two days ago, but he couldn't work up enough energy to care. Teeth brushed, faced washed, Steve stripped down to his boxers and undershirt, turned back the blankets, and froze in place when the ring of his cell phone broke the silence.

A glance at the display, sent his heart into overdrive.

The Adams Group.

He didn't bother with pleasantries. "Have you found them?"

"Not yet, Mr. Evans. We've only been looking for a week—"

"Look." Steve sat on the side of the bed. His knees suddenly refused to hold his weight. "My ex-wife died eighteen months ago." The hand that held the phone shook with frustration. Why couldn't these people understand? "I'm paying you good money, and I expect more than excuses."

"I understand your impatience. We're checking every place they've ever lived. It's just a matter of time before we find them."

Steve gripped the phone so tightly his hand ached. "What part of *we have no time* don't you understand? I don't need you to look in places where they've already been. Lee Anne was living in Austin when she died. It's where she was the last time I spoke to her. My daughters didn't disappear into thin air."

"Mr. Evans, you trusted our agency enough to hire us. Now you need to trust us to do our job. Looking for them in what they would consider familiar territory is the sensible place to start. We'll work outward from there."

Steve urged his heart and his temper toward calm. It was not this man's fault that he'd just now learned of Lee Anne's death. Not his fault that he couldn't locate his daughters. His voice was a defeated whisper when he continued. "I'm sorry. I don't mean to take my frustrations out on you. I've been a little crazy ever since I lost touch with Lee Anne. When I found her obituary two weeks ago..." His voice trailed off. "Eighteen months. She's already been gone eighteen months, and my daughters... Do what you can. Call me with a report again tomorrow. I'll be in Texas on Monday, but I can detour if I need to." He disconnected the call and picked up his wallet from the bedside table. It fell open to well-worn photos of his children. The faces in the pictures smiled up at him when he held them under the light of the lamp. His fingers stroked the images of the daughters he hadn't seen for ten years. Emotion clogged his throat, forcing tears past his eyelids. Every time he looked into the frozen features of his daughters, he asked himself the same question. *How? How did I let myself be so deceived?*

Steve slipped to his knees beside the bed. The regret of wasted years tore at his heart. "Jesus, please take care of my babies until I find them."

The glowing numbers of the dashboard clock read one fifteen. Samantha parked and dashed through a pouring rain to the front door of their apartment. Iris was probably frantic. Sam eased inside and flipped the light switch. Nothing. The thought of Iris and the baby alone in the dark during a storm made her heart sink. Her little sister was so terrified of storms since their mother's accident.

Sam nudged the door closed and stopped to listen. All quiet. She was relieved not to find Iris huddled in a petrified ball on their sofa. Hopefully her little sister had managed to sleep through the worst of it. After a moment to get her bearings, she shuffled through the dark to the kitchen and slid a large pan of lasagna into the fridge. The lights flickered back to life as the door closed.

"Thank goodness," Sam whispered. They couldn't afford to lose the power for too long. There were things in the ancient refrigerator that they didn't have the money to replace. Cash was tight, and even with the extra hours she planned to work next week, they couldn't afford to deal with any emergencies right now.

Daily schoolwork and her job at Pasta World kept Sam more than busy. But her little family couldn't survive without her weekly paycheck. Samantha cringed when she thought about the brutal week headed her way. The restaurant planned to be open extended hours during spring break. She had asked for, and received, some additional time on the clock. Working back-to-back six-hour shifts with only an hour off in the middle to eat and rest her tired feet, would be tough. But the restaurant paid a decent wage, and her tips were always good. The extra money would give them a much-needed financial break.

More than anything Sam hoped she could afford to do something special for Iris next Saturday. At eleven, Iris should be anticipating a carefree spring break. Instead she shouldered the responsibilities of an adult. Sam was grateful that she could count on her little sister to share the load of the life they were forced to live, but she wanted Iris to have the chance to act like a little girl once in a while.

Yeah, and what about you? A small voice of longing asked from deep inside. *This is your senior year. You're seventeen. You should be having a good time, not working yourself to death.* Sam pushed those thoughts ruthlessly aside. She did what she had to do. Period.

Sam already had one surprise waiting for Iris when she got up in the morning. The cook had sent home a whole pan of lasagna, one of Iris's favorite foods.

Expecting to find Iris asleep, but needing to check on Bobbie, Sam opened the bedroom door for a quick peek. Light from the living area cast a soft reflection into the other room. Her sister and the baby appeared to be sleeping. Sam took a deep breath of relief and caught the scent of lavender. "Oh, Iris," she whispered. She tiptoed into the room and picked up the candle from the table, held it under her nose, and inhaled. The heavy floral scent brought the warmth of their mother into the dark room.

The blankets rustled and Sam looked down to see her sister's eyes wide open. Sam sat on the edge of the bed. "Iris, I'm sorry. I didn't mean to wake you," she whispered, mindful of the sleeping baby.

Iris scooted up in bed. "That's OK. The storm was so bad." Her small shoulders lifted in a shrug. "I wasn't really sleeping much anyway."

"Oh, honey, everything's fine. Lie back down and get some rest. I'll be right here."

"Can we talk for a few minutes instead?"

"Sure," Sam answered. "Know what? I brought home a pan of lasagna. You want a midnight snack?"

There was no need for a second invitation. Iris scooted out of bed and sprinted straight for the fridge. She pulled out the pan, peeled back the foil covering, and leaned down to take a deep breath. "Oh yum, it's still warm. Smell that cheese and garlic."

"Yeah, the cook overestimated how much we needed for this evening."

Iris grabbed plates while Sam poured tall glasses of iced tea. They settled at the old Formica-topped table, their unexpected treat between them.

Iris nodded at the half-melted candle resting back in its original spot on the table. "Sorry."

Sam waved the apology away. "Did it help?"

"Lots."

"That's all that matters. I think we'll burn it more

often. Mom would like knowing that something of hers brought you comfort. What's up, kiddo?" Sam hoped to offer some quick assurances and get to sleep.

Iris chewed in silence for a few seconds. "Can I ask you a question?"

"Sure."

"Do we believe in God?"

"Do we what?"

"Do we believe in God?"

Sam propped her elbow on the table and her chin in her hand. Where did Iris come up with this stuff? "Is this something we need to talk about right now?"

Iris ducked her head and shrugged. "I just wanted to know."

Sam stared off into space for a few seconds. Having something to believe in would be nice, but experience had taught her to trust only herself. "I don't know," she finally answered. "With everything that's happened in the last year and a half, I can't tell you what I believe. Why is this important tonight?"

Iris toyed with the food on her plate. "I just get so scared sometimes."

"Of the storm?"

Iris took a deep breath "Not just that, of everything. Helen and Richard, the money Louis stole. I know you're doing the best you can, but we're just kids."

Sam laid her hand on top of her little sister's. "Helen and Richard are long gone, sweetheart. Richard is a letch and Helen refused to believe us. They never wanted to be foster parents. If they haven't found us after a year and a half, they aren't looking." Sam bowed her head. "I'm sorry about the money."

"You know I don't blame you for that. Maybe

Dad—"

"He's as dead as Mom."

"We don't know that," Iris insisted.

"He's been gone for ten years. If the drugs haven't killed him by now..." She allowed the thought to trail off with a shrug. "That's not a complication we'll ever need to worry about." Sam squeezed her sister's hand.

"I know these late nights are hard on you, and I know you aren't looking forward to next week. Taking care of Bobbie is a huge responsibility. I realize this isn't how you want to spend your spring break. But the money we'll save on day care next week is going to help us a lot this month. Do you understand?"

Iris nodded, but she still had a small frown between her brows.

What else was on her sister's mind? "Was Bobbie restless again tonight?"

Iris shook her head no. "She's a good baby." She stopped and looked into Sam's eyes. "Do you really promise things will be better in just a few months?"

Sam nodded her head. "I promise. Not perfect, but better."

Iris concentrated on her plate for a few minutes. "You still didn't answer my question."

Sam's energy and patience ran out. "Which question?"

"God. Do we—"

"Why are you hounding me about this?"

"Well, everyone at April's church—"

"Is that what this is all about?" Sam interrupted.

Tears sprang into Iris's eyes. She bowed her head over her plate. "I'm sorry. I don't want to make you mad. You always tell me I can talk to you about anything."

The sight of Iris's tears doused Sam's anger. "Of course you can. I'm the one who's sorry. I'm not angry with you, sis. I'm just tired." Sam closed her eyes and allowed her head to fall back. "Look, you asked me if you could go to church on Sunday mornings with your friend. I said 'yes' because, as long as you're careful about what you tell them, I want you to have friends. I didn't agree because I share their beliefs. I have more than I can handle dealing with our realities."

Iris pushed her empty plate aside without a word.

"Don't sulk. Who loves you most in the whole wide world?"

"You do." Iris's response was a mumbled whisper.

"*That's* the most important thing I need to know this evening. Now, let's go to bed."

They rinsed their plates and stacked them in the sink until morning. The baby started to cry the second they turned out the lights.

Callie lay awake in the dark and stared at the ceiling. The storm outside had blown over. The storm in her heart had received a new face. *Father, why are you doing this to me? Didn't you see the condition I was in just a few hours ago? I'm fifty-four years old; I can't do this again. Sawyer's death nearly drove me over the edge.* Her eyes closed and her chin quivered with the effort to stop the tears that would wake her husband. *And Benton? Even if I was willing to get involved in another child's problems, he'd never allow it.* She shifted under the covers, doing her best to strike a compromise with God, afraid of the consequences of losing this argument with her Heavenly Father. *I'll pray for her. I'll teach her about Your word. I'll be her friend. You* can't *ask me for more than that.*

No promise, no plea, succeeded in erasing Iris's face from her heart. Iris Evans, eleven years old, long brown hair pulled back from bright blue inquisitive eyes. Eyes shadowed with dark circles, reluctant to make contact with hers.

Callie considered the sixth graders who'd passed through her Sunday school class over the years. Young people poised on top of the rickety fence separating child from teen. Sociable, noisy, exuberant... occasionally shy. Could she really say that Iris's reticence was abnormal? She nodded in the darkness, answering her own question. Now that God had forced her to take a deeper look, she had to admit there *was* something in Iris's eyes that demanded attention. Callie didn't have a clue what lay under the child's cool demeanor. But like a treasure map where X marks the spot, Iris's hooded eyes marked a troubled heart doing its best to blend into the background—and failing. She needed help.

But not mine, God.

A snore interrupted her thoughts. She nudged her husband and instead of rolling to the opposite side of the bed, he turned toward her and pulled her close.

"Go to sleep," he whispered.

"You too." She forced herself to be still until her husband's soft snores returned. Even asleep, he continued to hold her.

Callie felt trapped instead of comforted. Physically trapped by the arms of her husband. She didn't dare try to get up. He'd want to know why, and she didn't dare tell him. Emotionally trapped by a tragedy she was sure she could have prevented. Spiritually trapped by her

Heavenly Father who refused to take *no* for an answer. She closed her eyes and waited for morning.

CHAPTER TWO

Callie shuffled the papers on her desk Sunday morning. The last few minutes of their class ticked away while the kids enjoyed a few moments of free time. She observed her students from under her lashes. Eight sixth graders, boisterous, outgoing, more than a little noisy, which wasn't such a bad thing considering her sleepless night. There appeared to be only one exception to the rule. Withdrawn, stingy with a smile or words, Iris drew attention to herself even though Callie was sure that wasn't her intention. In twelve years of teaching this class, Callie had never worried over a child being too quiet. Girlish laughter erupted from one corner of the room. She shook her head. Quiet didn't seem to be in the normal makeup of an eleven-year-old girl.

For the third week in a row, Iris sat quietly beside Callie's granddaughter, April.

April bent her head to listen to the girl on her other side then turned to Iris with an eager grin. The two girls huddled together, April whispering excitedly. Callie couldn't hear what the youngsters said, but she saw a split second of animation bloom on Iris's face before the child's reserved mask snapped back into place. Iris's shoulders slumped, and she shook her head at April. *I wonder what that's all about?*

Callie's mind went back to her conversation with God last night. Determined not to get involved, she pulled her resolve around her and shook her head. *I can't do it, Father. Please lay this burden on someone else's heart.* The five minute bell sounded over the babble.

"Ok, guys. Let's get everything put away." She waited a few seconds before continuing. "Anyone have a prayer request before we leave?"

Chase's hand shot up. "Remember my dad."

Abbie met Callie's gaze, her gray eyes bright with tears. "I haven't seen Baby for two days."

"Baby?"

Abbie nodded, her lip trembled. "My new kitty. Is it OK to pray for animals?"

A smile threatened, and Callie bit her lip to keep it from spreading. "Of course, Abbie. Anyone else?" She caught a slight movement from Iris, but Hailey spoke first.

"My grandfather is sick."

Callie nodded but focused her attention on Iris. "Iris, honey, did you have a request?"

Iris looked embarrassed at being singled out. She shook her head and lowered her eyes back to her folded hands.

The final bell rang before she could prod the child further. Callie went to the closed door of her room and prepared to dismiss her class. "I'll say a prayer. You guys be good this week." She watched them file out of the room. *Am I reaching them?* This was such an important stage in their lives. The choices they made, the problems they faced during the next few years would define the men and women they became. Glancing up to the ceiling, Callie said a quick prayer for her class and herself. "Father, watch out for those kids this week. Touch Hailey's grandfather, keep Chase's father safe while he's deployed, and bring home Abbie's kitten. Lord, sometimes I feel so inadequate for this job. Help me be someone who makes a positive difference in their lives. Help me understand what they need."

She began the familiar task of straightening chairs and folders. Colored markers and abandoned lesson papers littered the floor. Callie paused with her hands on the back of the chair that Iris had just vacated. "Jesus, she was so quiet again today. My heart aches for this child. I *am* worried about her. I know You want me to do something. I just don't know if I have the courage to go there. Father, grant me wisdom."

Callie glanced around the room a final time to make sure everything was back in place. Satisfied, she stepped into the hallway, hesitated, and returned to her desk to rummage through paperwork and craft materials. The visitor's card that Iris had completed three weeks ago was buried here somewhere.

That's odd, she thought once she found it. A phone number, but no address. *Why didn't I notice that before?* She tapped the card on her desk in consideration. Despite her hesitation, Callie's curiosity stirred. A little judicious snooping wasn't the same thing as getting involved. Was it?

Spring break started tomorrow. April would be out of school all week, and Callie could take a vacation day from her job at the clinic on Friday. Lunch, pedicures, a little Easter shopping. A girl day sounded like the perfect time for some information gathering. She'd talk it over with her daughter, Sophie, after church. Maybe April could provide some insight into her friend.

"Sometimes the things God leads us to do can seem hard or unreasonable. But those are the things that stretch our faith and make us grow."

Those words snapped Callie's attention to the front of the church and the message Pastor Gordon labored to deliver from behind the pulpit. Between the sleepless night, Iris's troubled eyes, and the concerned looks Benton kept directing her way, Callie had trouble keeping her mind focused on the morning service.

She looked at her husband from beneath her lashes. Callie could tell from the way he held her hand during the sermon, the way he'd hovered before church that last night's meltdown was still on his mind. What would he think if he knew God had placed another child on her heart?

Callie faced the platform and rubbed a thumb over Benton's knuckles, grateful for his steady presence. He loved her, but he'd never understood her guilt, never fully grasped just how devastated Sawyer's death had left her heart, mind, and soul.

Sawyer would have been two years old tomorrow— a fact she couldn't forget, despite Benton's desire that she move on. *Like that will ever happen.* She was stronger than she'd been six months ago. The crying spells, the sleepless nights, the days she stayed home from work and couldn't get out of bed were getting fewer and farther between. But she'd never forget. *God, how can you ask me to put either of us through that again?*

Just as soon as Valley View's morning service was dismissed, Benton draped his arm around Callie's shoulder. "Are you hungry? I thought I'd see if Mitch and Karla want to go for Mexican."

Callie studied her husband. "Tacos with a side dish of fish stories and boat talk?"

"Well..." Benton pulled Callie around into a full hug and leaned his chin on the top of her head. "Weren't you even with my bottom lip last week? I believe the lack of Mexican food in your diet has stunted your growth. I can fit you under my chin now."

Callie shoved him away, smoothing her blonde hair where his beard had tangled it. "You're a riot."

"I'll buy you some guacamole," Benton wheedled. He squeezed her upper arm. "I think you need more guacamole in your diet. Your muscles are just withering away."

Callie batted at his hands. "Don't mock the guac. The green stuff has powers."

Benton raised his eyebrows.

"Go ahead and ask them. I'll meet you at the car. I need to talk to Sophie for a minute before we leave."

Iris left April's house and walked two blocks to the designated corner. While she waited for Sam to pick her up, a black-and-white patrol car cruised the street in front of her. She fiddled with her bag and tried to ignore its presence. *Move on. Nothing important here.* Police made her nervous. She and Sam had been in hiding for a year and a half. No one had bothered them

21

yet, but things could change in a heartbeat. *Don't I know it?*

Fifteen minutes later, Iris was still waiting. Sam had looked so tired this morning after a night with the fussy baby. *I hope they're both getting a good nap.* She fingered the cell phone in her jacket pocket, a luxury they couldn't really afford, but necessary with Sam gone so much while she watched the baby. Her sister would be angry if she didn't call, but Iris didn't want to interrupt the much-needed rest. She hesitated for a few more minutes. The police car cruised by the corner a second time, forcing a decision by its simple presence.

Iris tugged her jacket a little tighter and looked at the sky. Dark clouds tumbled overhead, and the horizon looked even worse. They were in for another storm, but home was just five miles away. She could make in about an hour if she ran part of the way. Thunder rumbled overhead, and Iris bit her lip against the sound and the fear that came with it. *I can do this.*

Mind made up, she began the brisk trip home. There wasn't much she could do to make things easier on Sam, but an uninterrupted nap would do everyone good. *How angry can she be if I have lunch ready when they wake up?*

Mama Rosita's was maxed out with hungry after-church diners. The crowd included a large portion of Valley View worshipers. Callie waved to several people she knew while she stood in the line with her husband and friends. The aromas of cheese, peppers, and Mexican spices made her stomach growl long before a table became available.

Benton slipped his arms around Callie.

She leaned back against him. "I wasn't hungry when we walked in, but I'm starving now. My stomach just knows there's an avocado in this place with my name carved in it."

Benton kissed the top of her head. "I thought you'd started your spring diet."

"Are you implying that I need to be on a diet?"

From her place beside them, Callie's best friend, Karla Black, straightened to her full five feet, lowered her chin, and scowled at Benton over her glasses. "Are you?" Both her stance and tone telegraphed her intent to defend her longtime friend if necessary.

"Of course not, she's—"

Mitch stopped Benton in mid sentence. "You should probably shut up now. We're in a Mexican restaurant. Cheese sauce on top of shoe leather is an ugly combination."

"No," Benton objected. " I know how to take care of this one." He hugged Callie a little tighter to his six-foot frame, bending to rest his chin on his wife's head. "My wife is perfect in every way. She doesn't need to make a single improvement. Anything she wants, says, or does is fine with me."

Callie rolled her eyes and stepped away from Benton, hooking her arm through Karla's as they were led to their table by a young woman in an embroidered peasant blouse and full, ankle-length skirt. The restaurant was bright in a combination of red, yellow, and orange. Colorful woven blankets decorated the walls. Hand-painted pottery nestled in recessed nooks. Sombreros served as lampshades above each oversized booth and table.

The hostess motioned them to a corner table. A

second young woman appeared with a basket of crisp, warm chips and small bowls of salsa and cheese. She took their drink orders.

Callie studied her menu while she munched on salty chips and *queso* made spicy with a spoonful of Rosita's signature salsa.

The waitress returned, handed out iced tea all around, and waited while they made their lunch choices. Fajitas for the guys, enchiladas and tacos for the women.

"Top mine with an extra scoop of guacamole," Callie requested.

Once they were alone at the table, Mitch stretched and plucked another chip from the basket. He looked at Benton. "You gonna have some time to devote to our boat this week? We've only got a few weeks left to get it seaworthy."

Callie looked at her watch and glanced at Karla. "Sixty seconds."

"Hum?"

"It took them sixty seconds to forget we're here."

Karla snorted in response. The women angled their chairs together and focused their conversation on each other.

"I didn't see you in service this morning," Callie said.

"It was my turn to help in children's church."

Callie leaned forward. "Really? Did you see the little girl with April?"

Karla nodded. "Iris, right? Shy little thing."

"That's her. Have you noticed anything...strange about her?"

"She seems shy, like I said, but nothing other than

that. Why?"

Callie frowned. "Just curious. I'm worried about her. I wondered if anyone else was getting the same vibes."

"Worried why? What's wrong?"

"I don't know—for a fact—that anything's wrong." She paused when their server arrived and waited while she positioned hot plates of food in front of them.

Callie scooped guacamole onto a chip. "But I've taught that class for more years than I care to admit. I've never had a child sit for three weeks straight and say so little." *How can I make her understand?* "It's not being quiet that bothers me. Quiet is a nice change at their age. Its more about how she sits, with her head down, never making eye contact with anyone. Not participating in any of the gab sessions the other girls can't seem to live without. And when you do get more than three words out of her...you'd swear you were talking to an adult. Something's not right."

Callie expelled a long breath. "I hope I'm imaging things, but I feel like God's telling me to probe a little." She raised her hands in a shrug. "I'm not sure what I should do."

Karla tilted her head to the side and studied her friend for a few seconds. Callie smiled at the play of light on Karla's silver hair. Karla was fifty-nine, only five years older than Callie, but she mothered all of her friends equally.

"How long have we known each other?" Karla finally asked.

Callie grinned. "Almost forever."

"Exactly. I don't think you're imagining a thing. If something's bothering you, if you think God's directing you, you need to trust your instincts."

"I don't have many instincts left to trust. Besides, what I'm feeling is so vague." Callie lowered her voice even further and cast a furtive glance in Benton's direction. "I can't go through that again, Karla."

Karla didn't need an explanation. "Why are you still beating yourself up over that? You didn't do anything wrong."

"Nothing except send that little boy back into a situation that killed him."

Karla rubbed her forehead. "There were lawyers and a judge there that day. Plenty of people who testified on both sides of the situation. How is Sawyer's death your fault?"

A weight settled on Callie's chest and threatened to steal her breath. She took a drink of her tea. "If I'd stayed out of it..."

"Callie, I can't tell you how to feel or what to do. But if this child needs help, and you ignore what God is trying to tell you, how are you going to feel then? You need to let go of some of the past—that can't be changed—and open your heart to where God wants to take you now."

"I hear what you're saying, and I'm not ignoring the situation. I'm spending the day with April on Friday. I want to know what she can tell me about her little friend."

Callie directed the conversation down a safer path. "I know we're skipping Bible study this week for spring break. Whose turn is it to host next week?"

"Mine." Karla's smile was decidedly wicked. "And I found a new cheesecake recipe," she warned her friend. "I won't give away all the details, but it involves half a dozen Snickers candy bars. It's probably the most sinful dessert we've had since we started our study sessions."

Didn't Karla understand that some things couldn't be fixed, even with chocolate? *Some things can't be fixed at all.* Callie gave her friend a tight smile and the light comeback she expected. "You are a truly evil person."

The men paid for lunch, and the two couples stepped onto the sidewalk. Thunder rumbled overhead, and the first sprinkles dotted the pavement.

Hand in hand, Benton and Callie turned toward their vehicle. "See you guys at service tonight," she called.

"Later," Karla answered, "I'll be praying for God to give you some direction with Iris."

Benton unlocked the car. "Who's Iris?"

Callie looked at her husband and decided that now wasn't the time to mention her concerns about Iris. She had a more pressing issue to deal with today. Her answer was meant to distract and tease. "How can you guys sit right next to us and not hear a single thing we say?"

Her husband lifted his hands. "Respect for your privacy?"

Callie rolled her eyes, grabbed his shirt, and pulled him down to her level. She gazed into his tanned, bearded face. When his blue eyes met hers, butterflies tumbled in her stomach. He'd just turned sixty, but he could still tangle up her insides. "Thanks for lunch, handsome."

He closed the distance between them, placing a light kiss on her upturned mouth. "Anything to make you happy." His tone turned serious in the space of a heartbeat. "Everything OK today?"

Callie took a step back as the sky opened up, pelting them with rain. She ran to her side of the car and ducked inside. Benton settled in beside her.

"Home?" he asked as he turned the key in the ignition.

"The store."

Benton groaned. "On a Sunday afternoon? It'll be a madhouse."

Callie braced for her husband's response. "I need some flowers for tomorrow," she mumbled.

"Callie—"

"Benton, please. I know what you're going to say, so don't waste your breath. Take me to the store, or I'll just take myself once we get home."

Benton drove, staring straight ahead, his disapproval more than obvious in the set of his jaw and the thin line of his mouth.

CHAPTER THREE

Callie forced herself out of bed Monday morning. She sent a look of pure jealously at her husband, still asleep and snoring on his side of the mattress. Some mornings she almost despised Benton for staying in bed when she had to get up. *This* was one of those mornings. Nightmares had robbed her of sleep for the second night in a row. Every bump in the night became the sound of fist against flesh. The noise of the wind in the trees outside the bedroom window, a baby's terrified cries. Between the sleepless nights, her increasing concerns about Iris, and the stop she planned to make on her way to work... *Nothing like a day ruined before six AM.* If Satan wanted to convince her to stay out of Iris's problems, he was giving it his best shot.

Callie slipped on black slacks and an emerald green blouse in the muted glow of a small lamp. She functioned on autopilot, her mind still wandering through the fog of sleep deprivation.

Benton wouldn't stir for another hour or so. His

self-employed status allowed him to make his own rules and set his own hours. The first stop of his day would be the local coffee shop for waffles with a side helping of Garfield gossip. His remodeling business had always done well, but God had blessed it even more since his conversion three years ago.

Her feelings of morning disdain faded as the sunlight gathered strength outside. She smiled at her husband's still form. Marrying Benton had been both the smartest and the dumbest thing she'd ever done. Callie had been a Christian since junior high school. Benton never, until three years ago. The odds had certainly been stacked against them, but they'd been blessed. Callie gave thanks everyday for her husband's decision to follow Christ. Her thoughts saddened a bit. The last six months had tried their faith, both old and new.

Ready to face the day, she roused Benton just enough to kiss him goodbye and left the bedroom behind. Hot coffee waited for her in the kitchen. Callie chose sweetener instead of sugar, her smart choice immediately undermined by the addition of chocolate-flavored creamer to her cup. After a quick check of her e-mail and the morning headlines, she settled into her recliner to spend a few minutes in private devotion. In the early morning quiet, the house belonged to her and God, the perfect time to study her Sunday school lesson or review the current topic for their weekly Bible study.

The Monday night study group was Karla's pet project. The evening was open to any woman at Valley View Church who wished to attend, but Callie and Karla, along with two other friends, Terri Hayes and

Pam Lake, took turns hosting the sessions in their homes. Trial and error had yielded the unanimous opinion that cheesecake made the perfect Bible-study snack.

"Snickers." Her hands went to her stomach even as she smiled in anticipation. She'd need to kick up her treadmill a notch or two this week. Callie opened her worn Bible and started her daily devotion.

Twenty minutes later she placed the Bible on the small table next to her recliner and had her morning conversation with God. Callie gave thanks for the day and asked for wisdom as she navigated through it. She prayed for Benton, family, and friends, for God's will and direction in each of their lives.

"Father, please be with each of us today. Shelter our lives in Your hands and direct our feet on the path You've chosen for us. I know You're trying to show me something where Iris is concerned. I don't know if I can help her. I don't know how far I'm willing to go, but if You'll guide me, I'll take that first step. We'll see where we need to go from there." Callie's mind went to the white roses she'd purchased yesterday. Familiar tears stung the backs of her eyes. "Give me strength for today. Amen."

She gave her sleeping husband a final envious thought, finished her coffee, put her cup in the sink, and left the house with just enough time to make a single, heartbreaking stop before work.

Callie bumped her hip against the car door, slamming it shut. She picked her way across the uneven ground. Early morning mist hovered in clumps, resembling ghosts of souls long gone. The heels of her black pumps sank into the rain-soaked earth with every step she took.

Shifting the bundled flowers away from her wrist, she glanced at her watch. Six thirty. Enough time to stop, but not enough time to linger. *I will arrive at work on time. I will not start the day with red, swollen eyes.*

Her destination was easy to find, even through the disorienting fog. The stone bench was damp with dew and rain, but she ignored the moisture and sat, watching wispy fingers of vapor curl around the trunks of the trees and the evenly spaced grave markers. A single tear tracked down her cheek, blurring the edges of the granite monument in front of her. Callie swiped it away impatiently. *So much for my no-tears resolution.* She stooped to arrange the flowers at the base of the small stone. A dozen white roses. Sawyer would have been two years old today. "Happy birthday, baby."

Callie settled back on the bench, the silence of the morning unbroken except for the occasional twittering of waking birds. She closed her eyes, allowing her mind to wander.

Their office was a busy place. Patients came and went throughout the day. Some came alone, others with spouses. Some brought their kids. Multiply those days by eighteen years, and sometimes she had a problem remembering what happened last week. But Callie remembered, with single-minded clarity, the handful of times she'd seen Sawyer in their office. Every moment, frozen in her mind, part of the guilt she bore.

The memory of the first time she'd seen that precious baby still had the ability to make her smile, even while it broke her heart.

Callie had opened the access door to the exam area that day. Looking at the chart in her hand, she smiled and called for their next patient.

"Janette Baker?"

A young woman stood then bent to lift the infant carrier that rested at her feet. She walked back to the patient staging area, juggling everything from hand to hand. The young mother took a seat, placing the carrier on the counter by her side.

"Hi, Janette. Let me peek at this little guy. Sawyer, right?" Callie shifted fuzzy blankets from around the newborn to get a better look. "He's beautiful."

"We think so."

The baby's eyes stared up at her, a clear and attentive blue. Callie brushed gentle fingers over thick red ringlets. "Where'd he get all this red hair?"

Janette gave Callie an indulgent smile. "His father's sister has hair just about this color. We're blaming her."

"I'll bet she's horribly insulted." Callie took Janette's blood pressure and temperature and noted her patient's vital signs in the chart. "Climb up on the scales for me."

"Do I have to? I feel like such a cow!"

"You look great." Callie tapped the digital readout. "See there? You're down twenty pounds from your last visit seven weeks ago. That's fantastic."

"Twenty down, fifteen to go."

"Be patient, you'll get there." Callie made a few more notations in Janette's chart. "Are either of you having any problems Dr. Rayburn should know about?"

Janette shook her head. "I feel great. A little tired, but he's such a good baby, it's hard to complain." She touched her son's face with tender fingers. "We just take nice long naps together."

Diane, the office nurse, opened the door. "We're ready for you, Janette."

Janette picked up the carrier, and Sawyer let out a restless whine. "Isn't that just like a man? Give him a compliment, and he'll screw it up every time." She put the carrier back on the counter and dug a pacifier out of the diaper bag. "He probably wants his bottle."

"I'm going back to my office to clear up some paperwork," Callie said. "Why don't you leave this little guy with me? I'll take care of him while you visit with Dr. Rayburn."

"Are you sure?"

"Positive. We can keep each other company until you're done."

Janette surrendered the baby to Callie and followed Diane to the empty exam room.

Callie took Sawyer to her office and placed his infant seat in a patch of dappled sunlight next to the window. She returned to her desk and a stack of invoices they'd received with their medical supplies earlier in the morning.

Sudden outraged wails from the baby pierced the silence of her office. Callie dropped the papers in alarm, turning to see what had disturbed him so violently. She found his tiny fist tangled in his curly red hair. The harder he cried, the harder he pulled. Reflex kept his little fist knotted in his own curls. His face was screwed up into a furious mask. Tears of anger and pain puddled in his eyes.

"Oh, baby." Callie gently pried his little fingers apart, trying to calm him with his discarded pacifier.

"Poor little thing."

Callie struggled to clear her vision. She focused on the headstone that bore the dates of a life cut short by violence. "Baby, I'm so sorry about the way things worked out. I was trying to do a good thing for you. Babies should be with their mothers. I never meant..."

Callie jerked to her feet, brushed the wrinkles from her shirt, and headed back to her car. No sense going down that path again. Whatever courage or forgiveness or strength she'd hoped to find didn't exist in this place.

Iris climbed quietly out of bed. She always got up early on school days. There wasn't anywhere to be this morning, but she couldn't sleep any longer. If she stayed in bed she'd only disturb the others. Sam had come home late again last night, tired from a long shift at work and faced with a baby determined to fuss the rest of the night away.

Iris's bare feet hit the cold tile floor, and a shiver ran up her spine. She made her morning trip to the bathroom, grabbed her clothes, and hurried into the living area of the two-room apartment to get dressed in front of the old wall furnace. She bumped the thermostat just enough to trigger a rush of warm air, warmed her front, and then turned her back. Her eyelids closed in satisfaction.

After pulling on clean socks, she wiggled into her jeans and tugged on an orange T-shirt. Her stomach rumbled. She went in search of breakfast and settled at the table with a package of cold Pop-Tarts.

The apartment had come furnished and with all the utility bills included in the six-hundred-dollar rent. The necessities were provided, but that didn't include a microwave or toaster. The Pop-Tart made Iris thirsty. She opened the fridge and eyed what remained of a gallon of milk. With a quiet snort of resignation, she drank water instead. The baby would need the milk later in the day.

Samantha worked hard to provide everything they needed. They never went hungry, but what they had was often not what they—*she*—wanted.

Iris sat back down to finish her cold breakfast and noticed a note with some cash in the center of the table, anchored beneath their mother's lavender candle.

I need you to go to the store this morning. We need groceries for the rest of the week. Here's a list of what we need. Just do the best you can. This is all the cash we have until Friday, so please don't waste any of it. I love you and I'm sorry about being so late again last night. The car was acting up. Sam.

Iris fanned the four ten-dollar bills out on the table and looked at the list: milk, two loaves of bread, lunchmeat, cheese, teabags, sugar, one bag of chips, Pop-Tarts, bath soap, toilet paper, toothpaste, three pounds of hamburger meat, two boxes of Hamburger Helper, three cans of vegetables, and laundry soap.

After several months of experience, Iris was an expert shopper. She studied the list while she chewed and did some quick math in her head. If she paid attention and crossed her fingers, it might be possible to squeeze a package of cookies into Sam's list.

Iris thought about her morning. She had to do the laundry as well as the shopping. A quick check of their coin jar revealed five dollars in quarters for the coin laundry. The cookies inched a little closer to her list.

The grocery store was four blocks away, the laundry

two blocks farther. Even with the wagon she used to haul things back and forth, it would take two trips to get both chores done and be back home by ten thirty so Sam could go to work.

Why *does my spring break have to be such a dud?* A good book would help pass the time. Maybe she could sneak in a quick trip to the library while the clothes dried.

Her attitude bordered on resentful when she considered the mountain of daily chores that would keep her from enjoying a single second of the week ahead. *Things were so much better before...*

Iris sighed. Sometimes it was hard not to be jealous of other kids her age or angry about the way she had to live. She never got to have any fun. April had invited her to an afternoon pizza party later in the week. Would Iris be attending? *Not.* School, chores, and babysitting. Her life was just one big chore.

She slumped into the couch, flipping through TV channels with the ancient remote control. *Nothing.* Didn't these people know that spring break started today? Couldn't they schedule something interesting for the kids of the world who didn't have a life?

Her conscience pricked her, and Iris felt her cheeks heat with shame. Sam was doing everything possible to keep them safe. She shouldn't complain about doing her part. They knew from the beginning that it wouldn't be easy, but they loved each other, and they were determined to stay together. They lived with the fear of discovery and separation. Every day it got more difficult to keep their secrets.

Iris clicked off the television and listened for movement from the other room. All quiet. She went back to the kitchen and poured an inch of milk into her glass. She popped the last bite of her breakfast into her mouth and followed it with a single swallow of milk.

The office opened to patients at eight o'clock each morning. Dr. Rayburn was usually at his desk by the time Callie arrived at seven. The receptionist and the nurse came in later. Once the day started, there would be a constant flow of patients.

The practice catered to all phases of women's medicine, but Callie enjoyed the mommies most of all. Women in all stages of pregnancy filled the waiting room of their office every day. Watching them progress from those first few weeks of nervous anticipation to those last few days of waddling exhaustion made her job a joy.

Things had changed a lot since Callie's single pregnancy almost thirty-five years ago. In those days women went to the doctor and waited in tense expectation for test results to find out if they were pregnant, then suffered through nine months of impatience to see if God had blessed them with a boy or a girl.

Thanks to home pregnancy tests and ultrasounds, most of their patients knew they were pregnant when they came through the door. And the majority of them knew the sex of their baby long before it arrived, Three D pictures included. Callie had no argument with technology. It resulted in healthier mothers and babies, but it took a lot of surprise out of the process.

An early riser, Dr. Rayburn, sixty-five and widowed, almost always beat Callie to the office. A thin strip of light beneath his closed door told her that this morning was no exception. If she knew her boss, and she did, he'd be in there reading one of a dozen medical journals that came in during the month, waiting for coffee to materialize on his desk.

She announced herself with a quick knock of warning, and entered the doctor's private office. "Good morning, Norman." She placed charts for their first fifteen patients on the corner of his desk and fresh coffee on the coaster in front of him.

The doctor lifted his head at her approach. His thick, silvered hair and reading glasses made her boss look more like a wise old grandfather every day. The smile on his face triggered an automatic one from her in return.

"How was your weekend?" she asked.

"Busy." One hand reached for his coffee, the other moved the first chart from the stack to the desk in front of him. "Yours?"

"Not nearly long enough," Callie replied, only half joking. "Speaking of weekends, I need to take this coming Friday off."

"That's fine."

He reached into his drawer, brought out a container of chocolate cookies, laid three next to his cup, and offered the box to Callie. She declined. The promise of Karla's Snickers cheesecake replayed in her mind like a bad song. *Dang you, Karla.*

The doctor shrugged and returned the cookies to his stash. "Suit yourself. Your plans for a long weekend make me feel a little better about today."

"Today?"

"Chris called right before you came in. She'll be MIA today. Car trouble. Looks like you'll be manning the reception desk."

Callie shook her head. "Again? If you'd give that girl a raise she could afford some decent transportation."

The doctor grinned. "All in good time." He motioned to the charts. "How many are we seeing today?"

She consulted her memory. "Thirty-five, barring emergencies. Typical Monday."

"Will you be OK, or do we need to call a temp?"

"Don't be silly, Norman. It's just for one day. We'll be fine." She stood and stepped toward the door, turning with her hand on the knob. "We can discuss *my* raise in the morning."

Eight hours and thirty-four patients later, Callie's feet were killing her. The black pumps she'd worn that morning were far more suitable for a day spent behind her desk, dealing with the workings of the practice, than with the up-and-down, back-and-forth splitting of her time between her duties and Chris's.

Callie sighed in relief as she pulled the staging room door open and called for their final patient of the day.

"Lisa, come on back."

Lisa Sisko levered her belly out of the sofa. Five months pregnant with twin boys, she'd already gained more weight—and a few more inches—than she did in her entire pregnancy two years ago. Lisa's husband, Dave, was Valley View's youth pastor. While he held the official title, Lisa easily shouldered half of the responsibility. Watching Lisa struggle out of the chair, Callie found it hard to believe that this was the same young woman who'd taken their volleyball team to victory last fall.

Callie made room for her patient to precede her through the door. She couldn't resist a quick pat of

Lisa's stomach as she passed. "How are we doing?"

Lisa sat in a molded plastic chair, tossed her straight black hair over her shoulder, and counted items off on her fingers. "*We* have a constant backache, nightly heartburn, and swollen ankles. *We* have outgrown all of our clothes and still have four months to go. *We* have to pee fifty times a day. *We* are very glad that bikinis are not in our wardrobe, since the stretch marks are looking more and more like a map of bad country roads." She stopped and rubbed her belly with a smile. "Couldn't be better."

Callie laughed. "Bless your heart. You need to keep your feet up as much as possible. Let Dave deal with more of the day-to-day stuff."

Lisa laughed. "He does his part. I'll get my revenge when he has two active little boys to keep up with."

"Probably so." Callie made notes in Lisa's chart. When she looked up she found Lisa studying her with a small frown.

"Problem?"

Lisa motioned to her belly. "Not with this, but I do have a question if you have time to sit for a second."

Callie sank into the other chair and kicked off her shoes. "You are the last patient after a very long day, and I need a break. What's up?"

"I wanted to ask you about the little girl who's been coming to church with April. What do you know about her?"

Callie frowned. "Not a lot. Why do you ask?'

"I saw her at the grocery store this morning. She checked out in front of me. Her total wasn't all that much, but I guess it was a few cents more than she had." Lisa eyes filled with sympathy. "We all know how

41

embarrassing that can be. I tried to give her some change, but she wouldn't even talk to me. She just had the cashier take off a package of cookies and hurried out of the store. I looked for her when I was done, but I didn't find her."

"Poor baby..."

"Yeah, I really felt like someone should check on her. Do you know where she lives?"

The office nurse opened the connecting door to the exam rooms before Callie had a chance to answer. "Dr. Rayburn is ready for you, Lisa."

Callie offered a hand up to her pregnant friend, her mind once again at war with her emotions. She retreated to her office and searched her purse for her cell phone and Iris's visitor card. Checking on one of her students *did not* mean she was getting involved. She punched in Iris's number and waited.

"We're sorry, the number you have dialed is not a working number..."

Callie disconnected the automated response, checking the phone's display to make sure she'd dialed correctly.

Yep. There's something very wrong with this whole situation. She tapped the cell phone against her chin. There had to be a way to help Iris without putting her own emotional well-being at risk.

Her kitchen was a biohazard looking for a red bag. Callie stood in the doorway, the urge to kill her husband half-buried under the laughter that bubbled up at the pathetic scene that greeted her return home.

Pots simmered on the stove. Dirty utensils littered her countertops. Benton stood in the middle of the room with his back to her, a bag of dog biscuits in his hand. Sara, their blonde lab, and Opie, a two-year-old Irish setter, ignored the proffered doggie treats in favor of licking up the red spatters on Callie's kitchen floor.

"Sit," he told the two furry invaders. They refused.

"Come on, guys. Callie will be home in a few minutes. If she finds this mess and both of you in here, she'll hurt me."

Callie cleared her throat and grinned when she saw Benton's shoulder blades flinch at the sound.

Red spots gone and knowing there would be no further treats until they obeyed, both dogs finally sank down on quivering haunches. Benton tossed them each a snack. They snatched the bones from midair, swallowed without bothering to chew, and immediately sat for another.

Callie looked around her kitchen, her shoulders sagging at the mess. Benton had prepared dinner. It wasn't something he did neatly. Since the only thing he cooked was chili, she had no trouble guessing what was on the menu for tonight.

Her eyes went to the small breakfast nook in the corner of the room and the table set with her best tablecloth, sterling candlesticks, and tall blue candles. His effort made her smile despite the mess. Only Benton would set the stage for a romantic dinner and then serve chili.

She stepped to the stove and lifted the lid off the pot to take a quick sniff while her husband coaxed the dogs outside with a final treat.

"Smells good," she said when he came back to the kitchen. "What got into you?"

He dropped a kiss on the back of her neck on his

way to the sink to wash his hands. "Some of the guys at church were giving me a hard time about defending my title at the next chili cook-off. I thought it might be smart to stay in practice."

"Benton, its barely spring. The chili cook-off isn't until October."

"Yeah, but why wait 'til the last minute?" He dried his hands, and wrapped his arms around her from behind. "Not in the mood for chili?"

Callie folded her arms over his and leaned back against his chest. "I love your chili. After the day I've had, not having to cook dinner tonight is a serious blessing."

Benton turned her around and took a half step away so he could see her face. "I knew today would be hard on you."

Callie leaned against him. *You have no idea.* She deliberately changed the subject. "I think my feet are going to fall off. Chris had car trouble, so I did double duty today. I think I'm getting too old to be Dr. Rayburn's superwoman."

"You'll never be old. I have an idea. The chili needs to simmer for an hour or so. Why don't you go relax in a hot bath for a while? Put on your fuzzy robe and curl up with a book. I'll even clean the kitchen when we're done with dinner. Sound good to you?"

"Absolutely perfect. I knew I married you for a reason."

"You married me to be your kitchen slave? I thought you wanted my money and my body."

"Sweetheart, I want it all." She pulled him down for a lingering kiss. "After I unwind for a while we'll explore some of those other reasons, and it won't cost

44

you a cent." Callie headed for the comfort of their bedroom, leaving behind a properly motivated husband to deal with his mess.

CHAPTER FOUR

Callie took a sip of her chocolate-flavored coffee and savored the silence. Her Friday was off to a perfect start, one of those rare times when everything had fallen into place to give her the morning, and the house, all to herself. She loved Benton and her job and thanked God for both. But the opportunity to put husband and office aside for a few greedy hours and just *be* scored high on Callie's list of favorite things.

Benton had left for an out-of-town job at six in the morning. "Who had to leave whom in bed this time?" Callie whispered with a small, self-satisfied grin. She pulled up the footrest of her recliner and gazed out the open front door at a beautiful morning. Birds swarmed the feeders. Daffodils peeked shyly from their green pods. Opie and Sara chased squirrels from tree to tree. A breeze ruffled the thick green grass and reminded her of things she could be doing. The day off today would cost her a day of catching up tomorrow. The lawn needed its first spring mowing, and she should go grocery shopping...

"*She just had the cashier take off a package of cookies.*"

Lisa's words from Monday still echoed in Callie's mind. She tried to shrug it off. *I'm working on it, God. If April knows anything about the situation, I'll get it out of her today.*

Callie picked up her Bible and opened it to the book of Judges, the story of Jael. Of all the women in the Bible, Jael ranked as one of Callie's personal favorites. Any woman who could coax an enemy captain into her tent, lull him to sleep with food and promises of safety, then nail his head to the floor with a tent spike, was not a woman to be trifled with.

Callie read the familiar account. She could almost see Jael and Sisera that day. The enemy captain running for his life, looking for a place to hide, and expecting Jael's tent to be a safe haven.

"Come in here," Jael offered, so meek and subservient. "Why, you poor thing, you just look worn out. Let me get you a cup of cold milk and a warm blanket. Now you just lie down right here, and take a little nap. Of course I won't tell anyone where you are, even if they ask." Then *smack*. Lights out for the bad guy, a victory for God's army, and deliverance for God's people. All because of a crafty woman. Go Jael! Anyone who claimed the Bible bored them wasn't reading what she was reading. Callie placed her Bible on the small lamp table and closed her eyes in prayer.

"Father, help me have the courage of Jael. I don't need to nail anyone's head to my kitchen floor, but I need Your strength and wisdom every day. I don't know what Iris needs. I'm not going to give up on her, not as long as I feel You tugging on my heart, but I

SHARON SROCK

need You to guide me. If I can't help her, maybe I can find someone who can, once I know what the problem is."

Callie pulled into her daughter's driveway and honked for her granddaughter, April. The weather, always unpredictable at this time of year, had changed from morning sunshine to lunchtime clouds. A fine mist hung in the air, and with the temperature hovering around fifty degrees, it was cooler than she would have liked. She looked at the horizon and the streaks of blue amid the grey. The clouds had already started to break apart. It just might be a good shopping day after all.

April slammed out the front door and sprinted for the car, falling into the seat next to her grandmother. She kissed Callie's cheek and boosted the heat up to its maximum level in one smooth move. The eleven-year-old shoved her long blonde hair out of her face. "I wore shorts all week long. Why does it have to be so cold this morning?"

"The weatherman promised it would warm up later this afternoon." Callie examined April's outfit of white capris, a pink "GIRLS ROCK" T-shirt, and flip-flops. "Do you need to run in for a jacket or something?"

"Nope, I'm good." April fastened her seat belt. "Let's get this show on the road! I skipped breakfast this morning, so I'm double hungry."

Callie put the car in gear and laughed at April's enthusiasm. "What did you do with your spring break? Anything special?"

April smiled, opened her shoulder bag, and pulled out a handful of money. "Earned my keep." Unmistakable pride rang in her voice.

Callie glanced at the wad of cash in April's hand. "Wow, I'm impressed. Did you say lunch was on you today?"

"You *did not* hear that from me. I have forty dollars. I'm buying at least one CD. Maybe shoes. I'll have to see what else looks good."

Callie nodded as she drove. "What did you do to *earn your keep* so effectively?"

"Babysat the brat two days this week while Mom and Dad worked and Randy went to do whatever it is he does with his friends all day."

"Brat? Trent?"

"Is there another one?"

"April, he's your baby brother, not a brat."

"Grandma, you need to trust me on this one. The boy is a *brat*, all capital letters. But the way I see it, since he's just two, it's the only job he has right now, and he's really...really... good at it. So when I call him a brat, it's a compliment, not an insult."

"April." Callie laughed.

"Besides, it was practice for the summer."

"What happens this summer?"

"Randy has a job all summer with a landscaping service. Says he's saving for a car since he'll have his license in 'no time.'" April rolled her eyes in sisterly disgust. "Anyway, I asked Mom and Dad if I could watch Trent this summer so I could make some money, too. They talked it over and said I could try it this week to see how it went. We both lived through it, and I made forty dollars. I guess it went fine."

"April, don't you think you're too young to—"

April raised her hand. "Grandma, I'll be twelve by the time school is out. Please tell me the story about what you did the summer you were twelve."

Callie stole a look at April as she drove. "If anyone's a brat, it's you."

"I'm waiting."

"The summer I was twelve I watched three kids all day long. I made three dollars a day. For that grand sum of money, I was also expected to keep the house clean and the dishes washed. The family offered to pay me five dollars a day, but my mother wouldn't let them. I remember wanting to hurt her."

"I rest my case. Besides, I'm going to make a whole lot more than three dollars a day."

"And when your friends call and want to go to the pool or to a movie?"

"Please, give me a little credit," April insisted. "Mom and I have a deal. I'll watch Trent on Tuesday, Wednesday, and Thursday. He'll go to Terri's day care the other two days. That gives me all weekend to do things with my friends. Trent still gets to spend two days a week bonding with other brats his own age. Mom and Dad will save some serious money on their day care bill. And I'll make sixty dollars a week." She shrugged. "Everyone wins."

Callie drove a few miles in silence. "Sounds like you guys have it all figured out. Did you come up with this plan all by yourself?" They pulled into the crowded parking lot of the restaurant.

"Pretty much. I actually got the initial idea from Iris. I figured if she could do it, so could I." April released her seat belt and hopped out of the car leaving her grandmother to follow, pondering her first bits of Iris intel.

After a thirty-minute wait Callie scooted into the only vacant booth she could see in the whole dining room. If the aromas of garlic, yeast breads, tomatoes, and vinaigrette could be believed, the food would be worth the wait. Benton's favorite restaurant food was Mexican; hers was Italian. She tossed her jacket and her purse onto the bench beside her and faced April across the table. "If their food is as good as it smells, we're in for a treat."

April nodded and studied her menu. "I am officially triple hungry."

A waitress approached their table with a basket of breadsticks and warm marinara sauce.

"Hang in there. You're about to be rescued." Callie smiled.

April nodded but continued to read her menu.

The attractive young waitress gave Callie a brilliant smile. "Welcome to Pasta World. I'm Samantha. I'll be your server today."

"Thanks, Samantha. Could you give us a few minutes? This is our first time here." Callie patted the menu. "Everything looks so good. I think we're going to have a hard time making up our minds."

"Not a problem. If you wouldn't mind a recommendation, the lasagna is always terrific."

Callie shook her head. "I don't know how you work, and eat, here and keep that tiny little figure."

Samantha laughed and leaned down to share a soft whisper. "I stick with the salads."

"Sweetheart, when you're done there, could we get some dessert menus?"

The waitress turned to the table behind her. "I'll get those for you right away." She turned back to Callie.

"Can I bring your drinks while you're deciding?"

"That's perfect. I'll have iced tea, no lemon."

"Sweet or unsweet?"

Callie grinned. "Unsweet and lots of little blue packets."

"I hear that." She turned to April. "And for you?"

"Sprite," April said, finally looking up from her menu.

Samantha gasped. Without another word, the teenager scribbled a note and fled.

Callie watched their waitress depart with a small frown. *What was that all about?* The only label Callie could put on Samantha's expression was fear. Callie's gaze followed Samantha as she wove through the maze of tables and disappeared through the swinging doors of the kitchen. Something niggled at the edges of Callie's mind. Some hint of familiarity. *Have I met her somewhere?* A search of her memory yielded no results. The only thing she could say with any certainty was that the child was working way too hard. No one so young should have those dark circles under her eyes and such a drawn look on her pretty face.

The peculiar behavior of their waitress took a backseat as Callie studied the menu. The eggplant parmesan sounded good. She looked up at April. "What's your pleasure, sweetheart?"

April folded the menu and pushed it aside. "Spaghetti and meatballs for me."

"I think I'm going with the eggplant. We can share if you like."

Her granddaughter made a face. "Purple food? Thanks, but I'll pass."

Callie laughed. "Let me know if you change your

mind." She smiled across the table. "So, tell me about Iris. She seems like a nice girl."

April munched on a breadstick. "She is. She's smart, too. Most of the kids in our class think she's a nerd because she gets A's on all of her work. They give her a hard time about it."

"Have you gone to school with her for a long time?"

"No, she started right after Christmas break. I felt sorry for her at first because she seemed sort of lonely, but once I got to know her a little better, I realized she's just shy."

"Have you met her parents?"

April stared across the table at her grandmother, brows drawn together in a puzzled frown. "Nope, she never talks about her family. She mentioned someone named Sam a couple of times. I asked her if that was her brother. She said no and changed the subject." April shrugged. "But whoever he is, he seems to be the boss 'cause the few times she's mentioned him it's been like, 'I can't because Sam said—'"

A tray loaded with tall glasses of iced tea and sodas clattered onto their table, interrupting April in midsentence. Samantha managed to save all the drinks. "I'm so sorry."

"Sweetheart, are you all right?" Callie grabbed Samantha's arm and pulled her down into the booth beside her. "You're as pale as a sheet. Sit here for a second before you fall down."

The youngster gulped for air and hopped back to her feet "I'm fine, thanks. Just a little tired." She tossed her long brown ponytail over her shoulder. "Did you ladies decide on your lunch?"

Callie studied her with narrowed eyes and could

have sworn the child was holding her breath. "Eggplant parmesan for me, spaghetti and meatballs for my granddaughter."

"I'll send it right out," Samantha assured them and made her escape.

April raised her eyebrows. "How weird was that?"

"Poor thing's working too hard." Callie shrugged and pursued her original subject. "I thought your mom had rules about knowing the parents of your friends."

April rolled her eyes at her grandmother. "She does, if I want to hang out with them or go to their house. The only time I see Iris is at school or church. It's kind of strange now that you mention it."

"So Iris gave you the idea to babysit this summer?"

"Yeah. She babysits a lot for someone. From the things she says, the baby she's watching is a whole lot younger than Trent."

Iris sat on the couch reading her new library book. She loved to read. Thankfully, Garfield's library was within walking distance. Whimpering filtered in from the next room, and she put the book aside. Bobbie had slept for a long time. She'd want a bottle now that she was awake.

Iris poured milk into a baby bottle and put it in a pan of water on the stove to warm while she checked on her niece. The baby lay in the middle of the bed surrounded by pillows. Iris pushed some of them aside. "Hey, baby girl, did you have a good nap?" Bobbie gurgled as Iris checked her diaper. "You're wet, as usual."

Iris retrieved a freshly laundered diaper and baby powder from the small closet. She changed Bobbie's diaper and restacked the pillows. Leaving the baby on the bed, she put the cloth diaper in a pail, washed her hands, and went to see if the bottle was ready.

Bobbie started to fuss in earnest, but Iris took time to make sure the milk wasn't too hot. She dribbled a few drops on the inside of her wrist just as Sam had shown her months ago. The milk felt a little warm so she added some cold milk from the refrigerator to cool it off. The baby's crying grew more vigorous. "I'm coming," Iris called, testing the temperature a second time.

She lifted Bobbie off the bed and carried her to the couch. Settling into a corner of the threadbare piece of furniture, she fed the baby her bottle, holding her close, and rocking in a gentle motion. The baby nursed, blue eyes locked on Iris's face. When half the milk was gone, Iris laid the bottle aside and shifted Bobbie to her shoulder for a burp. The baby cried in renewed frustration. "Oh, don't act like such a *baby*, baby. Neither of us will be happy this evening if you get a tummy ache because you ate too fast." Iris continued to rub Bobbie's small back. Once the baby burped, she lowered her back down and allowed her to have the rest of the warm milk.

With a full belly and a second dry diaper, the baby was content when Iris propped her up on cushions at the opposite end of the couch. Iris entertained her niece by reading aloud from the Bible she'd checked out from the library at the beginning of the week.

While they meandered from store to store looking for dresses and shoes for Easter, Callie put together what she'd learned from April with what she already knew.

Iris had transferred to the Garfield school system after the Christmas break. She was shy but a good student both in Sunday school and her sixth-grade classes. She kept herself neat and clean and didn't have many friends. Callie sighed over the short list of details. Not a lot of justification for the concern she continued to feel. The bad phone number could be due to any of a dozen simple mistakes. Even the babysitting remarks didn't trouble her too much. Iris seemed like a mature, levelheaded girl capable of watching a baby for a couple of hours. What about the fact that she never mentioned her family? *The girls are eleven. I could fill a page with topics higher in priority than family for that age group.*

The Sam thing bothered her a little. *A boyfriend maybe?* Callie discarded the thought. Iris was too young, she hoped, for that to be much of an issue. Brother? Not according to April. Stepfather? Uncle? Dog? She shook her head. There wasn't a single concrete reason to be concerned but nothing to relieve her worries either.

By three thirty in the afternoon they'd walked almost the entire length of the mall and back. April tried on dresses at several clothing stores, rejecting them all for one reason or another.

They entered the Old Navy store, and Callie looked at her watch. "Sweetheart, I don't mean to rush you, but our pedicure appointments are at five. We have to look for shoes once we find your dress,and we haven't been to the music store for that CD you wanted either."

"I know." April stopped in front of a mirror and motioned at her eleven-year-old figure and the curves that had begun to form over the winter. "Nothing looks right on me anymore. Everything is either too grown up or it makes me look like a baby." She gave a dismissive wave to her long-legged reflection. "Maybe we'll find something in here."

They walked back to a small rack of spring dresses. April selected a purple print dress with a matching bolero sweater. She held it in front of herself. "What do you think?"

Callie tilted her head and studied the combination of girl and dress with a careful eye. "That's a lovely color. It'll bring out the roses in your complexion. Go try it on, and see how you feel about it."

April slipped into a fitting room while Callie looked through the other dresses. She found a mint green shift with a crocheted cardigan. Her granddaughter could try this one next if the purple one didn't suit her.

When April came out of the dressing room, Callie could tell by her expression that they *finally* had a winner.

"Do you like it?" April asked.

"I love it, sweetheart. Turn around, let me see the back."

April executed a quick spin. The skirt fluttered prettily around her knees. The length was perfect, and the way the sweater tied flattered those new curves.

"Beautiful," Callie said.

"I think so, too." April cocked her head and pointed at the green dress in her grandmother's hand. "What did you find?"

"Alternate choice, but if you like the purple one I guess we won't need it." Callie moved to replace it on the rack, but April stopped her.

"Do they have one of those in a smaller size?"

"Hey, girlfriend, I promised you one dress, not two. Besides, a smaller size wouldn't fit you." Callie continued to the rack.

"How much is it?" April insisted.

She looked at her granddaughter and back to the dress in her hand. "Thirty dollars. Do you really want this one, too?"

April chewed on her lip. "Not for me, for Iris. I want her to have something pretty to wear for Easter. I think she only has the one dress, and I want to buy this one. Mom and I are going to bag up some of the things I've outgrown, but I don't think she gets a lot of new stuff."

Callie thought back to her encounters with Iris. April was right. She'd worn the same dress three Sundays in a row. *So much for my powers of observation.*

"What about the CD and the shoes you wanted?"

April took the dress from Callie's hand, holding it up to examine it closer. "We can find shoes at Payless, and the CD can wait another week or two." Her mind made up, she walked to the rack and shuffled through hangers for the correct size. "I think this will look just right on Iris."

Callie put an arm around her granddaughter's shoulders. "You're pretty amazing. Do you know that?"

April headed into the dressing room to change back into her shopping clothes. "It's genetic."

Iris pulled the bedroom door almost closed. Bobbie had finally fallen asleep. Hopefully she'd stay that way all night. The furniture in their apartment included a queen-sized bed. Bobbie slept in the middle, surrounded with pillows. She and Sam took the sides for themselves. Things got a little crowded sometimes, but they'd gotten used to it.

Sam had made some mistakes over the last year and a half, but they were still together. Nothing else mattered to either of them. Sometimes Iris missed her mother so much she knew her heart was physically breaking. She hadn't exaggerated when she'd told Sam how scared she got sometimes.

Iris closed her eyes and remembered the first night Sam had gone to work after moving to Garfield. No way could they afford a sitter for Bobbie during the day, while Sam went to school, and again at night. Sam needed to work if they were going to survive. But staying in a new apartment, in a strange town, with a four-week-old baby had been the scariest thing Iris had ever done.

Sam's eyes had been bright with fear that night as well. They'd stood on the threshold of the apartment, door open between them, for what seemed like hours. Iris asked questions, and her older sister tried to reinforce answers and instructions. Finally, Sam closed the door between them and left for work. Everything had worked out fine that night and every night since, but things were so much better once Sam got home from work each evening.

They'd started out eighteen months ago with a promise of honesty between them. Absolute trust existed between the two sisters. If Sam said things would get better as soon as she graduated, Iris believed it.

Iris looked around the home they'd made for themselves. Today had been a good day, and Sam would be home from work soon. Iris picked up the television remote and tried to find something to watch while she waited.

Callie had a new blue dress, new spring sandals, plenty of new charges to her credit card, but nothing new to add to her information quest.

Benton was spending the night in a motel close to his job and wouldn't be home until late tomorrow afternoon. They'd had a conversation earlier to exchange the particulars of their day. She'd related details of the shopping trip, promising to treat him to dinner at Pasta World sometime soon. Admittedly more a treat for her than him. She'd made no mention of Iris and the concerns that continued to plague her thoughts. Callie wasn't keeping it from him, exactly, but there was really nothing to share. Iris was one of her students. Curiosity was normal, but that curiosity didn't have to mean that she was getting involved in the life of another child. *Nope, not gonna happen.*

Callie booted up her computer, went online, and ordered two copies of the new CD April had wanted. One for herself and one to be delivered to April with a note that said, "You're an amazing young lady." It was a wonderful thing to see your children and grandchildren putting the needs of others in front of their wants. That thought brought her mind full circle to Iris. Callie rubbed her face in resignation as God continued to stir her heart.

"All right!" The muttered response sounded a little belligerent, even to her own ears. "I'll talk to Iris after class on Sunday."

CHAPTER FIVE

When Callie finally opened her eyes on Saturday morning, sunlight danced from every corner of her bedroom. Pillows fell from the bed as she rolled over and squinted at the digital clock on the nightstand. Eight thirty. *Callie, you're a lazy slug.*

She took a few moments to stretch like a cat. Joints popped, and her mind drifted to the things she needed and *wanted* to do today. Trips to the office, the bank, and the grocery store were necessary evils for her Saturday. Mowing would be a treat for her and a nice surprise for Benton if she could find the time. Callie sighed. None of those things would get done from the warmth of her bed.

She scooted out from under the covers and padded into the kitchen to pour her first cup of coffee. The house had cooled overnight. Benton's old T-shirt and her bare feet provided little protection from the chill. Bracing against a sudden shiver, she grabbed her Sunday school lesson book and her Bible, wrapped three chocolate cookies in a paper towel, and retreated to the warmth of her blankets.

Callie read the printed text of her lesson along with a passage of Scripture in Matthew chapter twenty-six. She intended to emphasize two things to her class tomorrow. She wanted to make sure that her kids got the connection between the strength Jesus had shown during his arrest compared to the relative weakness of his disciples. Jesus spent an hour in prayer and found the strength to follow the will of His Father. The disciples spent the hour sleeping and ended up scattering in fear as the mob led Jesus away.

The second was the healing of the servant's ear. Callie considered this one of those wake-up moments in the Bible. This guy had come out with an armed mob to arrest Jesus because he didn't believe Him to be the Son of God. In the confusion that followed, Peter cut off his ear. Instead of bleeding to death, the servant received healing by the very person he'd come to arrest. Callie smirked. *I wish I could have been a fly on his wall that night.*

Her study complete, she laid everything aside.

"Father, help me find the words you want my class to hear tomorrow. Give me something to make an impression on them, something that helps them realize they can find the same strength Jesus found. Not to die, but the strength to look for Your will every day." Callie stopped and realized she needed to take her own prayer to heart.

"I'm going to talk to Iris tomorrow." She swallowed hard against the panic those words caused. "Please calm my nerves and help her to open up to me a little bit."

With a final joint-popping stretch, Callie threw off the covers and went to spend thirty minutes on her treadmill in penance for her cookies in bed.

The bank was the last stop in a busy morning of catch-up chores, the price paid for taking a day off. Callie took her place in the commercial lane at the bank and waited for her turn at the window. Her fingers drummed on the steering wheel in time with the music pouring from the stereo speakers. She sang along as the two cars in front of her completed their business, and new cars stacked up behind her. Once she pulled forward she powered down her window and tossed the deposit bag into the drawer.

"Morning, Ms. Stillman." The teller levered the drawer back to her side of the glass. "You're running a little late this week, aren't you?"

"A little bit. I took a day off yesterday, so I'm playing catch up today." Callie glanced in her rearview mirror as another car pulled in line behind her. She did a double take. *Iris?* She twisted in her seat to get a better look at the child walking down the street pulling a wagon piled high with... Was that laundry? What is she doing?

Deposit forgotten, she pulled forward, leaving her banking business behind. They knew where to find her. Her left foot tapped impatiently on the floorboard. "*Come on,*" she muttered to the heavy Saturday traffic. Out on the street she looked for the best place to turn around. Doubling back, she cruised the street that ran behind the bank. If it had been Iris, she was long gone. This just got weirder and weirder.

Sam sat on the edge of the bed Saturday afternoon

and balanced the checkbook. She allowed herself an exhausted sigh of relief. They'd survived the week of double shifts without incident. Well, almost. She shuddered when she thought about the scene in the restaurant yesterday. She'd never forget the shock of finding April at one of her tables. She and April had never met, but Sam had taken the time to check the girl out. Iris needed friends, but they would be friends Sam approved. April could have gotten a glimpse of her on any number of occasions. Sam managed to calm the tremor that raced up her spine. There had been no recognition on April's face. *Too close.*

She refocused on the checkbook, happily confident they could make it through the month without dipping into their dwindling savings. As a reward, Sam wanted everyone to enjoy a special treat today.

It was a beautiful day outside. Sam planned to take Bobbie to the park and enjoy some quality time with her daughter. She had other ideas for Iris. The local dollar theater was playing a new animated movie. The matinee would be packed with kids taking advantage of their final day of spring break freedom. On Saturday afternoons, the theater offered special pricing. You got the movie, large drink, hotdog, or candy for five dollars during matinee show times. Sam pulled some of her tip money from the back pocket of the checkbook and went to find her sister.

Iris sat on the couch, folding the laundry she'd washed that morning. Sam took a seat beside her and held out two five dollar bills.

Iris looked up. "Do you need me to go back to town for something?"

"Yep, but not for me," Sam replied. "I want you to

take this money and go to the movies. I want you to have a good time with kids your own age. Stuff up on junk food, and forget about Bobbie and me for the afternoon. If you have money left when the movie is over, I want you to go get a milkshake or something. I don't want you back here until every penny is spent."

"We can afford this?"

"Don't worry about it. I wouldn't give it to you if we didn't have it to spare." Sam took Iris's chin and looked into her eyes. "I want you to go be a kid for a little while."

Iris looked at the money in Sam's hand. "I can do anything I want with it?"

"Yep."

"I need to make a phone call."

"To?"

"The movie special costs five dollars. I want to see if April can go with me."

"Make it quick," Sam said. "The last matinee starts at three o'clock."

Iris returned with her jacket after making her call, bouncing with excitement. "She's meeting me at the theater, and since she got her allowance today, she won't let me pay for hers. We're going to go to the Pizza Shack after the movie. Can you pick me up when we're done?"

"Call me when you're ready to come home." Sam took the cell phone from Iris and examined it. "Your battery is low. You need to remember to charge it tonight."

Iris stuffed the phone and the cash in a pocket, but hesitated for a second at the door. "Sam, are you sure?"

Sam smiled at Iris. "I'm sure, but if you aren't out of

this apartment in ten seconds, I'm gonna change my mind."

The door slammed behind Iris with eight seconds to spare.

"You eat it."

"I'm stuffed. You can have it."

Iris leaned back in the booth and rubbed her stomach. "*You're* stuffed? I had a hotdog and half of your popcorn. If I eat one more bite, I'll explode."

April laughed and picked up the lone piece of pepperoni pizza. "If you're sure."

The girls sat in a corner booth at the Pizza Shack. Music from the old-fashioned jukebox boomed around them. Friends from school stopped by to talk about their spring break activities. Iris smiled and nodded but resisted April's attempts to draw her into these conversations. What would I tell them? *Oh, you went to the lake and three parties? I watched my four-month-old niece all week. Not!* They called her a nerd behind her back. They could all think what they wanted as long as they never found out the truth.

April finished the last bite of pizza just as the sunlight began to fade. She glanced at her watch. "Wow, Mom's going to be here any minute to pick me up. Do you need a ride home?"

Iris pulled out her cell phone, "Nope, I'm good."

"You have your own cell phone?" Genuine envy colored April's voice. "Mom says I can't have one until I'm fourteen. She says if Randy had to wait, so do I. How'd you talk your mom into letting you have one?"

Iris slipped the phone back into her pocket. "It's just for emergencies." She hoped April wouldn't notice her evasion of the *mom* part of the question. No such luck.

April propped her elbow on the table and rested her chin on her fist. She stirred her soda with her free hand. "Iris, how come you never talk about your family? I've never been to your house." She motioned to the pocket that concealed the cell phone. "I don't even have a phone number for you. I never see who drops you off for church. I'm really not trying to be nosy, but you look so sad sometimes."

Iris stared out the window for a few seconds. A single tear slid down her cheek. This is what she'd been afraid of. She knew in her heart that she could trust April with anything. But how could her friend understand?

"April, you're my best friend. I've had so much fun today." Iris stopped, almost grateful when she saw fresh headlights turn into the drive. "It's your mom," she whispered. "You better go."

April hesitated. "Are you OK?"

"I'm fine." Iris studied the concern on April's face. "If you'll ask your questions in July, I promise I'll be able to answer them then."

"Deal," April said, sliding out of the booth. She gave Iris a quick hug and ran to meet her mother. She stopped at the door and doubled back. "I forgot to tell you. You need to be at my house a little early in the morning."

"I'll try. What's up?"

"It's a surprise," April answered. "Eight thirty instead of nine. OK?"

Iris nodded and sat back in the booth. She emptied the pitcher of soda into her cup and stared out the window as her friend drove away. The last bubbles of soda rattled in her straw before she called for her ride.

Sam rocked the baby, watching Iris get ready for church. Her little sister was growing up so fast, faster than she would have under normal circumstances. They'd survived so much grief and change over the last eighteen months. Their first major goal was in sight. She didn't know whether to relax or brace for the next obstacle that fate threw in their path.

Mom, I don't know if you'd be proud of what we've accomplished or not. I know I've made some huge *mistakes, but we're still together, and if we can just hold out for another few months, no one can ever take that away from us. I wish you were here. I miss you so much. I...*

"Sam."

"I'm sorry, Iris. What did you say?"

"I said I was ready to go. April wanted me to get there a little early this morning."

"Right. Here, take the baby. She's finally back to sleep. I wish I could figure out what's making her so fussy and restless."

Iris took Bobbie while Sam gathered bags, blankets, and a jacket. After a quick stop to wrap the baby securely against the morning chill, they hurried to the car parked by the curb.

Sam opened the back door, took Bobbie from Iris, and strapped her into the second-hand car seat. Iris and Sam buckled themselves in for the five-mile drive to April's house.

Sam inserted her key into the ignition. The car made a clicking noise for a few seconds before coughing to life.

Iris looked at Sam with raised brows. "It didn't do that last night."

"It comes and goes," Sam said. "I'm going to have someone look at it soon, but I hate to pull the money out of our savings if I don't have to."

"How much do we have left?"

"The rent took a big chunk out of it," Sam reminded her. "We've had a few expenses that my check didn't cover, but we still have about three thousand dollars tucked away. If we're careful, we won't have any problem making it through the summer just fine."

"You're doing a good job, Sam. I wish I was old enough to get a job and help out more."

"Hey, you stop that right now. I couldn't have made it without you these last few months. You know that, right?" Sam let Iris out of the car a couple of blocks from April's house. "Go have fun with your friend. I'm going back home to catch a nap while Bobbie's in the mood to sleep. Call me when you need me to pick you up. Do not walk home again today."

Iris walked the remaining two blocks to April's house. Neither of them wanted to answer any questions about who was dropping her off, about her parents, or about the baby in the backseat, especially after April's questions last night. Sometimes their lives almost felt like a spy movie. She ran up the steps and rang the bell. April's father opened the door.

"Hi, Mr. Caswell." Iris stepped inside. "April said she needed me to come early this morning. Am I too early?"

"Not at all." April's dad put an arm around Iris's

shoulders, steering her past the stairs and into the kitchen. "April told us you'd be here, so we saved you some breakfast. Have a seat. I'll get April while you eat."

Her Pop-Tart breakfast faded from memory at the site of bacon and eggs. "Wow, you guys shouldn't have gone to the trouble—"

Mr. Caswell cut her off. "We didn't. Those are Trent's leftovers. He played with it for a while then decided he didn't want it. We thought we'd offer his plate to you before we gave it to our dog."

Iris studied his face. Would her father have made corny jokes? *I wish I could remember his face.* She must have hesitated too long.

"That was a joke, Iris. Sit, eat. April will be down in a few minutes." He started back to the living area but paused at the foot of the stairs and yelled, "April, Iris is here."

Iris ate her breakfast, relaxing in the comfortable confusion of her best friend's family.

Heavy feet pounded on the stairs followed by Randy's voice. "Dad, which one of these ties goes best with this shirt? Mom said the green one. I think the black one. And whichever, I need you to help me tie it because April untied them both!"

April's mom must have followed him down. "Paul, will you please help your colorblind son? I don't know why he asks for my opinion if he isn't going to listen to it."

Iris smirked. *Boys.* Her smirk changed to a sad smile. April had such a normal family. A house, a dog, parents, and aggravating brothers. Did she know how good she had it?

April's mother stepped into the kitchen, two-year-old Trent balanced on her hip. "Hi, Iris. April said to come on up to her room when you're done with your breakfast." She reached inside the refrigerator and pulled out a sippy cup for Trent. The little boy pushed it away.

"I big."

"You're a very big boy, T, but you're dressed for church. If you want juice, you get a sippy cup. Take it or leave it"

While Trent pouted, Iris finished her breakfast and took her plate to the sink. "Thanks for breakfast, Ms. Caswell."

"Anytime, sweetheart. Why don't you run on up and see what April wants? We need to leave in about twenty minutes."

Iris climbed up the stairs to her friend's open doorway. She entered the room as April came out of her closet with an arm full of clothes.

"Hey, just in time." April tossed the clothes on the bed with a pile of others.

"You have the greatest family," Iris said, crossing the room to see what her friend was doing.

"Yeah, for the most part, but if you ever get desperate for a big brother, I'll rent Randy to you, dirt cheap. Boys can be such a pain sometimes. He's bent out of shape 'cause I untied his ties. It's been months since he wore either of them. He loaned them to me for my two big stuffed bears. But today," April continued, her voice dripping with scorn, "since there's some girl at church he wants to impress, he wanted them back. I gave them to him. It's not my fault that they came undone in the process." April stopped to take a breath, looking her friend up and down. "These should do," she muttered.

"Huh?" Iris asked.

April waved a hand at the small mountain of clothes on her bed. "All yours, girlfriend."

"Huh?" Iris repeated.

"The clothes, they're yours."

Iris stared at the bed without saying anything.

April snapped her fingers next to Iris's ear two or three times. "Earth to Iris. Are you with me?"

"April, I can't take your clothes."

"Oh, yes you can," April corrected her. "Mom says I've grown four inches over the winter. We need to go shopping for new spring and summer stuff. These clothes taking up valuable space in my closet are the only things standing between me and a massive shopping spree." She grabbed Iris by the hand. "You have to take them, every single piece." April's look was pleading. "*Please.*"

Iris picked up a few things from the top of the stack. She could see shirts, shorts, capris, jeans, and a dress or two. "Are you sure?"

"Absolutely, they all have to go. You're doing me the biggest favor in the world by getting this stuff out of my mom's sight."

"All right," Iris said with a huge smile. "But just for you." She was already sorting things into stacks. She picked up a pink skirt with a matching jacket, walked over to April's mirror, and held them up to study her reflection.

"There's a shirt that matches that outfit somewhere." April dug through the pile.. "Here it is." She shook it out triumphantly

Her mother's voice came up the stairs. "Ten minutes, girls."

"OK, Mom," April yelled back.

"Iris, there's one more thing, but you have to promise me that you'll just say yes."

Iris glanced around her friend's bedroom. "Do you have a bag of shoes I need to take, too?"

"No," April said. "I bought something for you when I went shopping with my grandma the other day. I really want you to have it, and my feelings are going to be super hurt if you say no."

"OK..."

April went back to her closet and pulled out a green dress. She brought it over and held it up to Iris with a satisfied smile. "I knew it would be perfect. Do you like it?"

Iris put down the pink outfit and took the dress from April. "Oh, April..." She held it back out to her friend. "You can't spend your money on me."

April crossed her arms, her foot tapping the floor. "Remember my fragile feelings."

Iris took a deep breath and hugged her friend. "Thank you."

"That's what I wanted to hear. Besides, I already tossed the receipt so you're sort of stuck with it." She motioned to the pink outfit spread out on the bed. "The green one is for Easter, but why don't you wear this one today? It'll be a good chance to see if I guessed right about your size."

Iris started to get undressed. "That's a great idea."

April reached for the door. "You get changed. I'll go get a bag for all this stuff so we can take it to the van."

With the room to herself for a few minutes, Iris

changed into her *new* outfit. She stood in front of the mirror and smoothed the wrinkles from the skirt. The fit was perfect, and she had little doubt that everything else would fit just as well. She looked at the new green dress. Her single-word comment echoed in the empty room. "Wow."

CHAPTER SIX

For the first time in her life, Callie had no desire to go to church. Her nerves were in an uproar, her hands shook, and if she thought about talking to Iris, tears of anxiety came to her eyes. Making breakfast might have put off the confrontation she planned to have with Iris this morning, but it hastened one she was equally unprepared to have with Benton.

Callie broke eggs into the pan and looked at the clock. She grimaced at the time. Sunday school started in an hour and a half, and she was still in her robe. Stirring the eggs with one hand she sipped coffee with the other. *Is it too late to call in sick?*

She couldn't remember the last class she'd missed on short notice. Benton could go on ahead. She could bolster her courage with some prayer, and catch up with Iris after church. "That could work."

"What?" Benton stood beside her, pouring his own cup of coffee. *Where did he come from?*

Callie took a deep breath. "Nothing, just...thinking

out loud." She scooped eggs onto a plate, added half a dozen slices of bacon, and handed it to Benton.

He eyed the plate. "Thanks, I think. Did you wreck the car while I was gone?"

"Did I what?"

Benton waved the plate. "Breakfast on Sunday. I figure you're buttering me up for something." He looked back at the counter. "Where's yours?"

Callie reached up, placed her hands on his shoulders, and turned him toward the table. "Just for you. My stomach's a little queasy this morning. I—"

"Better get dressed then. We don't want to be late." Benton settled at the table in front of a glass of his favorite juice.

"I'm not sure I feel like going this morning." Callie reached around her husband with the coffee he'd left on the counter. When she set the cup down next to the juice, the steaming liquid sloshed onto her fingers. "Ouch!" She grabbed for napkins, and the full sleeve of her robe brushed the glass of juice and sent it crashing to the floor.

Callie stood in her kitchen, fingers red from the hot liquid, the hem of her yellow robe and her slippers stained with deep purple smears, while the grape juice that Benton favored spread in a puddle around her feet. She pulled her stinging fingers into her mouth and gave into the nervous tears she'd kept at bay all morning.

Benton ignored the mess and nudged out a second chair. "Sit."

"What?"

"Sit," he repeated. "I've watched you dance around something all week. At first I thought it was Sawyer's birthday that had you strung out. We both know it's

SHARON SROCK

more than that. You need to tell me what's going on."

Callie ignored the chair and her husband's *request* that she sit in it. She closed her eyes. "There's a little girl in my class."

"Iris."

"How did you...?"

"I'm not nearly as oblivious as you think I am."

"I think I need to help her." She watched closely, trying to gauge his response.

Benton sat back in his chair, crossed his arms, and stared up at his wife. "Please sit down."

Callie looked down at the purple stains on her robe. "I'm a mess."

"Is it gonna get worse if you sit?"

She stepped out of her ruined slippers, leaving them in the wine-colored puddle, and took a seat.

"Spill it. Why do you want to get yourself involved in another... situation?"

"It's not about what I want," Callie corrected. "It's about what she needs. There's something about her that worries me. I can't even explain it. I just know she needs help."

Callie reached across the table and picked up his cooling coffee. The bitter liquid made her shudder. He drank his black and strong. "Knowing she needs help but not knowing what she needs is driving me crazy."

She sat under Benton's scrutiny for several seconds.

"Let me make this easier for you," he said. "No."

"No, what?"

"Just no. I forbid it."

Callie scrambled to her feet, her voice barely a whisper. "You forbid it?"

Benton stood as well, pulling Callie into his arms,

grape juice, and all. He held her close for a few seconds before he answered. "I can't stand by and let your heart lead you down this path a second time." His arm's tightened as she tried to pull back. "Hold on." When he continued, his voice remained calm and reasonable. "I'm not saying you did anything wrong six months ago. I'm just saying that, good intentions aside, if you had stayed out of Janette's business, we both would have been better off."

She shoved against him, unaccustomed anger at his rational tone replacing the fear her plans had caused. "You're my husband not my father. You don't *forbid* me anything."

"Listen to me." Benton let her go and rested his hands on her shoulders. "I love you too much to think about you going through that again. The first round almost killed you. So, if it takes forbidding you to do this..." He squeezed her shoulders as he trailed off.

Callie watched her husband struggle for words.

"You don't get it, do you?" he finally said. "You blame yourself for what happened, and I blame me. I'm your husband. It's my job to protect you. It's what a man does, and I failed." He shrugged and ran his hands down her arms until he could link his hands with hers. "Don't do this to us again."

Benton's admission pricked Callie's conscience and drained her temper. "I'm so sorry. I had no idea you felt that way." She rested her head against his chest. "Don't you see, Benton? This isn't what I want either."

She took a step back and looked into his eyes, striving to match his rational tone. "I'm not trying to be stubborn and I'm not trying to be defiant. I don't want to be involved in this anymore than you want me to be involved. But there's a problem here, and God's telling me to, at least, look into it."

Benton opened his mouth and Callie laid a finger across his lips. "And look into it is all I'm planning to do. Will you at least pray about it before you say no? I can't imagine God leading me to do something without speaking to you as well. If God doesn't put us on the same page soon, we'll talk more about what needs to happen."

Benton closed his eyes and leaned his forehead against hers. "I'll pray about it, but I'm not happy about it."

Callie levered up and brushed a kiss across his lips. "That makes two of us." She turned to go.

"Where are you going?"

"I'm going to get ready for church. Clean up the juice, will you? I'll be ready in thirty minutes."

Callie walked around the room while her class worked on their lesson papers. She stopped here and there to offer help in answering some of the more difficult questions, but her mind and her eyes were on Iris.

The first bell rang. "OK, everyone, our time is almost gone. Let's get everything put away and take some prayer requests before we leave."

Kayle's hand shot up. "My baby sister was sick all night."

Chase went next. "We need to pray for my dad. He called, and he gets to come home next month."

"Oh Chase, that's wonderful news. Anyone else?"

Joshua raised his hand. "My dad needs a new job."

Callie waited a few more moments. "Is that it?" she

asked. "All right, let's all bow our heads. Jesus, thank You for a wonderful class today. We ask for Your presence with each of us this week. Help us apply what we learned today to our lives. Touch Kayle's little sister, and help Josh's father find a better job. Father, we are so grateful to You for keeping Your hand over Chase's dad while he's been deployed. Please bring him home safely next month. Amen."

The final bell rang and the stampede began. Callie called out to her granddaughter before she and Iris could get out the door.

"April, you and Iris hold up for a minute, please."

The girls stopped and waited for the classroom to clear.

Callie closed the door behind the rest of the kids. *Jesus, give me direction.* She sat back down at her desk. "Iris, I wanted you to know how happy we are to have you in our class. Are you enjoying yourself?"

Iris met Callie's eyes briefly before she dropped her gaze to the floor. "Yes ma'am."

"I'm glad." Callie allowed the silence to stretch for a few seconds. "I tried to call your parents. I wanted to tell them how much we've enjoyed having you in our class and invite them to come with you sometime. The number you wrote on your visitor's card doesn't work."

"I'm sorry, our home phone got disconnected. I guess I forgot."

"That's fine. I knew there had to be a simple explanation. Is there a better number I can use?"

"They have cell phones," April volunteered.

Iris's eyes cut quickly to April, but she maintained her silence. Callie frowned. *What is this child so afraid of?* She took a deep breath. "Could I have that number?"

"I'm not allowed to give it to anyone."

"You know, I can understand that. Those cell phone minutes can be expensive." Callie tapped Iris's visitor card on her desk. "I'd really like to visit with your mom and dad, Iris. If you could tell me a good time, I wouldn't mind coming to your house. I like to get acquainted with the parents of my students."

Iris fidgeted under Callie's gaze. "We haven't lived here very long. I can't remember the address. Besides, they both work really weird hours. I don't think it's a good idea for you to come to the house. I'll tell them what you said, and I'll be sure to invite them to church for you." She finished in a rush. "May we go to the gym now?"

The catch in Iris's voice made Callie frown. She stood and moved around her desk, putting an arm around the child's shoulders. The second she did, Iris began to cry in earnest.

"April, could you excuse us for a few seconds?"

Callie saw April hesitate for a second before she left the room. Her granddaughter finally stepped out and inched the door closed a centimeter at a time, eyes peeking around the edge until the opening disappeared.

"Iris, honey, I'm sorry. I didn't mean to upset you. Can you tell me what's wrong?"

Iris shook her head, maintaining her silence.

Callie stepped away and retrieved a blank index card from the stack on her desk. She wrote her cell phone number on the card and handed it to Iris, tilting the child's face up to make solid eye contact. "Iris, this is my cell phone number. I have it with me all the time. I want you to promise me you'll keep it. I want you to call me if you ever need anything."

Iris swiped at her face with a pink sleeve. "OK."

Callie handed her a tissue. "I mean that. I want you to call me, day or night, if you need something. Even if you just want to talk. All right?"

"OK."

"Promise?"

Iris looked at the card and slipped it into her pocket. "I promise," she answered before escaping through the door.

Callie watched her go. She looked up to the ceiling and spread her hands wide. "That went well," she told God with a shake of her head. "Now what?"

Iris climbed into the van with April and her family. Mr. Caswell looked at her in the rearview mirror.

"Where to, kiddo?"

"Hum?" Iris asked, confused.

"I saw that big bag of stuff you and April loaded into the van. You can't take off walking like you usually do. Point us in the right direction. We'll take you on home."

Iris's heart sank. *Oh no.* She'd been so excited about all the clothes, she hadn't considered how to get them home. *Think fast.* "Oh, I don't want to be a pain. You can take me back to your house. I can call my ride."

"Don't be silly, sweetheart." April's mother objected. "The bag's already in the van, there's no sense in hauling it back and forth. Just tell us where to go. We'll drop you off."

Iris didn't see any way out of the situation. *Sam'll kill me.* That thought echoed in her mind as she gave April's father directions to the small row of tiny apartments. Iris could feel April staring at her as they pulled to the curb. The van had barely stopped before she jumped out. "Thanks. Let me grab that stuff real quick." She went to the back of the van and pulled out the large trash bag full of clothes. "I'll see you at school tomorrow, April." She took a step away from the vehicle, waving a goodbye, leaving nothing for the Caswells to do except wave in return as they drove off.

Iris waited until the van disappeared around the corner before letting herself into their apartment.

Sam looked up from the couch where she sat, feeding the baby. "How'd you get home? I told you not to walk again."

Iris took a deep breath. A difficult morning was about to turn into a difficult afternoon. "April's parents dropped me off."

"Iris—"

"I know," she interrupted, "but I didn't know what to do." She explained about the bag of clothes and how April's parents had insisted on driving her home. "I didn't think about it when we loaded everything in the van." Iris kicked at the bag in frustration. "I should have told April no, but that would've caused questions, too."

"Iris, you know why we have to stay under everyone's radar for a little while longer. I've got a real bad feeling about this."

"Well I don't. OK? I knew you'd be upset, and I'm sorry, but you need to chill out. I covered over all their questions. I let them bring me to the curb, but they didn't see me come in. The only thing anyone knows now that they didn't know this morning is what building we live in." Iris threw up her hands in frustration. "They don't even know there's a *we*. They think I live here with very busy parents."

Iris heard Sam's deep breath, saw her stern expression. She closed her eyes. *Here it comes.*

"Iris, I told you that I thought it was a fine idea for you to get out more and go to church with your friend. Now, I think I made a mistake. We're too close. I won't risk everything we've worked for. I don't want you to go back to church with April, at least until after July."

"You can't do that!"

"I don't have a choice, Iris. And temper tantrums aren't going to change my mind."

Iris found she had nothing else to say. Feeling betrayed and defeated, she stomped into their bedroom and slammed the door with a loud bang. She threw herself across the foot of the bed for a good cry.

CHAPTER SEVEN

San Diego, Dallas, Houston, Tulsa, St. Louis, Denver, and now Springfield. Seven cities in ten days, and almost two weeks to go. Days spent in bookstores autographing copies of his second book. Nights spent at local missions and homeless shelters sharing his testimony with the hopeless, trying to restore hope.

Steve leaned his head against the headrest of his rental car. For once he was grateful that most bookstores didn't open until ten. He had a couple of hours to look for some closure in his own life.

Sunshine glinted through the windshield, bouncing prisms of reflected light around the interior of his car. The old neighborhood looked the same, even after eighteen years. A new generation of college students crowded narrow sidewalks, living in the same apartments, eating at the same restaurants. Life moved on. It was time for him to do likewise.

Steve looked at the key in his hand. He had permission to be at the restaurant before hours, but he lacked resolve. His heart was heavy with a mixture of conflicting emotions, but he didn't have all morning. Best get on with it. The key slipped into the lock, the door swung open, and he switched on the lights. Steve felt himself fall into a black hole of memories. The shrill beeping of the alarm brought him back to the present. He dug in his pocket for the slip of paper that contained the code and fumbled to disarm it while his eyes swept the room.

Obtaining permission to come here before business hours had been surprisingly easy. Celebrity status, even minor, had its perks. Steve had called the owner as soon as he'd seen the tour itinerary. Mac remembered him, had been following his writing career. Homeboy makes good, yada, yada, yada...

Steve had found a key to the front door and the alarm code waiting at the front desk of his hotel when he checked in last night. All Mac wanted in return was a signed copy of his new book. Steve laid the requested book, a very small price, on the ancient counter and stepped into the center of the room. The layout and décor hadn't changed. A table in the far corner drew his attention like a magnet. He closed his eyes for a second and allowed the heavy scents of garlic and pizza sauce to transport him back to another time. His breath caught at the old sensations. When he opened his eyes, he saw her there. She sat, head bent over a textbook. Long, honey-colored hair hiding her features until she looked up and met his eyes for the first time. His heart slammed against his ribcage at the memory.

Steve shook his head. She wasn't here. She wasn't in class. She wasn't at work. She wasn't at home taking care of their babies. She was dead. He'd come here, to this place of memory, to say goodbye. They'd met here. They'd studied and dated here. He'd proposed to her at that table.

Steve walked to the table, pulled out a chair, and sat. He cradled his head on his folded arms. "Lee Anne, I'm so sorry..." For Steve, minutes seemed like hours before he forced his head up in the shadowed room. He traced names carved into the old wooden table, his smile bittersweet when his fingers found the ones he'd left so many years ago.

"Hi, sweetheart." He paused, but the ghosts were silent. "There's so much I need to say to you." Since it seemed strange to sit at the table while he spoke to the walls, he got up to pace. "I was an idiot," he admitted. The image in his mind nodded and crossed her arms. A smile tugged at Steve's lips in spite of himself. "Yeah. I remember that look. I can see you agree with me."

He faced the table and shrugged. "You told me to stay away 'til I was clean. Well, here I am. I'm clean, have been for five years. I can't take any credit for that. God did it, and He's the one that keeps me strong. I never meant for things to turn out like they did. I have no excuses for what I threw away. I hope you can hear me when I say I never stopped loving you." His voice broke, forcing him to silence for a few seconds.

"We had it all, babe. I'd have given anything to come back home to you and the kids. I guess it wasn't meant to be." Groping for words, he raised his hands in surrender. "If only I could have made you listen once I finally found you." He took a mental step back. The path to *what if* could drive you crazy.

Steve went to the drink dispenser and fixed himself a large soda. He took several long gulps, trying to gather his thoughts. There had been so much on his heart when he came through the doors. In reality, coming here accomplished nothing.

Lee Anne was gone. She couldn't hear him much less forgive him. Only two people mattered to him right now. He closed his eyes. *Jesus, please grant me the miracle I'm looking for.*

Steve tucked two dollars inside the cover of his book to pay for his soda before crossing to the door.

He re-armed the alarm and turned for one final look. *Just an empty room.* He switched off the lights and closed the door, deeding the restaurant back to the ghosts.

As much as Callie enjoyed the tale of Jael, she found it difficult to keep her attention focused on the story during Monday night's Bible study. She caught Karla's studious gaze on her several times and silently vowed to try harder.

The women around her chattered and laughed as they read the account of God's instructions to the prophetess Deborah. Old guy jokes received new life when they came to the part where Barak wimped out and told Deborah he'd only lead the battle against Sisera if she went with him. The prophetess agreed to go but promised Barak that he'd get no credit for Sisera's defeat.

They finished with Sisera running from the battle and taking refuge in Jael's tent. The room filled with female cheers as God used a lowly housewife to dispatch the enemy in one of the sneakiest and most gruesome tales in the Bible. The women drifted out of Karla's house in twos and threes, uplifted by their study, stuffed with Snickers cheesecake, and ready to face the rest of the week.

At the end of the evening, two pieces of cheesecake and four friends remained. Callie and the others decided to share the leftover desserts over a fresh pot of coffee.

Laughter and conversation bounced around the table, four good friends sharing bits and pieces of their day.

Pam Lake finished her last bite. "Karla, this is heavenly."

Terri Hayes swiped her finger through the chocolate and caramel that remained on her plate. She allowed her head to fall back and rolled her blue eyes in obvious delight. "You have to write this recipe down for me before we go home. I think Gary would love it."

Pam pushed her empty plate aside. She raked red-tipped nails through her dark brown hair. "I need the recipe, too."

"Already taken care of," Karla assured them. "There are copies for everyone on the printer in the den."

"I'll make it for Gary on Friday night," Terri told her friends. "It'll be a nice way to end our dinner date."

"Time out." Callie leaned forward, grateful for some harmless girl talk to focus on. She propped her chin on her fist. "This is what, three or four weekends in a row you've had dinner with Gary? Is there something you'd like to share with the rest of us?"

Terri blushed and fluffed her shaggy brown haircut. At twenty-nine, she was the youngest of the four friends, and the only one still single. "I know we haven't been going out for very long, but I really like him," she confessed. "He's going out of town for a while on Saturday morning, but he promised he'll come to church with me just as soon as he gets back. I can't wait for you guys to meet him."

"All right!" Karla said. "Looks like Terri finally caught a live one."

Pam threw a balled up napkin at Karla. "Hush."

She turned narrowed brown eyes on Terri. "Details, Terri. Where did you meet him? What do you know about him?"

Terri smiled at Pam. "Stop with the third degree already. You'll like him. He works with computers."

"Computer nerds can be jerks, too, especially the male of the species." Pam frowned, always wary where men were concerned. "Promise me you'll be careful until you know more about him."

Karla rolled her eyes at her cautious friend. "Pam, leave the girl alone. She's old enough to take care of herself."

"I just want her to keep her guard up until she gets to know him better," Pam answered. "Men can be vile and sneaky creatures."

Callie shook her head. Two years after a painful divorce, Pam still carried the scars. Her husband had cheated on her, and no man was above suspicion. *She should get over it, already.* Oh really? Callie gave herself a mental shake. She had no right to talk about anyone dragging around old baggage.

The four friends sipped their coffee in companionable silence for several moments. Callie's mind drifted back to the problem of Iris and her disastrous fact-finding attempt yesterday. A day of contemplation and prayer had yielded no further direction. Maybe Benton was right."

"Callie." A hand waved in front of her eyes, drawing her attention back to the here and now.

"I'm sorry, Karla. What?"

Karla frowned at her friend. "I asked if you and April had fun on your shopping trip on Friday."

"Oh, we really did," Callie answered. "We bought dresses and got our toes done. We had a wonderful Italian lunch."

"Yes, but did you get the information you went after?"

Callie toyed with her cup. "No, and after yesterday, I'm more convinced than ever that there's something desperately wrong in that child's life."

Pam stacked their empty dessert plates in the middle of the table. "Wait a minute. Sounds like you have a better story than Terri. What's going on?"

"Not much of a story I'm afraid," Callie admitted. "April's been bringing one of her little girlfriends to Sunday school. There's something...off... about the way she acts."

"Is she disrupting your class?" Terri asked.

"Just the opposite. She's attentive and polite. She appears healthy and well cared for." At home in Karla's kitchen, Callie took the stack of plates to the sink for a quick rinse before loading them into the dishwasher. When she finished she turned around and leaned back against the counter. "You know what kids are like at that age. 'Quiet' is rarely a descriptive term." Callie crossed her arms. "Shy certainly applies, but I just feel like there's more going on than *shy*. God and I have been arguing for several days over how to handle it."

"Why would you argue with God?" Pam asked.

"He wants me to investigate. I want him to find

someone else."

Terri and Pam looked at Karla. Karla waved them ahead. "Give it your best shot. I had this conversation with her a week ago."

"If God's telling you to help this little girl, you can't sit by and do nothing." Terri said.

Callie felt her expression inch toward stubborn. "In case you've forgotten, I don't have a real good track record with *helping* children. I don't need another child on my conscience."

Terri gave her friend a sympathetic look. "Callie, what happened six months ago wasn't your fault. It was tragic, and I know it broke your heart—"

"Broke my heart?" Callie paced. "It broke a whole lot more than that. I still see that little boy's face every time I close my eyes. For weeks, every time I heard a baby cry, I imagined Sawyer's screams of pain as he was beaten to death. It's made me suspicious of every innocent bump and bruise I see on the kids at church or in the office. I thought I was finally getting over it until Iris came into my class. I can't...*won't*...go there again." Callie saw objections forming on three faces, and she raised her hand.

"I haven't told God no, completely. I'm willing to meet Him halfway."

Pam's brows drew together in a frown. "Halfway?"

"I'm digging and I'm praying. If I find out what the problem is, I'll turn it over to someone qualified to deal with it."

"If God's sending you in that direction, you are the person qualified to deal with it," Pam insisted.

Callie's answer was a single word. "No."

"Callie—"

"No."

Pam sighed. "Let's back up. What happened yesterday?"

"I realized last weekend that Iris hadn't completed her visitor card, and the information she did give me was wrong." Callie walked back to the table. "I wanted to get some contact information, so I held her up after class and asked for an address and a correct phone number. I told her I wanted a chance to visit with her parents, let them know how much we've enjoyed having Iris in our class, and invite them to church."

"Perfectly reasonable," Karla inserted.

"Well, I thought so." Callie sat back down. "First she made up all these wild excuses why she couldn't tell me anything, and then she started crying."

"Poor baby," Terri muttered, "and poor you."

"Yeah, poor me," Callie agreed. "I sent April out of the room. I hoped Iris might open up a bit if we were alone. By then she was *really* crying."

"Did you get anything out of her?" Pam asked.

"Not a thing. Once she calmed down, I gave her my cell phone number and told her to call me anytime she needed to talk or anything else." Callie paused to take a deep breath and rubbed her forehead. "That's part of my *halfway* strategy. I'm not ignoring what I feel, and I'm not turning my back on the situation, but I have a noninterference promise that I don't plan to break if I can avoid it." She started to get up, but Terri caught her hand and pulled her back down.

"Callie, I've never understood how you could blame yourself for what happened. You didn't do anything wrong."

Callie caught nods of agreement from Karla and

Pam at Terri's statement.

Terri continued. "I know that the thought of getting involved again scares you to death. But you aren't alone. I'll..."

Pam and Karla obviously saw where Terri was going because they reached out to join hands with Callie as well. "We'll," they whispered.

Terri grinned and nodded her head. "*We'll* stand with you on this. Ecclesiastes tells us that *a threefold cord is not quickly broken*. Well, we make four. Surely a force to be reckoned with. We won't let you fight, or fall, alone."

Callie bowed her head over their linked hands, touched by their support, but not surprised. "I just don't know what to do. Benton's against my involvement. My nerves are shot."

"Well, let's ask God." Terri led them in prayer. "Father, first of all, we give You thanks for time with our friends tonight and an opportunity to study Your word. Lord, please go with us through the rest of our week. Grant Callie the wisdom she needs to understand Iris's problem and the courage to go where You're taking her. We're so thankful that You have the answer to every situation. Let there be comfort, peace, and direction. We ask these things in Your name. Amen."

"Amen," they all repeated.

Callie squeezed Terri's hand. "Thanks."

Callie lay in bed next to Benton, wide-awake. A glance at the red numbers of the clock forced an inward groan. *Two in the morning. Good grief.* Maybe if she got up and got a drink or something, *maybe some hot tea,* she could go back to sleep.

The unexpected ringing of her cell phone made her jump. Callie grabbed it from the bedside table before it could ring a second time, slid out of bed, and hurried into the next room. She closed the door behind her before she spoke. "Hello."

"Miss Callie?"

"Yes," she answered automatically, "Who...Iris?"

"Oh, Miss Callie, I'm so sorry, but I didn't know who else to call." Callie could hear the panic in Iris's voice. She could also hear a baby crying, non-stop in the background.

"Iris, what's wrong?"

"I don't know," she wailed. "Bobbie's been crying for almost two hours. Nothing I can do will make her stop. I've fed her, I've changed her, and I've rocked her. Sam should've been home by now, and she isn't answering her cell phone." Iris stopped. "I'm gonna be in so much trouble, but I didn't know who else to call," she repeated. "I'm really scared."

"Iris, I need you to take a deep breath and calm down. I can hear the baby. Is she hurt, bleeding, running a fever?"

Callie heard a couple of ragged breaths through the phone. When Iris answered, she sounded a little calmer. "She feels a little warm but not very. I just can't get her to quit crying."

Benton came out of the bedroom. "What's up?"

Callie shook her head at him. "Iris, how old is the baby?"

"Four months."

"Oh, good grief," Callie muttered, pacing the hall, phone to her ear. She shuddered when she felt the foundation under her self-preservation instincts begin to crack. *God, give me strength.*

"Iris, give me your address." She went to her desk to make a note. "OK, I know where that is. Listen to me. It's going to take me about thirty minutes to get over there. Just keep rocking the baby. I'll be there as soon as I can." Callie handed the phone to Benton and went back to their bedroom to grab some clothes.

"Who was that?"

"Iris. She's in trouble. I'm going over there."

"At two in the morning? This is the little girl in your class, right? The one you know nothing about?"

She pulled a shirt over her head, answer muffled. "That's the one."

"Callie, I'm not comfortable with you going over there in the middle of the night."

Callie looked at her husband. "Benton, we've been through this. I know you're trying to protect me, and I love you for it. But there's an eleven-year-old child, alone, with a four-month-old baby at two in the morning. Do you really think I can just sit here and tell her that I'll see her in the morning?"

"No, of course not, but you can help without putting yourself in a dangerous situation. Call the police. Call social services. There's absolutely no reason for you to go running over there at this time of the night."

"You know, that's exactly what I'd made up my mind to do, but I can't do that before I know what's going on. I promised God I'd do this much before I handed the problem over to someone else. I've been looking for some answers. The fact that Iris called here shows me I've managed to establish some trust with her. I can't call the police and risk destroying that before I know what the situation is."

"But—"

She raised a hand to cut off his next objection, "Sweetheart, you can't say a thing to me I haven't already told myself. I shouldn't go, but I have to go." Callie retrieved her phone. "But I'm not going alone."

"Who are you calling?"

"Karla and the girls. They volunteered to help."

Benton plucked the phone out of her hand and held it out of her reach. "I don't think so."

Callie looked at him with raised eyebrows.

"It's two in the morning." Benton rubbed his face in obvious frustration. "You have no idea what you might be walking into."

She rested her hands on his cheeks. "I'm really not trying to override your good judgment. If I could think of another way to do this, I would. I've been praying for God to put this on someone else's shoulders. For reasons I don't understand, it looks like His answer is no. I was awake before the phone rang. God's trying to tell me something, and I have to be in a position to listen."

"I'll take you."

"Benton—"

"You have an eleven-year-old child, alone, with a four-month-old baby at two in the morning. Do you want to argue with me or get dressed?"

CHAPTER EIGHT

The headlights of their car swept the front of the ancient, single-level apartment building. Rundown, shabby. Those were the kinder descriptions that came to Callie's mind. Once the sun came up, the immediate landscape would be washed in shades of beige and gray. Dingy brick, patchy spots of green in the dirt that were more weeds than grass. A depressing place. She squinted, trying to read the numbers above the doors. A dim porch light illuminated the door to the last unit in the strip of four apartments. The two to the left were dark, windows bare, obviously vacant. The farthest one away was dark, but a pick-up truck was parked in front. Callie added *dismal* to her silent assessment.

Her husband turned off the motor. "This is your game. What's the next step?"

Callie studied him in the dark. Benton's face was a mask of disapproval. She jerked her head towards the dark building. "There's a frightened child on the other side of that door. You need to take the scowl off your face or sit here and wait for me."

Benton grabbed her hand before she could open the door. "What's gotten into you?"

Callie sat back in her seat and stared out the windshield. "I don't even know, Benton. I'm here because I have no choice. I—"

"There's always a choice."

"You know what I mean. We're human, we have a will and choices, but God has a plan. And sometimes He uses us to get that plan accomplished." She faced her husband in the dark. "When Sawyer died, I think I lost a little bit of my faith. My fault, not God's. I didn't pray about that situation. I was sure I had the facts. We saw what that got me."

"Callie—"

Callie shook her head. "I don't understand what I'm supposed to do for Iris or why. I just have to trust that this is part of the plan." She reached for the door. "Stay or come. That's *your* choice." She swung open the car door and started up the broken pavement of the walk. The frustrated crying of a baby filtered out of the apartment long before she reached it.

She knocked loudly. "Iris, honey, it's Miss Callie."

The door swung open. Iris stood there, both hands full of an angry, squirming infant. Both faces equally streaked with tears. The added look of defeat in Iris's eyes broke Callie's heart.

"Miss Callie..." The child's eyes cut to Benton. Callie saw Iris's arms tighten protectively around the baby. "Who's he?"

Callie glanced over her shoulder to find Benton looming behind her. His expression wasn't quite joyful, but the frown was gone.

She stepped in and wrapped both girls in a firm hug. "This is my husband, Benton. He's here to help me help you." She took the baby from Iris and sat down on the old sofa, motioning for Iris to join her. The baby continued to cry, exhausted, rubbing her little eyes with angry fists.

Callie held the baby's face to her cheek to feel for fever, agreeing with Iris's assessment. The baby felt a little warm but not hot. The old-fashioned cloth diaper was dry, pens securely fastened. She bundled the squalling baby to her chest and rocked. "OK, tell me what's been happening this evening."

Iris sat on the edge of the couch, elbows propped on her knees, face buried in her hands. "She woke up a little around midnight. I thought she wanted a bottle, even though I'd given her milk and some cereal before I put her to bed. I fixed another bottle and changed her diaper. She didn't want the milk, and she's been crying almost the whole time since she woke up." Iris straightened and brushed a hand over the baby's head. "I've kept her dry. I've tried the bottle a few more times, but she just spits it out." A fat tear slid down her face. "I'm so scared there's something's really wrong. I'm sorry I called you, but I can't find Sam. I didn't know what else to do."

"You did exactly right." Callie balanced the baby across her knees and pressed gently on the little tummy, relieved when the baby showed no signs of further distress. The baby grabbed Callie's hand and drew it to her tiny mouth. Callie grew thoughtful as her knuckles were gummed. "How old did you say she is?"

"Almost five months."

Callie nodded and looked at Benton who had been

standing quietly and helplessly to one side. "Sweetheart there's a first aid kit in the trunk of the car. Get it for me?"

"Be right back," Benton answered.

"I'll bet she's been fussy for a few days, hasn't she?"

Iris nodded. "A lot."

"Let's try something while we wait on Benton to come back." She shifted the baby to her shoulder. "Can you get me a couple of clean nipples and a cup of ice?"

"Ice?"

"Trust me. I think I know how to fix her problem."

Iris went to collect the requested items.

Benton came back in with the first aid kit, finally taking a seat next to his wife. "What are you thinking?"

Callie shifted the baby into his arms.

"I don't—" he objected.

She patted his knee. "Just hold the baby while I take her temperature." Callie dug the ear probe thermometer out of the box, held it steady in the baby's ear, and watched the digital readout. "One hundred point four."

Iris returned to the sofa with the items that Callie had requested. Callie put the nipples in the cup of ice and took Bobbie from Benton. "Come here, baby." She settled the infant in the crook of her arm, put a cold nipple on her finger, and rubbed it over the baby's gums. The silence was almost immediate.

Iris sighed in relief. Callie smiled, and Benton looked on with raised eyebrows. He cocked his head to the side. "Teething? That's what this is about?" Benton asked.

"Yep," Callie answered.

"At less than five months?"

Callie nodded. "I know it's been a while, and you're probably thinking of the grandkids who all got a later start. Think about when Sophie was a baby."

"Oh yeah." Benton nodded. "Her temp spiked, and we ended up spending a couple of hours in the ER with a screaming baby."

Callie shuddered at the memory. "Not something I want to re-live and not necessary in this case, thank God."

Iris came to stand next to the adults, reaching out to pat Bobbie's back while Callie continued to rub the ice-cold nipples over tiny irritated gums.

"What's wrong with her?"

"Nothing serious. She's starting to get some teeth, and that makes her mouth hurt. The cold makes it feel better. I've got some ointment in that box that'll fix her right up."

"Really?" Iris asked. "Thanks."

Callie looked down at the baby. Her little eyes were beginning to droop. "Bless her heart. She's worn out." She fumbled in the first aid kit for the teething gel, left over from Trent's first year, and applied some to the baby's gums. Bobbie fussed a little at the bitter taste, but relaxed once the medicine began to do its job.

Iris took the baby from Callie with practiced ease. She snuggled back into the corner of an old armchair, rocking gently until Bobbie was asleep. While the adults looked on, Iris carried her into the bedroom and laid her down in the center of the bed. After arranging some pillows into a secure nest, she came back into the living area.

"Thank you," she began in a small voice. "I'm glad you were able to figure out what was wrong. She's never acted like that before." Iris moved to the front door and rested her hand on the knob. "We'll be OK now 'til Sam gets home."

Callie looked at her husband, then back to Iris. "You know we can't walk out of here and leave you and the baby alone, right?"

Iris took a deep breath, fresh tears welling up in her eyes. "You really need to."

Callie led Iris back to the couch. She sat and took both of the child's hands into hers. She looked into Iris's frightened face. "Iris, I need you to tell me what's going on."

Iris looked at her feet and shook her head no.

"Sweetheart, I can't help you if you won't talk to me."

The child looked up at Callie. She bit her lip and tried one more time. "Please, you need to go before Sam gets home. I can't answer any of your questions. I got into so much trouble after church on Sunday. I promised Sam I wouldn't do or say anything else that could cause problems for us."

Sam again. *Who is Sam?* Callie studied Iris intently, a more important question heavy on her heart. "Iris, I need to ask you something. Just answer yes or no. *Please say no.* Is someone hurting you, physically?"

The child's earnest gaze never wavered from Callie's face. "No."

Callie released a sigh of relief. "I didn't think so, but I needed to know for sure." She glanced at her husband. "Iris, I appreciate the fact that you won't break your word to answer my questions. I hope you can understand that there are a whole lot of important reasons why I can't leave and pretend like nothing happened." Callie pulled Iris into a hug. "I promise you, we're not going to do anything to hurt you."

Iris jerked herself out of Callie's arms. "You don't understand! Sam's worked so hard since..." She stopped herself, pulling completely away from Callie. The child crumpled back down on the couch, her breathing short and shallow through parted lips. She fixed her gaze on the far wall, tears streaming down her face. "I've ruined everything," she whispered.

Five in the morning. Callie drummed her fingers on the table, her frustration building with every moment that failed to produce a responsible adult to care for these children. She amended her thoughts, deleting the *responsible*. No responsible adult would leave babies to care for themselves all night.

Iris had fallen into a fitful sleep on the couch. Her gentle breathing occasionally broken by a whimper or whispered groan.

Callie had nosed around the apartment while she waited. Only further confused by the combination of things she found and the things she didn't. She looked up as Benton came back through the front door. He offered her a large cup of convenience store coffee, his reason for leaving in the first place, and sat with his at the small table.

"Still nothing?"

"No, and I'm more confused than ever." She waved a hand around the quiet apartment. "There's no baby bed, no formula, and they're using cloth diapers. But take a look at this place. Everything's clean and neat. There's food in the cabinets. Not a wide variety, but no one's going hungry. Someone's making an effort to take care of the necessities."

"Times are hard right now, Callie. Maybe her mom and dad both work. Maybe it's a single parent situation—"

Callie narrowed her eyes at her husband. "What would you do if you found out that Sophie and Paul left April alone all night to care for Trent?"

Benton slumped in his chair. "Someone would die."

"I rest my case. There's *no* excuse for this." Callie shook her head, her eyes going back to the child sleeping on the couch. "I can't figure it out. I didn't feel like she was being abused." Iris thrashed around on the sofa, muttering in her sleep. "But she's so obviously terrified of something, I had to ask."

Callie reached across the table and took Benton's hand. "Thanks for coming with me. You have to know that this is not where I ever wanted to be again. I'm scared spitless. I keep saying no. God keeps dragging me deeper. I never knew God could *hogtie* me into a place with so few—" She cut herself off when the front door swung open to reveal a teenager standing in the early half-light. Long, dark hair pulled back into a ponytail, hands clenched into fists, tight faded jeans molded to narrow hips. The new arrival glared at the adults seated around the table, glanced at Iris asleep on the couch, and hurried to the bedroom, disappearing inside without a word.

"The mysterious Sam?" Benton asked.

Callie shook her head, just as puzzled as her husband.

The newcomer came back out, closed the bedroom door, and leaned against it. "You're trespassing. I need you to leave, right now."

Callie stood up and examined the room's newest occupant closely. Recognition stirred. "Samantha, right?"

"How do you—"

"Pasta World," Callie reminded her. "No wonder you were so nervous that afternoon. You heard me discussing Iris with my granddaughter."

Sam lost a little of her color but none of her fight. She pushed away from the door. "I haven't got a clue what you're talking about. I need you to leave."

Callie strove for a neutral tone. "No questions about who we are or why we're here? We're just supposed to go?"

Sam greeted Callie's question with an unpleasant snort. "I'm pretty sure you're from that church Iris has been attending. I have to admit I'm surprised to see you here so soon, but I knew when Iris came home on Sunday that it was just a matter of time before someone came to meddle in our lives. I'd hoped for some time to put a plan in place, but..." With a resigned sigh Samantha waved her *but* away. "Look, I've had a vicious night—"

Benton interrupted. "Hold up there, kiddo. Let me tell you about the night I've just had. I was in my bed, meddling in nobody's business, when my wife's phone rang at two o'clock. It was Iris, nearly hysterical because she was here, *alone,* with a baby who'd been crying for two solid hours. She couldn't reach you, so she called Callie for help. We've been here for several hours now, and your *vicious night* aside... I think we deserve an explanation before you simply order us to leave."

Samantha gave a sharp cry of dismay and rushed

SHARON SROCK

back into the bedroom. Callie watched through the open door as a sleeping Bobbie received a thorough examination. Sam re-joined them, her hostile attitude replaced with concern. "She feels a little warm, but seems all right otherwise. What was wrong with her?"

Callie laid a hand on Benton's arm and stepped between her husband and Sam. "She's teething."

Benton shrugged off Callie's hand. "The baby's fine, but the point remains she could have been ill or hurt. Now, we need to talk to your parents so we can make sure something like this doesn't happen again."

Sam's eyes shifted between husband and wife, clearly not sure who she should address. "Look, I appreciate your help tonight. I'm sorry if I was rude when I came in. My car broke down on my way home from work. It stranded me in the middle of that five-mile stretch of highway where there's no cell service and no houses. Someone finally stopped to help and went to call a tow truck for me. The man from the garage offered to take a look at my car if I wanted to wait. I know it took longer than it should have, but I've been trying to call Iris since three o'clock to let her know not to worry."

The teenager edged to the front door as her explanation continued. "I'm sure when Iris wakes up we'll find a dead battery on her phone. I reminded her to charge it the other day, but she forgets." Sam stopped to take a breath. "I'm really sorry for your trouble, but I'm sure you can see that this whole thing's just been a huge misunderstanding." Sam stood by the door, obviously waiting for the couple to give up and leave. "My parents work really strange hours." Sam offered when they refused to move. "There's no need

108

for you to stay. I'll let them know what happened just as soon as they get home. I promise. I'll have one of them call you."

"Wrong answer," Benton said without hesitation. He sat back down at the table and crossed his arms. "We'll wait."

The expression on Sam's face transformed from appeasement to frustration. The teenager's response was loud and angry. "What's wrong with you people?"

Sam's angry question woke Iris. The eleven-year-old jumped off the couch and grabbed Sam in a fierce hug. "Oh Sam, you're home! I was so scared. Bobbie was crying and crying..." Her voice trailed off as the tension in the room mounted. She took a step back. "I'm sorry," she whispered to Sam. "I've messed it all up. I know I shouldn't have called them, but I didn't know what to do." Fresh tears trailed down her small face. "I promise I didn't tell them anything. Please don't be mad at me."

Samantha pulled Iris back into a hug. "This isn't your fault, sweetheart," Sam assured her, looking from one adult to the other. "You did everything you knew to do." She issued a final plea. "Can't you see that you're upsetting everyone? Will you please just go? I've told you that I'll have our parents call you. We have class and work later..." Sam's voice dwindled away as Bobbie woke up, adding her hungry cries to the rapidly growing confusion in the small apartment.

Benton shook his head. "You're right. We probably should go." He stood and pulled his phone from a holder clipped to his belt. "Since we can't leave you three kids here alone, I'll just call the police. They can send someone over here until your parents come home.

Maybe they can get some sort of an explanation out of you."

At the mention of the police, Iris began to cry hysterically. Sam held onto her, reaching out to stop Benton. "Please, you can't do that," Sam pleaded while trying to comfort Iris.

From Callie's view point it was impossible to tell which one of the girls was holding the other up. She saw sheer exhaustion on Samantha's face, terror on Iris's, and grim determination on Benton's. The situation had come down to a stalemate, and Callie intended to end it before it went any further.

"Everyone just needs to stop." Three sets of eyes looked her way. "This isn't getting us anywhere. We're all tired, and our tempers are frayed." She stared at Sam for several seconds. Some of the discrepancies in the apartment began to make sense. Nothing she'd seen had indicated any adult presence. "There are no parents coming home from work, are there?" She nodded at Sam's stricken look.

Conflicting thoughts flew through Callie's mind. She couldn't leave these three children alone in this apartment, could she? *But they've obviously been living this way for a long time.* Stay here for the rest of the night? *Benton would strangle me.* Insist that Iris and the baby go home with her? *Look at the way Iris and Sam are clinging to each other.* Iris obviously looked to the older girl as a mother figure. Separating them might be worse than leaving them here. Her heart pounded in her chest. If she made the wrong choice and another child paid the price for her mistakes...

She felt tears threaten and pushed them away ruthlessly. Sometimes there were no right answers.

Sometimes you had to make up the rules as you went along. *Jesus, give me wisdom.* Callie felt her shoulders square with her silent prayer. Just the baby, she decided as she studied the older girl. *Samantha was old enough to drive and hold a job. She must be seventeen or better.* Iris would be fine here with her.

She focused on the girls. "We've all had a long, disturbing night. There's a lot to explain, but I think we'll deal better with each other after everyone's had some sleep." When no one objected, Callie continued, her focus on Samantha. "You don't know me, and you've no reason to trust me, but Iris knows me, she knows my daughter and granddaughter. Let me take the baby home with me—"

"Callie—" Benton began to object.

"Shh," she told her husband before addressing the two girls again. "I promise you, I'll take good care of her—"

Samantha began to sputter. "How could you..."

Callie looked at Iris. "Do *you* trust me?"

Iris nodded as she swiped at her streaming eyes with her sleeve. "She'll take good care of her, Sam."

Callie pressed her small advantage. "You two get some rest. Call me when you wake up later. I'll give you directions to the house. We'll sit down and see if we can wade through some of those explanations. Then we can figure out what needs to happen next."

The baby continued to cry for attention. Sam collected her from the other room. "We have work and school—"

"So do we," Callie reminded her, "but I've decided to take a day off. I think you two can do the same."

Something imperceptible passed between the sisters.

111

Callie interpreted it as a look of defeat. It almost crushed her. *What are these kids running from?* She didn't let her sympathy detour her. "That's the only way to get us out of here without calling someone else into this," Callie told them, locking eyes with the stubborn older girl. "Take it or leave it." Callie held Samantha's glare with an unblinking stare of her own. Lyrics from an old song filtered through her mind. Something about if looks could kill I'd be lying on the floor. *Soften her heart, Father. You've pulled me into this, now work it out in her heart, too.*

Sam finally drew an unsteady breath and surrendered the stare down. She lowered her eyes and crossed to the stove to prepare a fresh bottle for the baby "Iris, would you please go put a bag together for Bobbie?"

Once Iris left the room, Sam faced Callie. "I need you to understand that these two kids are the most important things in my life. I need your word that you'll give us a chance to explain what's going on before you bring anyone else into this."

"I'm not here to hurt you or cause you any trouble," Callie responded. "I only want to help if I can."

Iris returned with the bag, and they all walked to the front door. Callie held her arms out for the baby.

Samantha's eyes filled with tears as she handed Bobbie over.

"We'll see you later this afternoon," Sam promised.

"I'll be waiting for you." Callie bent to give Iris a quick hug. "Get some sleep, hon. Everything's going to be OK." She looked up at the teenager with what she hoped was an expression of reassurance and placed a hand on the slender, young shoulder. "Try not to worry, Sam. We'll get this all worked out."

The door closed between them, drowning out Samantha's response.

CHAPTER NINE

Callie hurried down the walk, Benton on her heels. She felt a hand on her shoulder and stopped, turning to face her angry husband.

"Have you lost your mind?"

"I hope not." The short statement sounded uncertain, even to her. "I know we need to talk, but I'd rather not have this conversation on the sidewalk." She turned back to the car. Benton opened the door for her, more she was sure, out of habit than design, and held it while she arranged herself, the baby, and the bottle in the seat.

"Callie, we don't have a car seat. What if we get stopped between here and home?"

"I suggest you drive carefully," Callie replied. "We need to stop by the office on the way."

Benton shook his head and shut the door with a little more force than necessary. He rounded the car and climbed into his own seat. "What were you thinking?"

"I don't really know—"

"You practically kidnapped that baby. What if we get stopped?" he repeated.

"*Kidnapped?*"

"Well…" he stopped, obviously searching for a word. "Well, blackmailed then. I don't even know who you are anymore. Can I please have my wife back?"

Callie narrowed her eyes at him from across the seat and waited for him to continue.

"You know, the sensible woman who respected my wishes and opinions. The one I've been married to for thirty-five years."

"Start the car. Drive to the office."

"Why the office?"

"For diapers and formula. We have more free samples than we can give away. I intend to load up the trunk. As for what I was thinking—did you take a good look at Samantha's face? That poor child is dead on her feet, and Iris didn't look much better. It will do them good to get an uninterrupted rest." She paused to cuddle the baby closer. "Having this little angel at the house for the day insures that Iris and Sam keep our afternoon appointment. I can't explain it, but I saw something in Samantha's eyes that warned me not to give them any options."

Benton drove for a few miles in silence. When he parked in front of Callie's office, he turned to face his wife. "Just for the record, I'm still against this whole thing."

Callie nodded and climbed out of the car with the sleeping baby, her response a confused mutter. "I'm right there with you."

Callie got Benton off to work and called the office to request the day off. The baby slept. Callie couldn't. She blamed it on the coffee.

Everything was under control for the moment. But every time Callie closed her eyes, she saw Samantha's expression when the door closed between them. There had been such resignation and defeat on that young face. Such an overwhelming sadness. Callie's mind reeled in turmoil over the direction her life was taking, but her heart broke for this young woman she knew nothing about.

Giving up on the idea of a nap, she decided to do something proactive about part of the situation. She picked up the phone and called her daughter at work.

Sophie answered on the second ring.

"Sweetheart, do you still have Trent's baby bed in your garage?"

"Sure do. I'm currently subscribing to the Erma Bombeck theory of birth control."

"The what?"

"You know, the theory that says as long as you keep the maternity clothes, baby bed, et cetera, you won't ever need them again. It's only after you throw them out that you should worry."

"Gotcha," Callie said. "Is there provision in this theory allowing you to loan an item?"

"I think I'm fully protected unless I completely dispose of the item. Why?"

"I can't say just yet, but, if it's all right, I might need to send your father around to pick it up in a day or two. I'll need to borrow some crib sheets and blankets as well, if you can lay your hands on them."

"Not a problem, I know right where everything is."

"Great. I'll let you get back to work."

"OK," Sophie responded, "but if this is your way of telling me I'm about to be a big sister..."

Callie laughed, disconnected that call, and prepared to make three more. She couldn't forget Terri's words from Monday night. *A threefold cord is not quickly broken.*

Benton had made his objections clear, and she understood his reluctance to get involved. But she needed help, and her friends had offered to stand with her on this.

Karla would likely be at home. She knew she could find Terri at the day care center she owned and operated, and Pam would be doing her usual computer guru thing at her husband's law office. Callie needed their take on all of this. Three calls and three explanations later, they all agreed to meet at Terri's house later that afternoon after Callie had a chance to talk to the girls. Feeling like she'd put some legs to her prayers, and with the caffeine seeping out of her system, Callie settled back on the couch to get a nap before the baby woke up.

The doorbell rang at two o'clock that afternoon. Callie opened the door, with Bobbie in her arms, to find Terri standing on the porch with a trash bag in each hand. The bags hit the floor at the sight of the baby.

"Ohh." Terri held out her hands. "Gimmee."

Callie laughed as she passed the baby into her friend's arms. "You could come in first." She picked up the bags that Terri had dropped. "What have you got here?"

"Baby clothes," Terri answered. "Lots and lots of

little girl clothes. I called Lisa Sisko after we talked."

"Terri…"

"Don't worry. I didn't give her any details. I just told her that I knew someone who could use them if she had anything she wanted to get rid of.

Karla and Pam arrived. Terri paused while they admired the baby. "Anyway, she bagged up Alex's old stuff for your new little princess. Bobbie, right?"

Callie nodded. "Right, but she's not mine." She faced her three friends. "What are you guys doing here? I thought we were meeting at Terri's later."

"I wanted to bring the clothes by early so you could send them home with the girls."

"OK," Callie said. "I arranged for diapers, formula, and a crib, but I didn't think about clothes. Calling Lisa was a great idea."

"That's not all." Terri's enthusiasm was palpable. She pulled an envelope out of her bag and passed it to Callie.

She held it in her hand and stared at her young friend. "What—"

"Just open it."

Callie opened the envelope and pulled out a single sheet of paper. Her eyes misted over when she read it. "Ah, Terri. A certificate for unlimited day care." She looked at the other two women. "And you two are here because…?"

Karla and Pam were grinning like Cheshire cats. "We have groceries," Pam answered.

"What?" Callie asked.

"For the girls," Pam clarified. "After you called, Karla and I went grocery shopping. We've got lots of goodies to stock those cupboards, extra heavy on the cookies."

"Plus," Karla added, "I called a friend of mine whose husband does some part-time mechanic work. He said he'd be happy to look at Samantha's car if necessary and only charge her for the parts."

Callie fought back tears. "You guys are the best."

Terri shook her head. "Nope, we're just stingy. We don't want you hogging this blessing all to yourself."

The tears disappeared in the face of Terri's lighthearted comeback.

"We told you, you won't stand alone in this." Terri reminded her friend.

"Thanks, guys." Callie realized that they were still standing in the foyer. She motioned to her living room. "You want to come in for a few minutes?"

Karla shook her head. "No, we aren't staying. You have a busy afternoon ahead. Just show us where you want to put everything 'til you can send it home with the girls."

Thirty minutes later Callie stood in the doorway of her spare bedroom. Cases of formula, boxes of diapers, stacks of folded baby clothes, and sacks of groceries covered every square inch of open space. A large ice chest sat in the corner holding what her refrigerator couldn't. She looked at the baby, asleep in her arms, and didn't know whether to laugh at the generosity of her friends or cry over God's provision.

When Callie opened the door at four, the tears of relief she saw in Samantha's eyes brought a lump of emotion to her throat. She handed over the baby. "Here you go. Safe and sound. Just like I promised." Sam's grasp on the baby reminded Callie of a drowning man with an inner tube.

"Thank you. I hope she wasn't too much trouble."

"She's an angel." Callie motioned for the older girl to precede her down the hall, gave Iris a quick hug, and led her guests to the dining room.

The room was sunny in yellow and white. French doors covered in gauzy panels opened into the lush backyard of their acreage. The table and china hutch were both a light oak. Callie had always found it one of the more homey rooms in their house. She hoped that Iris and Samantha could find some peace in the comfort of its walls.

"Have a seat. I made a snack so we could eat while we visited."

An uncomfortable silence settled around the table as Callie served sandwiches, chips, and sodas to her guests. She placed a plate of brownies in the center of the table for any comfort-food moments that might arise as the afternoon wore on. When neither of the girls made a move to touch their food, she helped herself to a sandwich, hoping the girls would follow her lead.

"Samantha, I don't want you to feel pressured, but I do have a lot of questions."

Samantha sat with her head lowered, a cheek resting on Bobbie's thick black curls. She released a heavy sigh and focused her attention on Callie.

"Iris and I had a conversation this afternoon. She's certain we can trust you. I'm not sure of that. Trust doesn't come easily for me anymore." Sam stopped and stared at Callie intently. "It's a long story. We're risking everything we have by sharing it."

"Iris has good instincts," Callie said. She left it at

that. Samantha would trust or she wouldn't. Callie couldn't force her hand either way.

Sam closed her eyes. Her voice a bare whisper when she began to speak. "Our mother died in a car accident a year and a half ago." Samantha stopped briefly when her voice broke. "Maybe I should start further back than that," she whispered and began again. "Our mom was an orphan. According to her, she was one of those kids who just never found the right family to fit into. She spent her childhood bouncing around from foster home to foster home. No one ever mistreated her, but she saw a lot of kids that weren't so lucky. She developed a real distrust of what she called *the system.*

"Mom was really smart." Sam wiped a stray tear from her face. "Not a genius kind of smart, but despite moving from school to school, she always made great grades. She graduated high school with a full scholarship and went off to college."

Sam rocked the baby in the stiff wooden chair as Iris took up the story of their family. "Mom met our father in her second year of school. She was sort of drifting, you know, trying to decide what she wanted to be when she grew up..."

Callie smiled as she listened. Iris was so articulate. If you closed your eyes, you'd swear you were listening to an adult. Now she understood where the trait had come from.

"... and she fell in love with a boy she met at the neighborhood pizza joint. They were both only twenty years old, but it was love at first sight."

Awww, there's the little girl, Callie thought to herself.

"He convinced her to marry him. From that point on she was determined to make the sort of home she'd always dreamed of having."

The baby began to fuss. "It's her nap time," Sam said.

Callie stood and came around to take the baby. "Let me hold her for a while."

Sam nodded and handed the baby to Callie. Sam toyed with the food in front of her, the sandwich on her plate more shredded than consumed.

"Did your mom finish school?" Callie prompted.

Sam took a drink, cleared her throat, and picked up where Iris had stopped. "Not 'til later. She got pregnant with me right away. Our parents decided on a more traditional family arrangement. My father knew Mom had never had those things. He wanted her to have a chance to be a full-time mother while he supported his family."

"That must have been great for you."

"Wonderful." Sam's smile was wistful. "I can remember my mom being at all the school things when I was small. Birthday parties she planned, homemade cookies in the cookie jar after school. We had dinner at the kitchen table every night..." Sam's voice dwindled. "Anyway, it was great. Iris came along right after I turned six. From my perspective, everything was perfect, until one night Dad didn't come home from work."

Callie leaned forward in her chair. "Excuse me?"

"I was seven, so my memory of that time is a little fuzzy." Sam pushed away her plate. "Iris doesn't remember our father at all. But, yeah. He left for work one day, and we never saw him again. I can remember some yelling behind closed doors prior to that but no real details. One day he was there. The next he wasn't."

"Your mother never told you what happened?"

"Not 'til much later," Sam answered. "At first, I guess she thought he might come back. Later I could tell it was a painful subject, so I didn't ask." She shrugged. "About three years ago I begged her to tell me the truth. Mom told me that our father got messed up on drugs. One afternoon while she was cleaning she found a stash of pills behind some books in his study. Mom told him to make a choice: the drugs or his family. He chose the drugs. Mom kicked him out, let him know that he didn't need to come back until he cleaned up his act. We haven't seen him since."

"What's your father's name?"

"Steve, Steve Evans. Our parents were Steve and Lee Anne Evans. Anyway," Sam continued, "Dad left. Mom went back to school, finished her business degree, and went to work at a bank. She was coming home from work one afternoon. A drunk driver hit her head-on in the rain." Sam closed her eyes and took a couple of deep breaths. "They said Mom died instantly."

Iris started to cry. Callie handed the baby back to Sam and held her arms open. Iris came around and snuggled into Callie's lap. "You poor babies."

"I miss her so much." Iris picked up the napkin next to Callie's plate, swiped at her eyes and blew her nose.

"Of course you do, sweetheart." Callie looked at Sam in amazement. "You've been living on your own all this time?"

Sam nodded, clearly fighting back her own tears. "Most of it."

"Most of it?" Callie asked

Sam sighed and darted a glance at Iris.

"All of it, just like we agreed," Iris said.

Sam shook her head in obvious disagreement, but continued. "Mom had a plan in place for us. She worried about our being alone if something happened to her. Our father's parents both died when I was a couple of years old. He was an only child. Mom was an orphan. We didn't have any family to turn to. She designated one of her friends as guardian for us."

Sam looked up at the ceiling of Callie's dining room, lips pressed into a thin line at the memory. "The afternoon it happened, cops came to our house to tell us Mom was dead." Her voice broke, and she paused for a few seconds. "They wouldn't leave 'til someone came to stay with us. We called Mom's best friend from the bank. Helen packed us up and moved us into her spare bedroom. She was great through the funeral and everything that needed to be done afterward."

"Then how did you guys end up on your own?"

"Helen was great at first. She and Mom were part of the same team at the bank. Right before Mom died, Helen got married." Samantha bowed her head, and Callie saw the hot blush that stained her cheeks. "Let's just say that her new husband, Richard, was anxious to be more than a father to the both of us."

Callie gasped indignantly. "Did you report him?"

Sam shook her head. "I tried to talk to Helen. That's when she stopped being *great*. She didn't believe me, and I couldn't risk going to the authorities. If we couldn't stay with Helen, they might place us in separate homes. We ran."

Callie looked from one girl to the other. This was the saddest thing she'd ever heard. "Your foster parents never tried to find you?"

"At first we were worried they might try, especially Richard. But why would they? He didn't get the chance to do anything, and we can't prove that he tried. We've never had any sign that they were looking." Sam traced drops of water down the side of her glass. "I'm sure they were just relieved to be rid of us."

Callie's eye's tracked from one child to the next. "How have you two survived?" She was having problems processing everything she was hearing. "You couldn't have gotten a job, at sixteen, that would have provided for the both of you."

Sam continued with visible effort. "Mom had a life insurance policy with Iris and me listed as her beneficiaries. College money. Not a fortune, but enough to see us both through for a few years, if we were careful.

"Someone to watch out for us wasn't Mom's only concern. She wanted us to be able to take care of ourselves if we ever needed to. When I turned fifteen, Mom added my name to her bank account. She said she was so frustrated by what she saw at work every day. People drowning in debt. Young adults who didn't have a clue about how to balance a checkbook much less live within their resources. She was teaching me to manage money by giving me access to our family budget and bills. After she died, I watched that account every day. Just as soon as the settlement arrived, Iris and I skipped school, closed the account, bought a car, and got out of Dodge."

She met Callie's gaze, her blue eyes bright with tears and full of pleading. "All we had left was each other. I wasn't going to let either of us get lost in the same *system* that bounced our mother all over the place."

Samantha sipped her drink and Iris continued.

"We moved to a new town where no one knew us. Sam found a small furnished apartment and signed us up in a new school. We were worried at first, but the lady in the school office hardly even looked at our birth certificates. I don't think she had lots of problems with kids trying to get into school" Iris laughed at her own joke then shrugged at the simplicity of their plan. "We're good students. Sam says we get that from our mother. We found out if you have enough money to get by, make good grades, and stay out of trouble, no one much cares what you do." Iris went to stand next to her sister. She placed an arm around Sam's shoulders. "Then Sam met Louis."

"Louis?" Callie asked.

"Bobbie's father." Sam got up to pace the dining room.

"When I found our apartment, I paid the rent for an entire year. The landlord didn't ask any questions. All he could see was the eight thousand dollars cash in my hand. I opened three bank accounts with the rest. Twelve thousand dollars went into a checking account for living expenses, the rest we split equally into two savings accounts. I was a little ahead in my studies, so I only needed to be in class four hours a day. I found a part-time job to supplement our expense account. We were careful with our spending. We were making it work."

Callie saw Iris nod in agreement.

"A couple of months after we moved into our apartment, the car started to act up. I took it to a local garage. Louis worked there as one of the mechanics. He was twenty-three and so sweet and handsome. He talked to me, made me feel special. When he asked me to dinner and a movie, I was flattered." Sam stopped pacing and looked at Callie.

"I was so lonely, a little scared of the future, and a whole bunch naïve. I made the mistake of confiding in Louis. I believed all the wonderful promises he made to me in return. Like I said, I was naïve. I was four months along before it even occurred to me to take a pregnancy test.

"When I told Louis about the baby, he seemed so excited. He promised to take care of us. We'd be a family." Sam snuggled the baby closer. "I believed him, right up to the day I found out he'd emptied our checking account and my savings account."

Callie shook her head. *I saw that coming.* "How much did he take?"

"Thirty thousand dollars."

"Oh, my."

"I know I was stupid," Sam said defensively, "but I won't call Bobbie a mistake, not ever. The second they put her in my arms I knew I wouldn't have changed a single thing."

"Oh, honey, of course not. So you had the baby..."

"Yeah, I had the baby," Sam continued, "but even before she got here, I knew we couldn't stay where we were. There were going to be too many questions once she was born.

"We spent a few weekends, before I had the baby, driving around to other towns to check out some new places. The first time we came to Garfield, it felt like we'd come home. We went back and started packing. I wanted to be ready to move just as soon as the baby was born.

"I couldn't work, go to school, *and* be pregnant, so we lived on the money in Iris's account. I was afraid to apply for any sort of medical aid. I paid the doctor bills as we went and left the hospital bills behind when we moved. After Bobbie was born, we loaded everything in the car and moved here. I rented our apartment, paid for it in advance like we'd done before. We settled in right after Christmas. I'd hoped we could live under everyone's radar until July." Sam was silent, her story told.

Callie struggled to keep everything straight. "What happens in July?"

"She'll be eighteen," Iris answered. "We won't have to worry about anyone taking me away from her."

Sam smiled at her little sister. "That and I'll graduate high school at the end of May. I can get a full-time job and support us a little better."

"How are you doing that now?" Callie asked. "Supporting yourselves."

"We don't have a car payment since we paid cash for it. We paid the rent for a year in advance, and all the utilities are included in the lease. We're very careful about what we spend." Sam answered. "I have school 'til noon each day, and then I have my job at Pasta World in the evenings. Iris watches Bobbie while I'm at work, so I only have to pay for day care when I'm at school. Between my job and using what's left in the bank for emergencies, we're making it. I have a really great boss. He knows about Bobbie but not about Iris. He thinks my family kicked me out when I got pregnant. He's promised me a full-time hostess position just as soon as school's out."

"She got a scholarship—"

"Not now, Iris!" Sam scolded.

"But it's important," Iris protested. "We agreed to tell her everything."

"Hold up," Callie said, leaning forward on the table. "A scholarship?"

Sam took a deep breath, "Iris," she said crossly before explaining. "I have a full, four-year scholarship to the state university, just like our mom. I've decided to turn it down. I can't do the mommy, work, and school thing much longer. I just want to graduate and go to work full time." Sam stopped talking and looked at her little sister. "That was the plan, until today." Sam picked up her glass and drank deeply. "There you have it. The whole truth."

"Do you swear to tell the truth, the whole truth, and nothing but the truth?"

Callie jerked in her seat at the memory. Breath caught in her chest and her throat threatened to close. Her hand shook when she reached for her own glass. She forced herself to drink deeply and breathe slowly. *I refuse to let the past dictate my future.* "Not this time," she whispered.

Sam looked at Callie, her brows drawn together in a puzzled frown. "What?"

"Nothing." Callie sat back and studied the girls from across the table. "I don't even have words," she said after several minutes. "I think you're both pretty amazing." Her gaze settled on Sam. "I know adults who couldn't do what you've done. But it's time to let me help you."

Sam sat back with crossed arms and narrowed eyes. "Help how?"

Callie came around and put an arm across Sam's

shoulders. "Sweetheart, I don't blame you for being distrustful. I would be too in your situation." She took the baby from Sam. "Follow us. Bobbie and I have a surprise for you."

Callie lead the way down the hall and threw open the door to her spare bedroom. "Ta-da..."

Sam and Iris looked inside. "What?"

"I have some clothes that should just about fit Bobbie," Callie explained. "There's disposable diapers and baby formula. I have access to more when you need it. I'll be bringing a crib by your apartment tomorrow evening so Bobbie has a safe place of her own to sleep. These groceries are for you, too. And if your car needs any more work, you let me know."

Callie picked up Terri's envelope. "And one last thing. Are you familiar with Tiny Tike Day Care?"

Sam nodded. "I checked it out when we moved here. I couldn't afford it."

"Well I know the owner, and as of now it's free to a select few."

Sam stood speechless for a few moments. "You did all of this for us? You aren't going to turn us in?"

Callie looked at Sam. "After all you've done to keep your family in one piece?" She shook her head. "You were honest with me, so I'll be honest with you. I had some help with all of this. Three good friends that want to help me help you. I'm not going to lie to you. There are some issues we'll need to deal with over the next few days. But I think for now, we all just need some time to think about what happens next. It's going to take some effort on everyone's part, but I'm going to help you make that July goal, if you'll work with me. All I ask," Callie added, "is a promise from you that you won't run again. That you'll let me bear this burden with you for as long as it takes. In return, I'll promise to work with you to keep your situation away from the authorities."

Sam was yet to be totally convinced. "Your friends?"

Callie waved her hand around the room. "They just want to help."

Sam's eyes filled with fresh tears. "Why would you do this for us?"

Callie took Samantha's hand in hers. "Sweetheart, the Bible tells us that we fulfill the love of Christ when we help bear one another's burdens. I care about what happens to you, and so does He. Let me prove that to you."

Sam reached for Bobbie and pulled Iris to her side. She held onto her small family, tears streaming down her face. A muffled "thank you" was the only response she could manage.

CHAPTER TEN

Callie approached the four-way stop three blocks from Terri's house and sailed right through it to the sound of blaring car horns. She cringed in the seat. *I'm glad You're paying attention, Father.* Her heart was heavy, but she needed to get her head in the game or she wouldn't be around to help anyone. The last twenty-four hours had left her emotionally and physically exhausted. A two AM wakeup call, followed by the events of the morning, topped off by an afternoon listening to Sam's story, had left her feeling overwhelmed. Callie shuddered at what those children had endured. For Samantha to shoulder such a responsibility at the age of sixteen and make it work as well as she had, was nothing short of a miracle.

Benton had arrived home from work, grumpy and short tempered from lack of sleep. Callie knew her uncharacteristic defiance only added fuel to the fire. There wasn't anything she could do about that. She turned into Terri's drive. God had her by the scruff of the neck and didn't appear to be in a hurry to let her go. *Jesus, please, if You're leading me to do this, speak to Benton, too.*

She knocked on Terri's front door and entered without waiting for a response. Pam and Karla's cars were already parked out front, and once Callie stepped into the hall, she could hear everyone's voices from the kitchen.

Callie accepted the glass of iced tea that Terri handed to her and took a seat at the table. She studied the expectant faces of her friends. How could she even begin to relate the story she'd been told?

She took a sip of her drink. "We're gonna need tissues."

Terri raised her eyebrows in response.

"If there's a dry eye at this table when I'm done," Callie said as she tapped the plaid placemat in front of her for emphasis, "I'll come do your dishes for a month."

"Oh wow." Terri stood and grabbed a roll of paper towels from the counter next to the sink.

Callie nodded, reached for one of the towels, and began to tell Samantha and Iris's tragic story. She watched, unsurprised to see the expressions on the faces of her three friends change from attentive, to concerned, to outraged, to full-blown sympathy. The table became littered with balled-up paper towels long before Callie reached the end of the story.

She took a deep breath, wiped moisture from her own eyes, and sat back in her chair. "I wish I could explain the look on those girls' faces when I showed them the stuff you brought. It broke my heart to see their amazement at such simple necessities."

"So they were OK that you'd shared the situation with us?" Karla asked.

Callie shrugged. "There isn't a lot of trust there."

Pam huffed. "Who could blame them?"

"But I convinced them that you guys just wanted to help." She looked at Terri. "Samantha was especially touched by the day care arrangements you offered. I think you'll meet them for yourself first thing in the morning."

Terri's nod seemed preoccupied.

"What's wrong?" Callie asked. "Second thoughts?"

Terri waved that idea away. "Good heavens, no. Anything we can do for those three girls...well..." She remained silent for a few seconds, indecision plain on her face. "I hate to be the only dissenting voice, but I need to remind you guys that my business is licensed by the state. The law requires me to report any situation where there are minors living with inadequate adult supervision.

"Samantha and Bobbie aren't really a problem. According to Sam, she's just another teenaged mother, disowned by a strict family, struggling to make it on her own. Her boss, teachers, and Bobbie's current sitter all buy that story. Yes, it's sad, but it happens. But Iris? That's entirely different. I could lose my license if this story ever sees daylight and the authorities find out I knew about it and didn't report it."

Callie placed a sympathetic hand on Terri's arm. "I have some ideas about that. Can you give me 'til the weekend to get the issue of Iris resolved?"

Terri brightened at the promise of a resolution. "Absolutely. I don't want to be the one to make their situation worse than it already is."

The women worked in companionable silence to clean up Terri's kitchen; then Callie took her leave with Karla and Pam right behind her. They stopped by Karla's car.

"What else can we do to help?" Karla asked.

Callie laughed mirthlessly. "Pray. Benton is not happy about any of this."

Karla shook her head. "Can you blame him? *You* didn't want to be involved in this forty-eight hours ago."

"If there was any way out of it, I still wouldn't be." Callie crossed her arms and leaned against the car while the light faded. She held up a hand, thumb and index finger a centimeter apart. "I came this close to a full blown panic attack this afternoon. I'm still not sure I'm the right person to be dealing with this. Benton knows I'm not, but God seems to disagree." She shrugged. "So pray, for both of us."

"Will do. Have been." Karla beeped her locks open and climbed into her car. Pam followed suit.

"Call if you need me," Karla reminded Callie as her car engine roared to life.

Callie nodded a goodbye to her oldest friend and leaned through the window of Pam's SUV. "I need another favor."

"Sure, what's up?"

"Actually, I need your computer expertise."

Pam grinned. "Geeks are us. What do you need?"

"Reassurance." Callie bit her lip. "I got in trouble six months ago for trusting too easily. If I give you some basic information, can you check out the girl's story?"

"I can try. How deep do you want to go?"

"Hmm. Enough to know that they're telling me the

truth. I need to make sure they aren't runaways or anything." Callie shrugged. "Well more than they've already admitted. Just dig a little, make some discreet inquiries if you need to. No names or locations."

Pam nodded. "I'll see what I can find out. Keep your chin up, Callie. You're doing the right thing."

Callie nodded and stepped away from Pam's car.

The lights still burned in Benton's shop when Callie made it home. She detoured in that direction and found her husband cleaning up after an evening's work on his boat.

"Hey," Callie said.

Benton looked up from stacking his tools back into the deep drawers of his tool cabinet. "Hey yourself."

"Are you in a better mood?"

He´ shrugged. "I'm not in a *bad* mood. I'm concerned about my wife." Benton returned to his work.

Callie wrapped her arms around him from behind and leaned her head against his back. "Your wife appreciates your concern." She felt his chest expand in a deep breath and knew that the sharp edge of his irritation had dulled as the evening wore on.

She released him and sat on a stool by the workbench to watch while he finished cleaning. Benton might be a total slob when he worked in her kitchen, but his shop would be in perfect order before he turned off the lights. "Did you and Mitch get much done tonight?"

Benton held up a wrench to the light to look for grease. He gestured to the trashcan at Callie's feet. "We stripped out the old wiring."

Callie peered at the twisted greasy mess in the can. "Yuck."

"All part of the process," Benton assured her. "We have to go back in with a new wiring harness, replace the carpet, and put in new seats. Then we'll get the motor remounted and put it in the water for a trial run. Mitch and I thought you girls might like a picnic at the lake once we're done. Give us a chance to see what she can do before the fishing trip." He picked up a screwdriver and gave it a wipe. "That's the plan anyway."

"It's always good to have a plan. Do you think you'll have time to do a favor for me tomorrow afternoon?"

"Oh, I think I could squeeze you into my busy schedule. What did you have in mind?"

"I need some help picking up Trent's crib from Sophie's."

"Callie—"

"Benton, I don't want to fight anymore. I know how you feel about all of this, but..." She squared her jaw. "You've been telling me for months that I shouldn't blame myself for Sawyer's death. Urging me to put it behind me and move forward. I know this isn't what you had in mind, but if it works, won't it be worth it?"

She reached out to her husband and Benton took her hand in his. "I'm not the same person I was six months ago. If nothing else, this whole miserable experience has made me tougher. Certainly, it's made me more careful."

"Careful?" Benton's eyes were creased with concern. "You're diving right back in."

"Not diving, wading. Testing the water with a cautious eye out for sharks. Don't be the undertow that pulls me down. I need something strong under my feet right now." She glanced at her watch. It was just after eight. "Did you guys stop for dinner?"

"Not yet. That's next on my list once I get things cleaned up."

She rubbed his arm. "Well, come on in when you're done. I'll make you a salad and tell you about my visit with Sam and Iris. There are some decisions that need to be made sooner rather than later. Once you know the whole story, you can decide if I'm sinking or swimming."

Steve sat on the raised platform in a rickety folding chair that threatened to collapse under his weight. He watched the faces of the men as the shelter's chaplain ran through some routine announcements. Steve's discouraged breath sounded harsh in his own ears. They were the same faces he saw every night. Different bodies, new city, but the same lost, hungry, haunted expressions as last night and the night before. If he could reach just one of them with the truth. *Father give me the words this group needs to hear. Clear their minds and open their hearts. Jesus, please work the same miracle in them that You worked in me.*

"We're honored to have a special guest tonight," the chaplain continued. "Steve Evans is here to share his testimony with us." The chaplain glanced around and motioned for Steve to join him next to the battered podium. "Let's give him a hand and our undivided attention."

Steve stood and shook the man's hand amid a smattering of lackluster applause. He stepped to the edge of the platform, allowing his eyes to track the faces in the first row of seats, trying to make eye contact and establish a sense of relationship.

"My name is Steve Evans and I'm a junkie. I wanted to talk to you tonight to let you know that there is hope and a better life for you if you'll just reach out and accept it. I'm not a preacher. I'm not here to tell you that God's gonna cure all your problems and addictions. That would be a lie. He could, but that's not the way it works. God loves you, and He's reaching out to each of you. He'll help you, but you have to meet Him half way."

Steve paced the width of the stage for a few seconds, allowing his words to sink in, warming to his subject. "I know what you're thinking." Steve looked down at his simple jeans and pullover shirt. Simple, but clean. He knew his face was full, his eyes a sharp blue beneath black brows. His gaze swept the small group seated before him, taking in the contrast of dirty clothes, unwashed bodies, hollow cheeks, and dull eyes. "How can I know? How can I possibly understand your pain, your problems, the demons clawing at you every day? I know because five years ago, I sat where you sit.

"Five years ago my thoughts rarely went beyond my next fix. I didn't have a job, didn't have a place to live, didn't have a single person I could call my friend." Steve reached for his hip pocket and pulled out the handkerchief he knew he'd need as his story progressed. "Let's go back farther than five years. Ten years ago, I had everything a man could ask for. A college education, a good job, and a bright future. More than that, I had a beautiful wife who loved me and..." His voice broke and he leaned against the small podium for support. Would this ever get easier? *Jesus, protect them wherever they are.*

Steve used the handkerchief to swipe at his eyes. "And two little girls who were the center of my universe. I gave it all up the day my wife found my drugs and kicked me out of our house. She forced a choice on me that night. It took me five years to figure out I'd made the wrong choice. Five years to understand the choices were still mine to make."

He paused. *Are they hearing me?* "I'm not going to lie to you. Every day is a struggle. But every day it gets a little easier to ignore the lies Satan whispers in my ears. I *can* live without the drugs. I *can* reclaim my life. I *will* find those precious children that have been lost to me for ten years. I will do those things because the friend I found five years ago, the Christ that became my Savior and my hope that night, is stronger than any lie Satan can come up with. God makes a difference in my life every day."

Steve stopped pacing to look back out over his audience. Some were asleep in their seats, some were staring at the wall behind him, but some were nodding, and he saw the shine of a tear on a sunken cheek here and there. "I'm not special. God doesn't love me more than He loves you. You just have to take what He's offering. Hope, salvation, a fresh start. He's holding those things out to you. Will you accept them? Is there anyone here who's strong enough to challenge their future to a fight?"

Iris brought bags of groceries in from the car while Samantha got Bobbie ready for bed. Both girls had been quiet on the short ride home, their emotions more than a little raw from all the unpleasant memories they'd confronted that afternoon.

For the first time since their mother's accident, Iris felt better. She took a deep breath. Her chest didn't feel so heavy. She couldn't explain it. *Does Sam feel the same way?* Maybe now they could relax a little. Sam came out of their bedroom, closing the door behind her as Iris came in from another trip to the car.

"All done?" Sam asked.

Iris stacked the bag she carried on the floor in front of the sink. "There's a couple more cases of formula."

"I'll help you finish up."

The girls carted the final two cases of formula into their small kitchen and looked around for a place to put it.

Sam got her first real look at everything Iris had unloaded. "Wow."

"Totally wow. Take a look at this." Iris threw open the fridge to reveal shelves groaning under the unaccustomed load.

Sam picked up the final bag. "Better go get your shower. Tomorrow's a school day."

Iris studied her big sister with experienced eyes. *Something's wrong.* After the day they'd had, there were about a ga-zillion reasons for the look on her face. Iris reached for one of the bags of cookies she'd just unpacked and took down a couple of glasses. "Snack first?"

Sam shook her head, her answer short. "I'm not in the mood, Iris."

Iris continued the comforting act of assembling their snack. Their mother had established the ritual of cookies and milk at the kitchen table years ago. It was the setting she'd chosen whenever she had a need for a serious conversation with her daughters. New job assignments, trouble at school, or occasional money problems. All were discussed with their mom, and resolved, over cookies and milk. Chocolate cookies and cold milk would always be their comfort food of choice. Iris fully expected the tradition to filter down to Bobbie just as soon as those teeth came through.

Ignoring her sister's objections, Iris broke the seal on a new carton of milk. Now that they had formula for Bobbie, milk wouldn't need to be such a luxury. She placed their snack on the table and took her seat, leaving Samantha little choice in the matter. With a harassed sigh, Sam sat opposite her and snatched up a cookie. Without a word she twisted it apart, licked out the cream, and dunked the cookie in her milk. With perfect timing, she transferred the soggy cookie from the glass to her mouth before it disintegrated in her fingers. Iris waited while Sam properly dispatched two cookies before she spoke.

"I know today was really hard, and I can tell you're still upset." Iris shrugged. "I guess I get that, but I hoped you'd be happy when we didn't have to hide anymore."

"Of course I am," Sam agreed.

"We agreed that we had to trust them. You said we can't afford to move." Iris stopped to search her sister's face. "Sam?"

Sam sat back and closed her eyes. "This is home. We're not going anywhere."

"Then what is it?"

The older girl rubbed her face with both hands. "Iris, it's stupid and petty. I know it is, and since I don't want to *be* stupid and petty in front of you, I just need you to let me work this out for myself."

"Sa-am"

Samantha shoved away from the table. She stood and waved her hand around the apartment bulging with clothes, food, and formula. "It's all of this."

"What?" Iris didn't bother to hide her confusion.

"All of this stuff."

Iris was confused by Sam's attitude. "I thought we should be, like, grateful."

Sam sat back down and cradled her head in her hands. "Oh, Iris, of course I'm grateful, it's just...I don't even know how to explain it."

Iris continued to stare at her sister.

"I've worked so hard the last few months to find ways for us to get by. I know we didn't always have what we wanted, but we had what we needed.

"Bobbie's spent more time with you than she has with me. She thinks you're her mother most days because of the schedule I'm forced to keep. Now, it just seems so pointless. Your Sunday school teacher and her friends have swooped into our lives like fairy godmothers and with a single wave of their magic wands, accomplished more in one afternoon than I have in six months." Sam sighed. "I can't explain it, Iris. I *am* grateful that things are going to be better now. Maybe neither of us will have to work quite so hard. I guess my pride is just a little bruised because it seems like the best I could do wasn't quite good enough." She ate another cookie. "I told you it was petty and stupid."

Iris chewed her own cookie, struggling to understand her sister's feelings. "Sam, that's just goofy.

We wouldn't be together tonight if it weren't for you. There's nothing anyone could do or say to make what you've done less *amazing*. *You* did that, not them. Do you remember Saturday when you told me to 'go be a kid'?"

Sam nodded.

"I know you're not a kid like me, but now you have the chance to be seventeen. You missed prom, but now you can enjoy the rest of your senior year. Work a little less. Go on a date with a nice guy." Iris paused when Sam snorted at her comment. "It could happen. Not everyone is a loser like *Louis*. Miss Callie can help us have those things if we'll let her.

"I just want to be eleven for a little while. I want to have friends over, talk on the phone, and eat junk food." Iris cocked her head as she continued to look at Samantha. "Who loves you most in the whole wide world?"

Sam's lips twitched in a small smile as Iris repeated their family motto and awaited the proper response. "You do." She studied Iris. "How did you get to be so smart?"

"I've had great examples. Are you better now?"

"I think so. Go get your shower. I'll clean up our snack."

"Okeydokey." Iris headed for the bedroom. Sam stopped her as she reached for the knob.

"Iris, I love you. What we have, what we made together, we would never have come this far if you'd ever refused to do your part."

"That's me," Iris replied with a cheeky grin. "Wise beyond my eleven years." She neatly dodged the dishtowel Sam aimed at her head. "Dweeb." Iris laughed as she ducked.

"Brat!" Sam responded.

Later that night the three girls lay in bed. Iris looked toward the ceiling of the darkened room.

God, Miss Callie says You can hear what we think. I hope she's right, and You can hear me right now. I just wanted to say thanks. Tonight is the first night in a long time that I'm not afraid of what's going to happen to us tomorrow. I'm not sure how You fixed it, but I know it was You. If You could help Sam understand, I think, maybe, things would get even better. Anyway, I just wanted You to know that I know it was You and I appreciate it.

Iris had her answer. God really did listen.

Samantha lay awake far longer than Iris. She was having her own internal conversation with God.

God, Iris has been asking me if we believed in You. I've brushed her off because I didn't know what to tell her. I still don't. Do you have any idea how weird this is? Lying here, having a conversation with myself in the dark.

That lady you sent over here told me she cared about us because You cared about us. I don't understand. I don't see how You could possibly care about us when You've taken so much away from us. I'm not blaming You, I'm just saying.

I'm sorry if I acted like an ungrateful brat earlier. I am grateful, but I'm really confused. Please, help me understand...

That request for help was Sam's last conscious thought as she faded off to sleep.

Callie shifted under the covers, careful not to disturb Benton. She couldn't call what had awakened her a nightmare. It was something heard not seen. In the April wind that whistled outside the window, in the whirring of the ceiling fan above her head, in the gentle snores of her sleeping husband. God help her, she could hear Sawyer crying, and it battered at her resolve. With an internal groan she pulled a pillow over her head to block out the noise.

CHAPTER ELEVEN

Samantha sorted through all the outfits Callie had sent home with them the day before. There were so many clothes. Bobbie would never wear them all before she outgrew them. Oversized T-shirts, diapers, and socks had always been Bobbie's normal uniform of the day, but not today. Sam passed over all the play clothes, feeling a twinge of quickly suppressed foolishness when she dressed Bobbie in a spring dress with a matching bow for her hair. The dress might be a bit much for a morning spent at day care, but her daughter looked adorable in the pink and white ruffled gingham.

Sam yelled into the next room. "Iris, are you about ready to go?" Sam wanted to leave a bit earlier than normal so she'd have a few minutes to speak with the owner of Tiny Tikes Day Care. Callie had been clear in her assurances that the proposed day care would be free. Samantha had agreed because, hey, it was the best day care center in Garfield, but free wasn't really an option for her. They could never afford the normal fee, but Samantha was determined to pay a fair price toward her daughter's day care expenses.

Iris came in with her backpack slung over her shoulder. "Did you write my note for yesterday?"

"On the bedside table. Don't forget your phone. I need to be able to let you know what my boss says about leaving early this afternoon. I want to be here when they bring the crib."

Iris checked the zippered pouch on the side of the pink backpack. "Phone's in there. Since I don't have to come straight home this afternoon to sit with Bobbie, can I go to the library after school?"

Samantha didn't answer. She hung the diaper bag from a shoulder, picked up her own book bag, and juggled Bobbie into the crook of her arm. She snagged a blanket for the baby and a light jacket for herself and walked out the door.

Iris locked the apartment behind them while Sam buckled Bobbie into her car seat. Both girls stowed their bags in the backseat before climbing into the car.

"Can I?" Iris repeated.

"What?" Sam asked.

"Go to the library after school?"

"Oh, sorry. My mind's on other things." Sam started the car. "Let's see how this goes first. I know Callie said this offer included morning and *evening* child care, but I need to meet her before I decide."

Iris nodded. "No more bad feelings?"

Sam gave the question careful consideration before she answered. Was she better today? "I think it's going to be all right. I guess I really was being goofy last night. It's just so much to take in all at once." She drove a couple of miles in silence. "It won't be easy for me to take a step back and let someone else worry about things. But I do feel better this morning." *I guess my subconscious gave my head a good talking to overnight.* Sam parked the car in front of the day care center.

Two houses stood on the end of the block with their backyards fenced into one large play area, complete with jungle gym, sandboxes, and two large swing sets. As she walked up to the porch of the smaller dwelling, she spied an assortment of toys to ride, push, and pull scattered across the spring green grass behind the fence.

The door to the center opened into a large room bustling with activity. Bright primary colors warred with stark black and white. Children played in groups or enjoyed breakfast at a small table along the back wall. The occasional cry of an unhappy child overrode the sound of cartoons playing on the TV. A woman, dressed in blue jeans and T-shirt, her brown hair cut into a casual shaggy style, looked up with a wide smile. She hurried in their direction.

"Welcome to Tiny Tikes. I'm Terri Hayes. Samantha and Iris, right?"

The girls nodded, and Terri focused her attention on Bobbie. "Come here, sweetheart. Look how pretty you are today."

Sam shifted possession of her daughter and looked around the center. "Busy place this morning."

"Oh, this is calm compared to an hour ago. Let's go back to my office where we can visit for a few minutes. I know you guys have school, but I figure you have some questions for me." Terri led the way to a small corner room and closed the door behind her visitors. The silence was complete and immediate. The girls looked around in bewilderment.

Terri laughed at their obvious confusion. "I had this room soundproofed when I remodeled. This can be a noisy place sometimes. I needed a quiet place to make phone calls and do paperwork." Terri took a seat behind her desk, settled Bobbie on her lap, and motioned for Sam and Iris to take the other two chairs. "Fire away."

Sam picked at the sleeve of her sweater with nervous fingers. "I just wanted to make sure I didn't misunderstand yesterday. You want to keep Bobbie in the mornings while I'm at school and again at night when I'm at work?"

"That's right."

"I get out of class at eleven every morning and I have to leave for work every afternoon at four thirty. I don't get home again until eleven. That's about ten hours a day."

Terri snuggled the baby closer. "I understand."

Sam was skeptical. "Eleven o'clock every night? I know you have to open early. That won't interfere with your mornings?"

Terri's grinned. "I'm older than you, but I'm not ancient. I'm a night person. I never go to bed until after the late news. Then I usually relax with a book before I go to sleep. I'm going to love having a baby all to myself for a little while each evening. If you'll pack some night clothes and her baby food, I'll make sure she's bathed, fed, and ready for bed when you pick her up."

Sam relaxed at the sincerity in Terri's voice and a few more of her concerns slipped away. "We need to talk about your fee—"

"Free, my treat," Terri interrupted.

Sam shook her head. "I know that's what Callie said, and I really appreciate the offer, but no. I can't afford to pay you anything close to your normal rate, but free just doesn't work for me. Bobbie is my responsibility. I need to know I'm providing for her." Samantha held her ground under Terri's scrutiny. She watched Terri reach into her desk drawer and draw out an envelope.

"You don't disappoint me, Samantha Evans. I figured we were going to have this conversation. I gave it a lot of thought last night, and I printed up a special contract for us both to sign." She handed the envelope across her desk. "If free won't work for you, then this is my only alternate offer. It's not negotiable."

Sam accepted the envelope. Her fingers trembled when she broke the seal. *Just can't leave well enough alone, can you?* Iris leaned over to read the single sheet of paper with her sister. The girls looked at each other with raised eyebrows when they reached the section outlining Terri's proposed payment arrangements.

"You can't be serious," Sam whispered.

"Completely."

"This is *so* unacceptable."

"Like I said," Terri pointed out, "it's not up for debate."

Sam took a deep breath before she continued. "Fifty cents an hour? Five dollars a day for ten hours of day care? For an infant?"

"Those are my terms." Terri cuddled Bobbie closer. "This really will be a treat for me." Terri's expression was solemn when she finished.

Iris grinned while Sam shook her head in renewed confusion. "I *really* don't understand you people." She raised a hand before Terri could answer. "You want to help us, I get that, but..." her voice dwindled off for lack of anything else to say.

Terri handed a pen across the desk. "Hon, just sign the contract. Go to school knowing that I'm taking good care of your daughter. She'll be here, waiting to see her mommy, when school's out."

Sam signed her name to the bottom of the page. "Thank you." She stood up and went around the desk to kiss her daughter goodbye. "Mommy will be back soon."

Iris walked out, but Sam lingered in the doorway for a final second. "Thanks."

"Shoo," Terri said as she bounced the baby on her lap.

Callie was dead tired when she got home from work. A small patient crisis had delayed her departure from the clinic, the office deposit had to be taken to the bank before they closed, and the dresses she'd left at the dry cleaners were ready to be picked up. On top of everything else, it was raining, again. *No way we're going to get everything done on schedule.* She got out of the car, juggling her bag and a large hamburger and mushroom pizza. No home-cooked meal tonight.

"Guys, get back," she pleaded with the dogs as they danced around her legs. Their noses lifted to sniff the air. Pizza was a favorite with them as well. The hopeful expressions on their doggy faces made Callie smile. Her mood lifted a little at their antics. She sprinted for the porch, a promise thrown in their direction. "You'll get the leftovers in a bit."

Benton opened the door just as she reached for the

knob.

"Thanks." She slid the purse off her shoulder, handing it and the pizza box to her husband. "Take this. I have stuff out in the car."

"Welcome home. I—"

"I'll be right back," she said, dashing back through the rain to get her dresses. By the time she got to the kitchen, Benton had plates and their pizza on the table. She went to the refrigerator and retrieved cold cans of soda and then dropped a kiss on the top of his head on her way to a chair. "Sorry I'm late. We had a small crisis at work this afternoon."

Benton opened the box, and the aroma of pizza filled the kitchen. "This looks good. Can you talk about your small crises?"

"Not really," she responded as he placed a slice of the aromatic pizza on her plate. "It's a patient thing." She glanced at the clock. "Oh man, we're going to be so late getting everything done tonight."

Benton sat back with a grin. "Callie, take a breath. We're good."

"I told the girls seven o'clock. It's almost six. We still have to get the crib." She started to get up. "Maybe I should call and let them know we're running late."

"I have the crib," Benton said.

"You what?"

"I already have the crib in the back of my truck. I finished early today, so I picked it up. Sophie says 'Hi.'"

"Oh...thanks." Callie chewed through a whole slice of pizza before looking up at her husband.

"What?" he asked.

"I thought you were mad at me."

Benton shook his head. "Not mad. Just not happy

with your decisions. I told you last night, I'm worried about you. But I like to think I'm not a jerk. They need a crib. We have access to one."

Callie linked her hand with Benton's. "I wouldn't have survived the last six months without you to lean on. I get the fact that you don't want me involved in this. I'll be honest with you. I've done everything I know of, including flat telling God *no*, to get Him to leave me out of this whole situation. He won't, and even if he gave me permission to walk away tonight, it's just not in me to stand by and watch those kids struggle while I do nothing. I know you'd protect me from everything bad in the world if you could, but as scary as this is, I think I have to do it." Callie selected another slice of pizza. "I feel like I know what God wants me...wants us... to do for these kids. I'm waiting for Him to provide some confirmation."

Benton's eyes narrowed at her choice of words. "What, exactly, do you feel like God's asking *us* to do?"

Callie shook her head with a nervous chuckle. "I don't think either of us is ready to go there yet. Besides, if I told you what I'm feeling, we'd never know if you followed what I suggested or what God wanted. Continue to pray about it, OK? I'll have my answer when you have yours."

Benton looked into Callie's eyes. He took a deep breath and bowed his head. "Jesus," he began, his tone a bit uncertain. "I'm still real new at this, and this might not be what Callie had in mind, but we're both here, and I guess You are too. I don't know what You've laid on Callie's heart, but I'm asking You to give us both the direction and confirmation we need to know what You want us to do for these kids. Thanks."

Callie wiped her eyes as Benton opened his.

"What's wrong now?"

She shook her head. "Nothing, it just takes me by surprise sometimes. This easy relationship you've developed with God. I prayed for it for so long, it still seems like a dream." Callie squeezed his hand. "Have I told you today how much I love you?"

"Nope, but I figured it out."

"You did?" She smiled. "How'd you do that?"

"You brought home my favorite pizza. Now sit back and eat while it's hot. Then we'll go take care of your errand."

They pulled to a stop in front of the apartment building at seven o'clock. The rain had passed, turning the sun into a fuzzy orange glow through hazy clouds.

Callie shook her head at the bleak surroundings.

"Something wrong?" Benton asked.

"Not really. It's been months since I was out this way in the daylight. When we were here the other night I thought about how dismal it would look in the light of day. I was right."

The apartment door flew open before they even had a chance to get out of the truck. Iris ran down the walk to greet them.

"Hi, Miss Callie," Iris said with an excited grin.

"Hi, right back. Did Samantha make it home?"

"Yeah, she's inside. Bobbie is fussy again today. I think her mouth is still sore."

Callie put an arm around Iris's shoulders. "Probably so."

Iris rubbed her hands together. "This is going to be so much fun. I'll go tell Sam you guys are here. Then

I'll come back and help carry stuff in." She ducked from under Callie's arm and raced away, leaving the adults standing next to the truck.

"Is this the same sullen child that wouldn't even speak to me two days ago?" Benton asked.

"I don't think I've ever heard her say so much at once. I—"

Iris came running back. "Sam says she'll be right out." She looked up at Benton, "What can I do to help, Mr. Stillman?"

Callie pulled a sack of crib sheets and blankets out of the truck and handed them to the exuberant child. "You can take these inside and then you can calm down. What's got you so fizzed up?"

"You're our first company."

"We were just here two nights ago," Callie reminded her.

"That didn't count. Now we're friends. I cleaned up this afternoon, and I even made cookies," she said proudly.

They followed Iris back inside.

"You made cookies?" Benton asked. "What kind?"

"Just slice-and-bake chocolate chip," she admitted. "I wanted to do something to show you guys how much we appreciate what you're doing."

"Iris, you shouldn't have gone to all that trouble. We're glad to be able to help," Callie said.

"Shush woman." Benton studied Iris while dodging Callie's attempt to smack him. "You did good, kiddo. Slice-and-bake chocolate chip cookies are my personal favorites. I didn't have time for any dessert at home. Where are they?"

Iris actually giggled. She pointed to a plate of

cookies on the counter. "Right there."

Sam joined everyone in the small living room. "Sorry. Bobbie's having another bad night."

"Not a problem. Iris made me cookies." Benton helped himself to a second cookie before heading back to the truck. "Come on, ladies. Let's get this show on the road."

Callie stood in the bedroom doorway, watching as Benton prepared to get to work. He swept his arm toward the corner Iris had cleaned out for the crib.

"This is perfect, Iris." He opened his toolbox and began to lay out some of the things he'd need.

"Can I help?" Iris asked.

Benton glanced up. "I don't know. You make a pretty mean cookie. But do you know the difference between a wrench and a screwdriver?"

"Yes, sir," she assured him, her blue eyes serious.

"Well, the first thing you can do is stop calling me sir. *Sir* is my dad."

"Sure thing, Mr. Stillman."

Benton shook his head. "I can see we're going to have to work on more than the crib."

Her husband's teasing words received a childish giggle. The interaction between Iris and Benton took Callie back to Sophie's childhood. Before their daughter realized she was a girl, she'd spent many afternoons out in the shop helping her father with one project or another. Callie crossed her arms and leaned against the doorframe as nuts and bolts were tightened across the room. Did those days ever last long enough? *Jesus, please help Benton understand what You want from us.*

"Hand me a screwdriver," her husband requested.

"Flat or Phillips?" The child asked in response.

157

Benton's quick bark of laughter filled the small bedroom. "Flat." He accepted the tool with an amused shake of his head. "Has anyone ever told you that you're cheeky?"

"What's that mean?"

Fresh cries from the room behind her interrupted Callie's musings. She pulled the door closed and held her arms out to Sam. "Let me take her for a while." Taking the baby from Sam, Callie walked and bounced and otherwise tried to soothe Bobbie to no avail.

A few minutes later the bedroom door opened and Iris and Benton came out. "Finished already?" Callie asked.

"Yep," Benton said. "The bed is put together, and Iris made it up. It's ready to receive a baby." He walked over to stand next to his wife and reached out a hand to stroke the fussy infant's cheek.

Callie shifted the baby into Benton's arms. Bobbie stopped crying, her eyes fixed on Benton's beard. Her little fingers brushing his rough whiskers.

"Wow," Iris said at the baby's reaction. "She likes you."

Benton shifted the baby to his shoulder. His large calloused hand rested firmly on the tiny back. "What's not to like?" He joked.

Sam smiled at the picture they made. "You're the only guy that's ever held her. That's sort of sad when you think about it. At least I'll know who to call the next time she's unhappy."

Bobbie's eyes drooped. Benton walked back into the bedroom and laid her in the freshly assembled crib. He covered her with a light blanket and rubbed her back until her eyes were completely closed.

"Nothing to it," he whispered to his female audience. Callie smiled behind his back, reminded of nights when he was the only one who could get their daughter to go to sleep. He'd always been a pushover where little girls were concerned.

Benton drove home in the rain, unusually quiet. "Something on your mind?" Callie asked him.

"I've been thinking about what you said earlier, about what God wants us to do for these girls."

She closed her eyes, crossed her fingers, and offered up a quick, silent prayer.

"How would you feel about asking Iris to come live with us between now and Samantha's birthday?"

Callie felt an invisible load shift off of her heart. "Benton, are you sure?"

"Now don't go getting all teary eyed on me, but yeah, I'm pretty sure." He hesitated. "It's the answer you were looking for, isn't it?"

"Yes. It's the perfect solution. It'll take the pressure off Terri and hopefully the girls as well. Maybe they won't worry so much about being separated and Sam can spend as much time at the house as she wants."

"Agreed. You know I wasn't in favor of any of this, but I think I'm feeling what you're feeling. They need help, and for whatever reason, God seems to want us to take care of it."

"When did you...?"

"When Iris was making up the crib. Except for the dark smudges under her eyes she looked like a little girl playing house. Except this isn't a game for them. It made me think of Sophie and April and how I'd feel if it was them. I'd want someone to be there for them. We have plenty of room. Why don't you talk to them and see how they feel about it?"

"I will, I just have to figure out how to go about it. Samantha's still a little suspicious of my motives."

Callie thought about her schedule for the next few days. "We've got such a busy weekend ahead of us with the party Friday night at the gym." *I need to invite the girls to that,* she reminded herself. "Then Sunday is Easter, and we have dinner planned with Sophie and her family." Callie chewed her lip. "Maybe I can get Sam to go shopping with me on Saturday. I could offer to help her do Easter baskets for the girls, maybe some Easter pictures of Bobbie."

Benton laughed. "Sounds like a plan. Everyone knows you girls do your best thinking at the mall."

Callie punched his shoulder playfully. "I really appreciate your help this evening, but if you don't behave yourself, those chocolate chip cookies will be all the dessert you get tonight."

Benton's eyes narrowed at his wife's thinly veiled suggestion. He nodded, patted Callie's knee, and focused on his driving.

Callie grinned in the darkness as she watched the needle on the speedometer creep up to fifty in a forty-mile zone.

CHAPTER TWELVE

Callie took her lunch to a nearby park on Friday to enjoy some fresh air. The flowerbeds lining the footpaths were bursting with rainbow-colored tulips and sunny-faced daisies. Young mothers with toddlers took advantage of the sunshine, turning the playground into a beehive of activity.

She took a seat on a vacant park bench and watched in amusement as the sight of live rabbits in a small fenced pen attracted some of the children. The kids waited in an excited, noisy line for their turn to enter the enclosure. The bunnies, obviously not so thrilled to be a part of the day's entertainment, huddled together in a trembling mass of multicolored fur. *Poor little things.* An enterprising young photographer took pictures of the preschoolers as they each got their chance to play with the timid animals. Callie's love for children knew no bounds, but any sympathy she had today rested solely with the nervous animals as they waited for their turn to be manhandled.

Callie glanced at her watch. Samantha should be home from school by now. She punched in Sam's number on her cell phone and waited for the call to connect.

"Hello."

"Samantha, its Callie. How was your morning?"

"Busy, just walked through the door."

"Is it a bad time?"

"No. What's up?"

Callie bit her lip. "Do you girls have any plans for the weekend?"

"I don't, and Iris hasn't said anything to me about doing anything."

"Great, I have some invitations for you if you're interested."

Sam's reply was hesitant. "OK."

"I had some errands to run after work last night. I found the most adorable little dress while I was at the mall. I couldn't help myself. I bought it for Bobbie."

"You shouldn't have done that," Sam admonished Callie mildly. "You guys have done way too much already."

"Too late." Callie laughed. "I can't wait for you to see it. Anyway, I thought we could dress her up and go have her picture made with the Easter Bunny tomorrow."

"I'm not sure..."

"Please," Callie wheedled. "They do wonderful pictures. I know it's something you'll treasure when she's older." Callie waited in silence for a few seconds.

"Do you offer classes?" Samantha finally asked.

"What?"

"You know. Getting Your Way 101?"

Callie snickered. "I don't need classes, sweetheart. I have a natural gift. Do we have a date?"

"Sure, why not? What time?"

"Why don't I pick you girls up at eleven? We can grab some fast food and then go to the mall for pictures. Just be prepared to be patient. The line is always a long one."

"OK, we'll be ready. What else?"

"Well, since Sunday is Easter and Bobbie has this beautiful new outfit, I wanted to invite you to attend church with us on Sunday morning. We always have such a lovely Easter service. I know having you there would be a treat for Iris."

Sam sighed on the other end of the connection. "Let's take it a day at a time. I'll give you a yes for Saturday and a *maybe* for Sunday."

"That works." Callie hesitated, reluctant to make Sam feel pressured, but tonight would be fun for everyone. "There's one more thing. Are you working tonight?"

"No, now that spring break is over I'm back to my normal schedule. This is my free Friday."

"Oh, good. The youth group is having an Easter party at the church gym tonight. Lots of free food and fun. I wanted to invite you and Iris. I know Iris would enjoy it, and I think you would, too."

"I don't know."

"Just think about it. It starts at seven. I thought it might be something you could share with Iris."

"I'll think about it. We'll see you for sure tomorrow."

Callie snapped her phone closed with a sigh of relief. She looked up to the brilliant blue sky. *Father, please soften Sam's heart. This is going to be a difficult conversation. Help me present it to her in a way she can accept.*

Callie spared the bunnies one last sympathetic look, packed up her trash, and walked back to her office.

Friday night Callie decided she was getting old. At fifty-four, she'd wrestled with this question for quite awhile, and tonight she had the answer. She was old, and she had the perfect test for anyone else faced with the same troubling possibility. Put them in an echoing gymnasium with one-hundred-plus screaming kids and see how long they kept their sanity. Grading could be done on a scale. Survive all night, you were fine. If you still knew your name and what day it was after six hours, you weren't quite there yet. If, after three hours, you'd forgotten either one of those things, you were on the verge. If you were ready to bolt in two hours or less, you were old. End of discussion.

Christian music poured through the speaker system at a decibel level she was afraid to consider. Balls flew through a hoop at one end of the basketball court. On the flipside, a group of kids engaged in a serious game of dodge ball. Video games beeped, pinged, and exploded in direct competition with the clatter of balls on the pool tables in the gaming alcove. Callie imagined someone passing by on the outside would see a cartoon building with the roof bouncing and the walls pulsating in and out.

Pam Lake passed her a tray of loaded nachos, and Callie slid them through the raised glass of the serving window where a trio of girls waited. They chattered to each other nonstop while they sent text messages from their cell phones. How could they even think in this noise?

"Here you go, girls. Enjoy."

"Thanks," they said in unison, picking up their snacks and disappearing back into the swirling mass of young people.

Callie took a deep breath and wiped her hands on a towel tied around her waist. For the first time in an hour, no one waited at the window for food. She found herself watching the big double doors of the gym. Sam hadn't promised that she and Iris would come tonight, but...

Callie shook herself out of her self-imposed sentry duty. If they came, they came. The lull at the window continued, and she took advantage, fixing a hotdog for herself and leaning back against the counter to enjoy it. "Whew."

Pam drizzled cheese on a bowl of chips and leaned next to her friend. "I'm too old for this."

Callie looked sideways at her. "You're too old? Don't be a wimp," she teased. "I've got fifteen years on you."

Pam munched a chip and grinned. "Be mean to me and I won't tell you what I've found out."

Callie took in Pam's smile. Relief washed over her. *A smile meant good news. Didn't it?* "What—?"

The kitchen door swung open to admit Callie's fourteen-year-old grandson, Randy. *Dang it.* She pushed the thought aside. This probably wasn't the time or place. "Hi, sweetheart. What's up?"

Randy grinned and shot a thumb over his shoulder. "Someone was looking for you."

"Samantha." Callie hurried forward to greet her guest. "You made it."

Sam shrugged. "Once I mentioned your invitation to Iris, I didn't have much choice. I haven't seen her so excited in a long time. Between tonight and our trip to the mall tomorrow, I may have to tie her to a chair."

Callie grinned in response. "I'm so happy you guys came. Where is Iris?"

Sam motioned behind her. "Who knows? April met us at the door and pulled her away."

"She'll be fine," Callie assured her. "Come on in and keep me company." Her attention went back to Randy. "Thanks for showing her the way, but I have to kick you out. You know the rules, no kids allowed in the kitchen."

"I know," he answered. "I have a pool game to get back to." He turned at the door. "How long are you planning to stay tonight?"

"My shift ends at nine. Why?"

Randy grinned slyly. "The annual basketball challenge. Sisko and his staff don't have a clue what they're up against this year. We need some reliable witnesses to their defeat."

Callie laughed at her grandson. "You know I'll take your side, sweetheart. Win, lose, or draw." She watched him leave then put her arm around Samantha's shoulder. "Did you lose the baby, too?"

Sam replied with a small shrug, allowing herself to be steered to an empty barstool. "Terri saw us come in. You think she'd be tired of babies after spending the whole day with them."

"Not a chance," Callie said. "Have a seat. I want to introduce you to a friend of mine." She waited while Pam scooted a few more bowls of nachos out the window.

The other woman turned and blew heavy dark brown bangs off her damp forehead. She smiled at Callie's visitor. "You must be Samantha. I'm glad you guys made it. Callie's been watching the door like a hawk."

Sam produced a small wave as a roar sounded from the gym floor. "Noisy place."

Pam chuckled and passed Sam a soda and a hotdog. "It keeps them off the streets for a night. I'm Pam, by the way. Pam Lake." She held her hand out to the younger woman.

Sam put the soda on the counter and dried her wet hand on the leg of her jeans before holding it out. "Nice to meet you. Call me Sam." Pam nodded and glanced at Callie. "You haven't heard about the *big game*? That's all Jeremy's talked about this week. The boys have practiced almost every night for a month."

Callie shrugged. "I—"

The door swung open a second time. Dave Sisko stepped through, interrupting Callie's response.

Sisko served as Valley View's youth pastor. The kids had shortened his name to Sisko years ago, and it stuck. Callie grinned. Some days Dave looked more like one of the kids he ministered to instead of their leader. Not quite six-feet tall, pale blue eyes permanently creased at the corners with laugh lines, in a baby face that wouldn't look old at sixty. His hair was a light sandy blond and rarely visible under the baseball cap Callie figured he slept in.

Dave held the door open to allow his wife, Lisa, to precede him. In addition to the pregnant bulge of twins around her middle, Lisa carried their sleeping daughter in her arms and sank down gratefully on one of the barstools that lined the wall.

Callie watched Lisa closely as the younger woman brushed the waterfall of straight dark hair away from her face. Her brown eyes were bright, but some of the color was missing from her Hispanic complexion. "Are you all right?"

Lisa nodded. "Yeah, just tired. Dave's taking us home early. I hate to desert him, but the babies and I are worn out."

Callie nodded. "That's probably a good idea, but before you go, I want you two to meet someone." She motioned to Samantha. "Samantha Evans. Dave and Lisa Sisko. They're our youth pastors and responsible for the party tonight."

Samantha held out her hand to Dave. "Sam," she said.

Dave clasped her hand in both of his. "Sam it is. I'm Sisko to everyone around here. It's great to meet you."

She nodded and extended her hand to Lisa with a shy smile.

Callie stood back. It was good to see Sam interacting with people closer to her own age. She did her best not to eavesdrop as Sam exchanged a few comments with Sisko and Lisa. Sam seemed shy, but at ease. Brushing the hair from the toddler's face as she talked with Lisa, and even allowing her hand to be pressed to Lisa's swollen belly. This was just the sort of thing Callie wanted to encourage.

When conversation between the three young people lagged, Callie looked at the clock. "What time's the big game? I'd like to be out of here by ten. But I promised to stick around to witness your defeat."

The answer to Callie's question was lost under the

racket of a dodge ball slamming into the Plexiglas serving window. The adults cringed, and then looked out the window as a teenage boy retrieved the ball. The youngster mouthed a muffled "sorry" through the glass and returned to his game.

Sisko shook his head at the interruption before answering Callie's question. "Defeat?" He removed the ball cap and brushed the hair away from his forehead before settling it back into place. "You've been listening to your grandson's propaganda. You shouldn't believe everything you hear." His blue eyes danced with mischief.

"Maybe not, but according to my grandson, you and your staff are in for a serious whoopin' later this evening."

"Oh, there's gonna be a whoopin' later, but *whose* remains to be seen." He glanced at his wife. "Ready, sweetheart?"

Lisa nodded and handed the sleeping child to Dave as business at the serving window picked up again. Sisko shifted his daughter so that her head rested on his shoulder then laid his free hand on his wife's back. "Looks like the natives are hungry again. I'll be right back. Give a yell if you need anything. One of my staff will take care of you."

He winked at Callie. "Whoopin' starts at nine. Glad you're planning to stick around. Randy and company are going to need all the support they can get after we wipe up the court with them." With a nod in Sam's direction, he ushered his family out the back door.

Samantha found a place in the bleachers between April and Iris. The big game was about to start. Her

169

eyes moved across the crowd. She spotted Terri on the other side of the court with Bobbie cuddled in her arms, baby bottle tucked under her chin while she juggled a tray of nachos and a bottle of soda.

I'm having a good time. She sat back, just a little surprised by that admission. Fun...with church people? The kids seemed to be having such a good time, and everyone she'd met had been super nice. She hadn't expected to be so comfortable in this group of rowdy strangers.

Her attention shifted to the basketball court as Sisko, sneakers squeaking on the wooden floor, stepped out in white athletic shorts and a red T-shirt. The crowd around her settled into their seats as he motioned for silence.

"Is everyone having fun?" A deafening roar answered him from the bleachers. He laughed, motioning for quiet one more time. "I'll take that as a yes." He rubbed his hands together. "As you know, my staff and I have been challenged to a round of basketball. Allow me to introduce you to tonight's *losing team.* They're tall, they're lanky and they're wearing green shirts. I call them the Valley View Green Beans." Sisko rattled off a list of names as the crowd laughed. The boys ran out onto the court, waving to friends and family.

Samantha cheered with the crowd, laughing when the boys turned their backs on Sisko in a well-practiced show of dismissal.

"Whatever," Sisko continued. "Now for tonight's victors. Let's give it up for my staff." Five of the more *senior* members of the youth department, all dressed in red shirts, joined Sisko on the court. Callie had explained that the definition for *senior* tonight meant they'd graduated high school but were still under the age of thirty. Sisko took a few seconds to high-five his teammates. Chests were bumped, and muscles flexed, while Randy and his friends blew raspberries at the adult posturing.

"Let's pray before we get started." Sisko bowed his head as the crowd around him settled down.

"Father thanks for allowing us to be here tonight for some fun and fellowship. We ask You to give us a good game. Keep Your hand over each of the players. May the best team win. Amen." He carried his microphone over to the sidelines. The teams took their places at midcourt and the game began.

Never a sports fan, Sam still found herself caught up in the frantic action on the court. Her throat grew hoarse from cheering and laughing long before the game ended. The score bounced back and forth with neither team ever leading by more than four points. The boys had the speed, but the men had more experience. Pranks abounded, including several balls that completely disappeared from the court, and calls by the referee that could best be described as *creative*. There was much shoving and bluster, along with plenty of good-natured trash talk from both players and spectators. The crowd in the bleachers, consisting mostly of people under the age of eighteen, cheered loudly for the boys while they booed the men in malicious good humor.

Sixty seconds remained in the thirty-minute game. Sisko's team was ahead twenty-six to twenty-four. The men were breathing hard, drenched in sweat. The boys called their final time out. After a brief conference, they signaled for the return to play. Sam held her breath when, with the clock ticking down to zero, Callie's grandson passed the ball to a teammate. In a desperate bid for the win, the green-shirted young man tried to sink a three-point shot from midcourt. The buzzer sounded as the ball sailed through the air, bounced several times on the rim of the hoop, finally slipping over the outside edge to the floor. The youthful crowd groaned in defeat.

Sam clapped, sorry the action was over so soon. She put her arm around Iris's shoulder. "Time to go, sis."

"I know. Go get Bobbie. I'll meet you at the front door."

Samantha found her sister a few minutes later standing at the door with Callie.

"Did you girls have a good time?" Callie asked.

"Awesome," Iris answered.

"I did," Sam said. "Thanks for inviting us."

Callie gave both of the girls a hug and dropped a kiss on Bobbie's dark curls. "I'll see you tomorrow at eleven."

Callie stood at the door and watched the red of their taillights fade. Tonight had been a success. Iris had been more animated than Callie had ever seen her. And Sam? Callie had seen some definite cracks in her reserve as well. Callie rested her head on the door. Her deep breath fogged the glass panel.

Tomorrow? Anxiety gripped Callie's heart when she thought of the conversation she needed to have with the girls the next day. Was it even possible to build the sort of trust she planned to ask for...*demand*... in less than a week? She pushed away from the door and went back to the kitchen to collect her things. *Jesus, grant me wisdom.*

CHAPTER THIRTEEN

Callie knocked on the apartment door. Iris answered, her eyes sparkling a clear blue in an unusually animated face.

"Hi, Miss Callie. Come on in. Sam's almost ready to go to the," she raised her voice in mid-sentence, "place where all the stores are."

Callie frowned at Iris in confusion. "The place where all the stores are?"

Samantha carried Bobbie into the living area. "Ignore her, she's trying to be cute," Sam explained. "She was so excited about going to the mall this morning I finally told her if I heard the word *mall* come out of her mouth one more time, we'd leave her here."

"Well, we haven't been *there* in months," Iris pointed out with a pout.

The older girl followed her own advice and ignored her sister, her eyes focused on the bag in Callie's hand. "Is that the dress you told me about?"

Callie sat down on the couch and opened the bag. "I

thought we'd wait until later to dress her, but we need to make sure I guessed right on her size." She held the mint green dress up for inspection. The tiny skirt had three layers of ruffles topped by a bodice embroidered in a bouquet of small, multicolored flowers. There were matching socks and a headband attached. "Do you like it?"

"Ohh." Samantha took the dress from Callie, holding it up to get a better look. "It's perfect. She's going to look beautiful. Thank you so much!" The young mother paused. "She'll need new shoes."

"We can pick up a pair once we get to the mall."

"I'll find her a pair of shoes at the mall," Sam corrected her. "You've done way too much for us already."

"Whatever works for you is fine with me. I'm glad you like the dress as much as I do."

"It's a really great dress, Miss Callie." Iris turned toward the door in a transparent attempt to get the two older women to follow. "Can we go now?"

Samantha watched her sister walk out their door. "I'm sorry," she apologized. "I gave her twenty dollars last night. She's impatient to get to the bookstore."

Callie put Bobbie's dress back in the bag. "You don't have to explain anything to me. Don't forget I have a granddaughter just like her. If April didn't get out to the mall at least once a month, her whole social structure would probably collapse."

They followed the younger girl out the door and stopped short. Iris already had Bobbie's car seat out of Sam's car. She leaned against Callie's car, her foot tapping a rapid beat.

Callie laughed and nudged Samantha down the walk.

"I think we should hurry. This may be the worst case of mall withdrawal I've ever seen."

Iris bounced from foot to foot, impatient to get to the fun stuff. She loved her niece, but pictures with a dorky looking, six-foot Easter bunny just didn't interest her. She could almost hear the bookstore calling her name. "Can I go now?"

Sam shook her head. "Wait for us."

Iris rolled her eyes and shuffled forward two feet as the next person in line got their bunny time.

Callie grinned at Iris and turned to Samantha. "Any reason you have her chained to the stroller?"

Iris didn't allow Sam time to answer. "She doesn't want me to be rude."

"Rude?"

Sam narrowed her eyes at her little sister. "Yes, rude. You invited us to the mall. We're your guests. She needs to stay with us."

Callie put an arm around each of the girls' shoulders. "Well," she told Sam, "I appreciate your thoughtfulness, but I can't imagine this is as much fun for Iris as it is for us. If courtesy is your only reason for making her stay, it's fine with me if she goes."

"Are you sure, Miss Callie?" Iris asked.

Callie nodded. "Sam's the boss, but I don't have a problem if you want to go explore on your own for a few minutes." She motioned to the escalator just a few feet away before pointing out a store on the next level. "That's the bookstore right there. Looks like they have quite a crowd in there today."

Sam shook her head as she faced her sister. "Do you have your cell phone?"

Iris patted her pocket in response.

"Bookstore *only*. You meet us in the food court in an hour."

Iris didn't wait for Sam to change her mind. "Great, see you in an hour." She skipped away and raced to the escalator. Halfway up, she turned to wave down and saw Callie raise her phone. Iris planted a hand on her hip, and gave a wide smile for her friend's camera. Callie had been taking pictures all day. *I should ask her for a couple.* She hopped off the stairs and threaded herself through the crowd at the front of the store.

Curious about what was going on, she skirted around the group and watched from the sidelines. A dark-headed man sat, bent over a table, signing copies of a book.

"Cool," she whispered. A stack of books rested on a rack next to where she stood. Iris picked one up and started to thumb through it when the man looked up, straight at her. Goosebumps prickled her arms and a shiver ran up her back. *Too weird.*

Uncomfortable under the intensity of his stare, Iris smiled and shelved the book. She took a step back and allowed the crowd to close the gap that separated her from the man at the table.

What's up with that? She shrugged and continued back to the young-adult section.

Steve caught himself staring at the little girl and shook himself back to the business at hand. Something familiar...

He shrugged off the thought. He'd lost track of the times over the years when he'd seen a girl that fit the age or general description of what he imagined one of his daughters would look like and felt this urge to reach out. Following that impulse would likely land him in jail, famous author or not.

He returned his attention to the stack of books in front of him. He signed a few more, posed for a couple of pictures, and listened intently to the remarks of his readers. But he couldn't stop himself from glancing around from time to time, hoping to get a better look at the child who had vanished into the crowd.

Three hours after entering the mall, an exhausted Bobbie slept in her rented stroller, still dressed in her frilly green dress and new white shoes. Callie was pleased with the outing so far. She and Sam had watched the computer monitor as the photographer snapped the pictures. If the finished prints were as nice as what they'd seen on the screen, their nearly ninety-minute wait in line would be worth it.

Iris joined them in the food court, a bag of books clutched in her hand. She pulled out two new mysteries by one of her favorite authors, eagerly sharing the plot of the continuing series with Callie.

"So you see," Iris explained, sipping her smoothie, "these eight kids all live out in the middle of nowhere so they form a club to have something to do. They go to all of these great places together and everywhere they go, there's always some trouble or some mystery to solve. Their parents are always cool about all the stuff that happens to them. The books are full of these wonderful descriptions of places I'll probably never get to visit. It's kind of like traveling when I read them."

Sam grinned over the top of her cup. "She's leaving out the part where she has a crush on the red headed boy in the book."

"Do not."

"Oh, whatever. Tell it to someone who hasn't heard you mumbling in your sleep."

Callie shook her head at their sibling bickering while she read the flyleaf of one of the books. "These sound like a lot of fun. You should share them with April. She likes to read, too." Callie slid the book back to Iris. "What else did you buy?"

Iris fingered her bag with a sheepish grin. Callie didn't hear her whispered response.

"What?" Callie asked.

The youngster pulled the remaining item from the bag. "A Bible," she repeated. "Now I won't have to keep renewing the one I checked out from the library."

Callie shot Iris a quick wink. "Always a good choice. Extra points for you in class tomorrow."

Callie studied the girls seated across from her. How could she destroy their carefree mood? She took a deep breath, mentally preparing for the storm to come. *Get on with it.*

"We need to discuss some things," she told them. Her heart began to ache as she watched their lighthearted expressions change to guarded in the space of a heartbeat. They linked their hands on top of the table and waited for Callie to continue.

"When we were all together on Tuesday, I agreed to do what I could to keep you girls together."

Samantha nodded. "You promised that if we'd stay put, you wouldn't turn us in."

"That's right. But we have a problem, and I'm going to need your help to keep our bargain. Terri's day care business is licensed by the state. Part of her contract requires her to report situations like yours to Child Protective Services. We've been looking for ways around that regulation, something that allows me to keep my promise to you and keeps Terri out of trouble down the road. I think I have a solution." Callie paused. She felt Sam's cynical gaze intensify. "Benton and I talked it over. We'd like Iris to come live with us until July."

Samantha sat back, arms crossed, blue eyes turning to frost. "Now this all makes sense. This is why you brought us here, right? That whole speech about Easter dresses and pictures was just a smoke screen."

"Sam—" Iris interrupted.

"Just hush, Iris!" Sam turned to Callie. "I knew all of this was a little too good to be true."

Callie shook her head wearily at Samantha's predictable response.

"You can't even deny it, can you?"

"I'm not going to try. But if you think I'm insulted by your reaction, you're wrong. It's natural. I expected it, and I understand it. But you need to listen to what I have to say before you dismiss it as a solution. I'm not suggesting a permanent arrangement, just during the week. Iris can still spend every weekend with you and Bobbie in your apartment."

Samantha got to her feet, her answer to Callie coming in a single clipped word. "No." She took hold of the stroller. "Iris, get your things. We're leaving."

"It's a long walk home, Samantha." Callie's voice was calm, but stern. "You will sit, and you will hear me out."

"What gives you the right...?" Samantha hissed.

"Sit down," Callie repeated, "and listen. If you don't

like what I have to say, I promise I'll take you home and give you guys a chance to come up with your own solution." Callie didn't continue until the girls were back in their seats.

"Look, girls. I need you both to take a deep breath and look beyond your initial knee-jerk reaction to my suggestion. This isn't a betrayal of your trust or an effort to take over your lives. Sam, when's your birthday?"

"July eighteenth."

"Think about that. This is Easter weekend. You're just twelve short weeks away from having everything you've worked for. All I'm proposing is that Iris come stay with us during the week between now and then. You can pick her up every Saturday morning. She can stay with you and Bobbie, in your apartment, until Sunday night. You get what you want, Terri's conscience is clear, and her business stays out of trouble."

Callie looked into Samantha's unwavering gaze. "You've struggled so hard to hold things together. Isn't it worth this short-term sacrifice to reach your long-term goal?"

"What I want," Samantha said, "is to keep my sister with me. That's all I've ever wanted. I'm not going to let you take her away from me. You can dress it up any way you like, but that's what you're trying to do."

Iris sat through the verbal battle without speaking a word. Callie looked at her. "Iris, how do you feel about my suggestion?"

"Miss Callie, you've done so much...I don't want to hurt your feelings or anything, but like you said earlier, Sam's the boss."

Callie nodded. She reached into her purse and pulled out a ten-dollar bill. She slid it across the table to Iris, motioning to the arcade across the aisle. "Why don't you go see if you can win a stuffed animal for Bobbie? I want to talk to Sam alone for a few minutes."

Iris didn't move from her seat until she received a small nod from Samantha. Iris placed a hand on her sister's shoulder and bent to whisper something in her ear before leaving the table.

"You do," Sam responded.

Silence settled over the table as they watched Iris walk away.

"You've done a great job with her," Callie observed. "You have a lot to be proud of." When Samantha didn't answer, Callie tried again. "Sam, I know how you feel—"

"How could you possibly? You, with your wonderful husband, perfect friends...your...stable life..." She trailed off, her frustration obvious.

"Samantha, please look at me." Callie waited until her request was granted. "Sweetheart, you're right. God has blessed me with those things, but I didn't always have them. I could tell you stories that would curl your hair. Have I ever stood in your exact shoes? No, but I know what it feels like to be hurt and let down by people I thought I could trust. I know what it feels like to be scared to take the next logical step."

"I don't think—" Sam started to speak.

Callie held up a hand to stop her. "Wait a minute. I want to ask you a couple of questions, and I want you to think carefully before you answer. OK?"

At Sam's nod Callie continued. "I know how much you've depended on Iris over the last few months. But

Terri's watching Bobbie for you now. Do you really need her there at night? I said need, not want."

Sam looked away, shaking her head slightly.

Callie continued, "With the schedule you keep between work and school, how much actual time, *awake time*, would you be sacrificing with Iris if she spent Monday through Friday with us?"

Sam's gaze shifted to the table. Her shoulders hunched in a small shrug.

"Do you worry about Iris spending so much time by herself?"

"You know I do," Sam responded.

"Isn't it worth this little compromise to get that worry off your shoulders?"

Sam's expression remained petulant, her voice soft but harsh. "You just don't get it, do you?" She paused, gulping in a few deep breaths before she continued. "Everyone Iris has ever depended on has vanished from her life. Dad, Mom, the foster parents we thought we could trust, even the promises Louis made to me and broke, were betrayals for her as well. Iris is my responsibility now. I'm all she has left. This isn't about what I need or what I want. She belongs with me, not you. I love her. I can't just pass her off to you and go about my business. How can you not understand that?"

Sam stared across the table, eyes bright with emotion. She rubbed her face. "I knew this whole thing was a bad idea. Why are you even asking me? If you decide to turn us over to the authorities, there's nothing we can do to stop you."

Callie took a deep breath. *Jesus, give me words.* "Because I respect the extraordinary effort you've made to this point," she replied. "Sincerely respect. I don't want to minimize what you've accomplished. I don't want to make you feel punished for anything you have or haven't done because it's impossible not to see the love you've put into keeping your family together." She reached across the table, taking Samantha's hand in her own. "You've been so strong, worked so hard. Can you be strong enough now, to let go just a little? Would you do me the honor of allowing me to help you and your sister for the next few weeks?"

Samantha pulled her hand away. Her eyes closed, her voice a mere whisper. "It's so hard."

"I know that."

Callie gave her some time to consider the proposed arrangement. When Sam looked up, the emotion in her eyes had translated into tears. "Your solution feels like I'm giving up. I hate that."

"Sam, sometimes winning requires a small retreat." Callie felt some of the tension ebbing. "Honey, I don't want to be the person who forced you into a decision you didn't want to make. I want to be a friend you can lean on in a difficult situation."

"I'm seventeen," Samantha began.

"And I'm old enough to be your grandmother," Callie finished for her. "But you're more mature than some adults I know. I think there can be friendship between us. I'll bet there are lots of things we can teach each other." Her voice softened. "Let me be your friend."

"I haven't had a real friend in a long time."

Callie took a step through the door Samantha had just opened. "If you'll accept my invitation to church tomorrow, I can promise you'll hear about Someone who'll be a better friend than I could ever be."

Samantha cocked her head. "Why do you always do that?"

"Do what?"

"Everything you do or say. You always manage to circle it back to your church and what you believe."

Callie took a moment to think. "You're right. I probably do. I don't even pay attention to it. My faith is so much a part of my life I guess it just comes out." She paused and stirred the remains of her smoothie. "There are so many verses in the Bible that tell us to speak of the Lord in everything we do, to tell everyone about His love and mercy. That was His final commandment to us. To take the message of His love everywhere. Haven't you ever attended church?"

"Not really. Mom took us on special occasions, but it wasn't a big part of our lives. Since she died, I've been so busy..." She looked steadily into Callie's eyes. "You've definitely made an impression on Iris. She's hounded me for a couple of weeks about what we believe. Quite frankly, I don't know what to tell her. I have a hard time understanding how a God who's supposed to love me so much would take so much away from me." Samantha shrugged. "I don't get it."

"I know how hard it must be for you to understand my feelings about God. Benton lived with me for more than thirty years before he finally got it." Callie studied the young woman across the table. "You know, there's a song we sing at church about God being *holy*. Well, I've found that He is also w-h-o-l-l-y. He's wholly everything I need in my life. Will you accept my invitation to church tomorrow? Give yourself a chance to hear about God's love firsthand?"

Sam's expression remained skeptical. "I don't

know." She rested her elbows on the table and buried her face in her hands. The young shoulders shuddered with a heavy sigh. "I need to talk to Iris about your idea. I really do see the logic of it, but I need to see how Iris feels. I won't make her move. I can't have her feeling like I'm deserting her too." When she raised her eyes back to Callie, there was pleading in their depths. "Can you give us a couple of days to decide what we need to do?"

Callie was thoughtful as she searched the blue eyes across the table. "Is running one of the options you'll be discussing?"

Samantha shook her head. "No, I promise."

Callie nodded. "I can buy you a little time, sweetheart, but we need to do something by midweek."

"I understand." Sam's voice caught for a second.

Callie reached for the teenager's hand. This wasn't part of the plan, but the pain in Sam's eyes broke her heart. "Sam, there's a third option. Our spare room is big enough for the three of you."

Sam shook her head. "It means a lot that you'd ask, but I can't. It hasn't always been easy, but I like providing for me and my daughter. Do you understand?"

Callie nodded and squeezed the hand she still held. *Independent little thing, aren't you?* "Completely. But it's an open invitation if you ever change your mind."

Sam cleared her throat and glanced at her wristwatch. "That ten dollars you gave Iris should be long gone by now. If you'll watch Bobbie, I'll go drag her out of the arcade."

Callie looked over Sam's shoulder, her eyes growing round with surprise. "I don't think that'll be necessary."

Iris returned to the table, and the tension gave way to laughter when she dumped not one, but four large stuffed animals onto the table.

Dinner time was long gone by the time Steve sat down in the food court of the mall to enjoy a hamburger and fries. The signing had been successful, more successful than most in these smaller stores.

Steve's shoulders slumped with fatigue. His agent had told him, even before the tour began, that several independent bookstores around the country were holding a contest to win a personal appearance. When the winner was announced a couple of days ago, he'd rolled his eyes in response. Hadn't he just been in Oklahoma a few days ago? Can you say ping-pong ball? He'd never understood why the cities he visited couldn't follow some sort of logical pattern.

He didn't really mind, and since he wasn't paying the airfare, he couldn't complain too much. Steve swiped his last fry through the ketchup on the paper plate before gathering up his trash and dumping it in the nearest can. *I'm just tired.*

His gaze traveled to the second level and the bookstore. Pretty quiet now, but the crowd had been a good one. That little girl... Steve forced the thought from his mind, doing his best to surrender his weariness and his melancholy to God. He was doing all he could do. The agency he'd hired had given him nothing new.

Jesus, give me strength for the rest of the tour, and wherever my babies are tonight, please keep them safe.

Callie slid the cake into the oven and wiped her

hands on a dishtowel. She checked her to-do list to make sure nothing remained. Ham in the slow cooker, timer set for later tonight, check. Potato salad, chocolate cream pies, and last, but not least, the cake. Check, check, and check. They were all having Easter dinner at Sophie's after church tomorrow. Preparing and transporting the food always presented a challenge, but having everyone in one place for the afternoon made it worth the effort. The whole family hadn't been together since Christmas, busy schedules taking everyone in a dozen directions. It would be wonderful to slow down for a while, take her mind off the ghosts from the past and the problems of the present, and just enjoy her family.

She turned out the kitchen light and made her way to the living room. Benton was on the sofa, glued to the latest offering from the History Channel. Callie shook her head. Could he really care about the origins of toilet paper? She flipped on the lamp at the other end of the sofa, grabbed her book, and snuggled into the cushions. The book remained closed as the show caught her attention as well.

Benton laughed as the show drew to a close with previews of next week's episode, an hour on the history of the toothbrush. "Contagious, isn't it?"

Callie considered the screen. "Not contagious, but it is distracting when you have things on your mind."

He muted the TV, motioned to Callie's feet, and patted his lap. "Want to talk about it? You've been so busy in the kitchen since you got home. You haven't said anything about your conversation with the girls."

Callie turned sideways on the sofa and took her husband up on his invitation. She propped her feet in his lap. Her head fell back in bliss when his fingers began to knead her tired arches. A whimper of contentment echoed through the quiet room. "Bless you."

The room remained quiet for several minutes. Benton finally prompted the conversation. "Samantha and Iris?"

Callie lowered her feet, shifting on the couch so that she could lean against Benton's sturdy shoulder. "There's nothing to tell. Samantha is afraid to trust us. I don't know that I blame her, but she's going to have to start somewhere. I proposed our solution. She opposed it and asked for a couple of days to think it over. End of discussion."

"You aren't afraid they'll take off?"

"Not really. I asked her about that, point blank. She denied that as an option. I'm asking her to trust us, so I need to show I trust her. She's worried about Iris feeling abandoned. I think...hope...once they talk tonight, they'll figure out that's not what this is about."

Benton snuggled her closer. "How are you handling this whole thing? I know you aren't sleeping. I wake up, and you're either gone or tossing."

"The nightmares are back. I'm sorry if I'm restless."

He squeezed her shoulders. "I didn't ask you to apologize. I love you, and I'm concerned about you."

"I'm trying to take it day by day. If I stop to think about what I'm doing, my heart beats hard, and my neck gets sweaty. Time has not dulled the way I feel about Sawyer's death—"

"Callie—"

"I know, Benton. I know all the arguments. I heard all the assurances that his death wasn't my fault. My brain accepts the logic, but my heart just aches for the life of that little boy." Callie sighed. "My head understands the need to help Sam and Iris. My heart is scared to death. It's like I'm caught in a loop. You're praying. I'm praying. My friends are praying. Just like Sam and Iris need to trust me, I have to trust that God knows what He's doing. If anything should go wrong this time...I don't think I can take another child on my conscience, much less three."

Callie smiled when she felt Benton's lips brush her hair as the kitchen timer sounded for her cake. "We'll see what Sam and Iris have to say tomorrow."

CHAPTER FOURTEEN

Callie made her way up the aisle of Valley View Church in her new blue dress on Easter morning. Her eyes roamed the crowded sanctuary, anxious to locate Samantha and the baby before they could get lost in the swarm of people. She greeted visitors along her path with mixed emotions. It always made her happy to see so many new faces in service, but sad at the same time. So many people would attend church this morning and consider their religious obligations fulfilled until Christmas.

Iris and April waved as she walked by. Callie's smile faded a bit when she didn't see the older girl sitting with them. Iris had been so sure Sam planned to be here this morning.

Iris. The child had been a contradiction in emotions this morning. On the outside, a pretty picture in her green dress, hair left straight and hanging below her shoulder blades, just a hint of eye makeup and lip gloss, but a bundle of nervous energy on the inside. She'd fidgeted her way through class, her eyes darting to the clock every few minutes, fingers tapping the table, knees bouncing. Clearly wound tighter than a spring.

Lagging behind once the dismissal bell sounded, she'd waited until the room was clear to thank Callie for her "generous" offer and to let her know Sam would be bringing her stuff when she came to church this morning. Callie shook her head at the memory. Such a grown-up speech negated by Iris's terrified expression, unshed tears, and the smallest tremor around her lips. Iris had resembled a man sentenced to face a firing squad instead of the carefree sixth grader she should be.

Callie's involvement in this situation had destroyed her peace of mind. She was, obviously, in good company. With God's help, maybe they could both get their smiles back when this was over.

She scooted in next to her husband. The praise team began to lead them in familiar Easter choruses. Callie closed her eyes in an effort to focus her mind on the service ahead. She felt Benton move and glanced over to see Samantha crowding in between them.

"Sorry I'm late."

"You're right on time." Callie breathed an internal prayer of thanks and reached for the baby. "Come here, precious."

The music stopped as Pastor Gordon stepped to his place behind the pulpit.

"I'm so glad you chose to join us in God's house this morning," he said. "I want to welcome all of our visitors to our Easter service. I have a special message prepared for you today," he continued. "I've delivered a lot of Easter sermons over the years. What they all boil down to is God's love for us and the sacrifice He made to show it. That's my topic today. I'll be taking my text from a very familiar Scripture, John 3:16." He paused as he stepped down from the platform. "But first we have an extra treat for everyone. Cindy and Ron Grey will be presenting their new son to the Lord today. Guys, why don't you bring Jalan, and come on down to the front?" On the screen behind the pulpit pictures of the parents with their new baby scrolled as music played softly in the background. The family arranged themselves in front of the platform while Pastor Gordon offered an explanation to the visitors in his congregation.

"The Bible teaches us that babies are a unique gift from God. We like to take a few minutes to honor that gift by praying for the baby and the family. To ask God's special blessing and direction on everyone as this child grows. The Bible tells us Mary and Joseph brought the newborn baby Jesus to the temple in a similar manner." The pastor reached for a bundle of items lying on the pulpit behind him. He handed them to the new father as he continued to address the congregation. "This is a certificate of dedication and a New Testament with Jalan's name engraved on the front."

"This is so cool," Samantha whispered.

Callie smiled at the young mother's spellbound expression.

The pastor took the baby from his mother, looking across the gathered family. "You guys have got quite a crowd. God has certainly blessed Jalan by giving him so many people to help guide him through life. Shall we pray?"

Callie stood at the open patio doors and watched the Easter festivities taking place in her daughter's backyard. Her oldest grandson, Randy, had hidden a couple of dozen brightly colored eggs around the large area. Two-year-old Trent scrambled on chubby legs, trying to find them ahead of April and Iris. Samantha, not about to let Bobbie be left behind, rushed around with the baby on her hip, an Easter basket in hand, laughing with each egg she picked up.

The voices and laughter filtered through the screen. Sam bent down to claim another prize and held it in front of Bobbie before dropping it in the basket. "Purple," Callie heard the young mother tell the baby before racing for the next one. "Green."

Callie glanced to the side when her daughter Sophie joined her at the door.

"I still can't quite wrap my mind around what you've told me about Iris and her sister." Sophie said. "I'm so glad you talked them into joining us.Looks like everyone is having a good time,"

Callie shrugged. "For now." She leaned her head on Sophie's shoulder and slipped an arm around the younger woman's waist. "You were just about Bobbie's age on your first Easter. I dragged you around just like that. I know you don't remember, but I just knew you'd be scarred for life if you missed your first Easter egg hunt."

Sophie laughed. "I may not remember, but I've seen the pictures." She hugged her mother. "Have I told you today how glad I am God chose you to be my mom?"

Callie returned her daughter's embrace. "You were always a joy. Let's get dinner on the table."

Sophie stood where she was. "Speaking of scarred for life..." She motioned to the yard. "You're doing a good thing here."

Callie moved away with a shrug. "What dishes are we using?"

Sophie held her ground. "Mom, talk to me. I'm not twelve. I know you still hurt over what happened. You never talk about it, but I know this has to be a gigantic emotional stretch for you."

Callie sank down on a bar stool, propped her chin on her fist, and stared out the door. "I'm scared to death. I'm not sleeping. Everything I eat tastes like straw. Your father is watching me like I might fall apart any second, and my friends are convinced this is a situation sent from God to help me heal. I thought I had healed, at least mostly. Then Iris came to my class. I'm still not convinced I'm doing the right thing."

"How can helping these kids be the wrong thing?"

Callie sat up and waved the question away. "Helping...that's a good thing. Involving myself in their problems. Taking Iris into our home. Keeping this situation out of the hands of the authorities, where it probably belongs." She sighed. "If one thing goes wrong, this whole house of cards is going to fall down around my head. And I'll have not just one child on my conscience, but a whole family. It's a daunting prospect."

Sophie studied her mother. "You taught me, my whole life, that God has a plan for me. For each of us. When I was old enough to start dating, you encouraged me to pray for the right guy. When I began looking for a college, you told me to listen for God's direction. When I cried on your shoulder about not being able to have a third child, you told me to wait for God's will. When the kids were ten and twelve and I came to you in a panic because I'd just found out I was pregnant, you quoted Scripture to me that reminded me God had my life planned before I was born and everything was going according to plan." She raised her brows at her mother. "Did you mean those things?"

Callie fished a tissue from her pocket and dabbed at her eyes. She managed a nod.

"Then, Mom, have the courage to go where God is leading you. He won't let you down."

Callie smiled when her daughter packaged up her own advice and served it right back to her. "Have I told you today how blessed I am to have you for a daughter?"

Callie stood on her front porch as Samantha and Iris walked out to the car together. The dogs frisked around their legs. The girls obliged their bid for attention with pats and rubs. Opie dropped a ball at Iris's feet, and Callie smiled when the youngster lobbed it into the backyard. Both of the dogs raced for ownership of the slimy toy.

Callie couldn't hear what the sisters were saying to each other, but she could tell by their expressions that this was a difficult parting for them.

The storm door squeaked behind her. Benton's arm came around her shoulders and a kiss brushed her hair. He turned her back toward the house. "Let's give them a little privacy, shall we? I'm sure Iris will be in shortly."

Callie gave them a final look and allowed herself to be led inside.

Iris took Bobbie from Samantha and gave her a tight squeeze. "Be good for Mommy this week, OK?" She kissed the baby's face a half-dozen times before bending into the backseat and strapping the infant into the car seat. Iris's fingers ruffled her niece's silky, dark curls. "Don't grow too much between now and Saturday."

Iris turned to Sam. "I left her extra pacifier in the top drawer of the dresser."

Sam brushed her own long hair away from her face. "I'll find it."

The silence stretched between the sisters. Iris couldn't remember a time when there'd been nothing to say.

Sam broke the quiet. "Call me if you forgot to pack something, I'll bring it by."

Iris shrugged. "I think I'll be good for five days."

"Five days isn't all that long. I'll pick you up bright and early on Saturday morning."

The dogs finally decided the battle over the ball and crowded between the girls, dropping it at the toes of Iris's shoes, obviously hoping for some more play time. Iris scooped it up and hurled it away.

"Don't forget to put the leftovers April's mom sent home with you in the fridge. You won't need to cook dinner all week."

"I'll remember."

"Save me a couple of slices of ham for the weekend."

"Will do."

Iris glanced to the vacant porch. Sam fiddled with the strap of her shoulder bag.

"You should probably—"

"I guess I need to—"

They stopped, surrendering to the need to hold onto each other.

"Five days," Sam whispered.

"It'll go fast." Iris assured her.

CHAPTER FIFTEEN

Callie stowed the groceries in the backseat of her car after work Monday afternoon. Terri was hosting their Bible study tonight, and Callie needed to hurry if she planned to get everything put away and dinner started before time to leave. She didn't normally cook dinner on their study nights, a small concession to the cheesecake calories. But she wasn't comfortable leaving Iris to suffer through Benton's limited culinary abilities on her first full day with them.

She beeped the horn at the dogs as they darted back and forth in front of her car. The second her door opened, Opie rushed over to lay his head in her lap. He looked up at her with his liquid brown eyes and whined a soulful greeting. Her heart melted. How could anyone resist such unconditional affection? "I missed you too." Callie scratched the soft red fur between his eyes before grabbing her purse and two bags of groceries. Iris appeared on the porch as she stepped from the car.

"Need some help?" Iris asked.

"Sure. There's one more sack in the backseat. I'm not sure where they put the eggs, so be careful."

Benton met her at the front door, took the sacks, and followed her to the kitchen. "Groceries on Bible study night?"

"Iris has to eat while she's here."

He grinned as Iris carried in the remaining sack. "Iris, we need to revisit this arrangement. If it means I get dinner every night while you're here, you just became a permanent part of our family."

Callie looked at her husband. "Funny guy," she said. "I said *Iris* needed to eat, I didn't say anything about feeding you."

"Cool," Iris said. "What am I having?"

Callie stacked food onto the counter. "Do you like tacos?"

"Oh yeah."

"Great." Callie tossed her an onion. "Look in that top drawer and grab a knife. You know how to chop an onion?"

"I think I can figure it out." Iris chose a knife and got to work.

Benton grabbed Callie from behind, swinging her around to face him. He danced her around the kitchen. "If I help, will you feed me, too?"

"Depends."

"On..."

"On how fast you kiss me hello and let me get back to work."

Benton pulled her closer and brushed her lips with his. "Hi, how was your day"?

"Busy. Yours?"

He let her go. "I finished up the Williams' job. They

have a shiny new kitchen with all upgraded appliances. Mrs. Williams said she was making Mr. Williams take her out to dinner to commemorate the occasion. Go figure."

"Congratulations," Callie said, opening a package of hamburger meat. "Does that mean you'll be celebrating with a day off tomorrow?"

"Nope. Mitch is coming over tonight. We're going to work on the boat. We're probably going to have to push our trip to the lake back a week or so."

"That's fine. We'll go when you guys get it finished." She looked at Iris. "You settling in all right?"

"Yeah, the room's great. I'm all unpacked."

"Do you have homework?"

"All done, it's always the first thing I do when I get home from school."

"Wow. Do you think you could teach that trick to April? Sophie hasn't had much success in that area."

Iris giggled. "I'll see what I can do." She looked around. "If you'll tell me where you keep your plates, I'll set the table."

Callie nodded to a set of cabinets. "Right over there. Help yourself."

Noting the time, she turned the meat down to a simmer. "Benton, you're going to have to come finish this. I need to go."

Iris turned with the plates in her hands. "You aren't eating?"

"Nope. Bible study starts in thirty minutes. Besides," she added with a smile, "it's like Jesus told His disciples. I have food you know not of."

Benton aimed a swat at her backside as she breezed past him. "I don't think he had cheesecake."

Callie grabbed her keys. "I am weak, but He is strong," she answered. "Be back in a while."

Callie frowned when Terri came back to her living room, alone. "Still no Pam?"

"Not yet."

"What, exactly, did she say when you talked to her?" Karla asked.

Terri shrugged, "Just that she was waiting on an important phone call, and for both of you to stay put until she got here."

Callie twisted her watch band. Could Pam have uncovered something important? She'd hinted at it Friday night before they'd been interrupted. Then Pam and her family had left Saturday morning to spend Easter weekend with her husband's family. *I may die if she doesn't get here soon.*

"What?" Karla asked.

Had she said that out loud? "Oh, nothing. I'm just anxious to talk to Pam. She's been doing some research for me and I'm curious to see if she's found anything."

"Research about what?" Terri prodded.

"Iris and Samantha, I—"

Callie looked at her two friends expectantly when the front door opened and Pam's voice filtered down the hall. "Knock, knock."

"Come on back," Terri called.

Pam came in and leaned against the doorjamb, a smile on her face. "I found him."

Callie's heart jumped beneath her ribs.

"Who?" Karla asked.

"Steve Evans," Pam clarified. "Iris and Samantha's father. I found him. I just got off the phone with him."

Oh, dear God, help... "Pam." Callie's voice was a whisper.

"Where did—" Terri interrupted.

"Why did you—" Karla wanted to know.

Callie's breath caught in her throat. She leaned forward to put her head between her knees as darkness threatened to snatch away her consciousness. Karla's voice came to her through a tunnel.

"Callie, what's wrong?"

Somewhere in her fight for breath, Callie felt Karla's cool hands clasp her hot sweaty ones. "Terri, get her some water." Karla chafed her hands. "Callie?"

Callie felt a cold glass pressed into her hands. She took a small sip, more out of reflex than desire; then she set the glass on the floor at her feet. Her voice was a croak from her constricted throat. "Pam, why?"

Pam knelt down. "Callie, you asked me to dig into their background. I thought—"

Callie rested her forehead against Pam's. "To check out their story, make some anonymous inquiries." She shook her head. Had she ever been in control of this situation? Weeks of anxiety poured out in an angry flood. "I knew something like this would happen."

"What something?" Karla asked.

"This...this whole thing." Callie surged to her feet and paced Terri's living room. "It wasn't enough to give them groceries and support. I've got Iris living with me. I just get that hurdle cleared and Pam snoops out their father. A man with a drug habit who walked out on his family ten years ago. How much deeper can we...*I* go?"

Callie sighed at the shocked look on the faces of her friends. "That came out wrong." She struggled to find words to express her feelings. "You guys know I didn't want to get involved in this. But once I got a handle on their situation, how could I stand by and do nothing? Those girls have been through so much. They need trustworthy people to lean on, to take part of the burden off their shoulders. But this? This is too much. We're getting wrapped up in something we have *no* business messing with. Iris and Sam are just beginning to trust us. If we destroy that, they'll run again. Then what happens?" She looked at her friends for an answer and found none. "Trust me. Those are not consequences you want on your shoulders for the rest of your lives."

"Then why did you ask?" Pam took a step back.

"I didn't ask you for this. What I wanted you to find," Callie frowned at Pam, "was some simple validation of their story. Something that would put my heart at ease about what I was getting into. Newspaper articles about the crash that killed their mother, an obituary. I needed to know that these girls weren't on the run from living parents or the law."

"I found all of that," Pam whispered.

Callie rounded on her dark-haired friend. "And you just couldn't leave it—"

"Callie, let her talk," Karla interrupted. "Let's listen to what she found out. Then we can decide what to do with the information."

"Like I said," Pam began as Callie sank back into her seat. "I located some articles from one of the Austin newspapers that covered the accident. Everything I read pretty much ran along with what

Samantha told Callie. I followed up with Lee Anne's obituary." She shrugged, and accepted the glass of tea that Terri handed her. "I found enough info in her obituary to track down where she'd originally gone to school. I went through some old college records and found four men named Steve Evans that were the right age. I eliminated three of them right away. I've spent the last couple of days playing phone tag with the fourth. His latest message to me said that he would call me back tonight at eight o'clock." Pam lowered her eyes to the floor. "It was him."

"And you never once thought to tell me what you were doing?" Callie tried to gentle her tone and failed.

Pam's expression was crestfallen. "Callie, I'm sorry. I guess I should have told you, or asked you. But you said you needed to know the truth. To me that included the truth about their father. I talked to a plumber, a news anchor, and an aircraft mechanic. They all had no clue what I was asking them about. The odds that the last name on my list would be any different were pretty long."

Callie retrieved her glass and took a long drink. When she spoke again, her voice shook with the effort to be calm. "You're sure it was their father?"

"Oh yeah," Pam confirmed. "Once I started asking some general questions, he filled in the blanks faster than I could keep up with. He gave me both of the girl's names and their ages. He said he's been looking for them for almost three years. Frantically, since he learned about their mother's accident."

"What did you tell him about the girls?" Terri asked.

"Nothing other than I *might* know where to find them if he was interested."

"And his response was?" Karla prompted.

"He was crying so hard he could barely answer me, but I think he's pretty interested in finding them." Pam faced Callie again. "You know me. I don't have a lot of trust for the male of the species, but the relief in his voice sounded genuine."

"Then where has he been for the last ten years?" Callie asked.

"Stoned out of his mind for the first five," Pam answered. "That too agrees with what Samantha told you."

"And now?" Terri inquired.

Pam smiled at her friends. "Ladies, I think what we have here is the tail end of a certifiable miracle," she told them. "I found this man on the Internet, but I contacted him through his literary agent. He's on a book tour right now, promoting his new novel *Back from Hell*. Mr. Evans got saved at a street mission five years ago." Pam drank more tea. "He told me he's been clean for five years and looking for his family ever since."

"Wait a minute," Callie shook her head, disbelief evident even to her own ears. "You found him in a matter of days. I find it hard to believe he's been looking for very long."

"Well," Pam conceded, "that's what I thought at first, but he explained—"

"I'll bet," Callie muttered, stopping when Karla put an arm around her shoulder.

"He told me he was so guilt ridden over the way he'd treated his family, it took him a while to work up enough courage to try and contact them," Pam explained. "Then once he got his nerve up, he had to find them. Lee Anne didn't just work at a bank. She was part of a four-person troubleshooting team for a major banking chain. They'd only been in Texas for a year or so. They'd lived in Ohio before that and Colorado before that.

"Mr. Evans said he had them tracked to Texas. He actually spoke to Lee Anne on two occasions, but after more than seven years...she pretty much told him to go away and leave them alone. According to him, he was so discouraged he didn't try again for several months." Pam stopped in front of Callie. Her excited explanation dwindled to gentle pleading. "He just found out about Lee Anne's death a month ago, Callie. He's frantic. He's got a team of private investigators looking for his daughters. It was just a matter of time before he found them. Please don't be mad at me."

Callie sank back into her seat. She didn't trust herself to speak.

"That's incredible," Karla whispered.

"So, what happens next?" Terri asked.

"I told him I'd call him back by Thursday. I think we have to meet this guy," Pam said.

"You can't be serious," Callie whispered. "We *cannot* do this."

"Callie, he says—"

Callie cut Pam off. "I don't care what he says. Don't you get it? I trusted Janette and everything she told me, and a little boy *died* because of *my* misplaced trust."

"Callie," Karla's tone was gentle. "Take a deep breath. We're not going to do anything to put those girls at risk. All we're going to do is go talk to the guy."

Callie shook her head. "No, *we* aren't going to do anything." She held out her hand to Pam. "Give me the number. I'll discuss it with Benton." Her insides quaked at the thought.

Pam dug in her bag and extracted a card. "Callie, I'm sorry," she repeated.

Callie's conscience pricked her at her friend's apology. Her misgivings remained, but she felt the irritation draining away. "No, I'm the one who's sorry. You did what I asked you to do. I can't fault you for being thorough." She took the card and pulled Pam into a hug. "Forgive me?"

Pam nodded. "Callie, I opened this can of worms. If you decide to meet with him, I'll go with you."

"Thanks, I'll keep that in mind."

"Are you going to tell the girls what's going on?" Terri asked

"I wouldn't," Karla answered.

"I second, third, and forth that motion," Callie said, resignation and left over irritation mingling in her voice. "Samantha is already waiting for betrayal. Telling her that we just took it upon ourselves to track down her long lost father, and oh, by the way, here he is..." Callie pinched the bridge of her nose.

"Eventually—" Pam began.

"Let's cross that bridge when we come to it." Callie stopped her.

Callie prayed while she drove home. Her recent acceptance of what she *thought* God had been asking her to do was replaced with fresh doubts and renewed arguments.

God, this can't be right. This can't be where You want this

whole thing to go. Reuniting these girls with their father sounds really good, but we don't know anything about him. Even once I meet him, there's no way to be sure he's on the level. How can I betray the trust Iris and Samantha have put in me by doing something like this?

She pulled into the driveway at nine thirty and sat in the darkened car. She sat, staring at the stars through the windshield. *Father, please show me what You want me to do.*

The voice she heard startled her when it came, soft but distinct. *Trust me.* Reflex whipped Callie around to look behind her. There was no one there. She switched on the dome light and looked again. The backseat was empty. Callie peered around the yard through the windshield. Lights burned in the shop and out by the boat, casting long shadows over everything. Mitch's truck sat in the drive but nothing moved. Even the dogs were absent.

Callie held her breath and waited. She didn't hear anything else, but as spooked as she should have been at voices in the dark, she felt a strange sense of calm settle around her. *God?* She picked her way across the yard to check out the progress on the boat. "I'm home," she called.

Iris popped up from the boat like a newly released jack-in-the-box. Callie jumped back, hand over her heart, a shocked scream locked in her throat. *So much for calm.* The child wore a pair of Benton's grimy old coveralls rolled up at her wrists and ankles and bagging through the seat.

"Sorry," Iris said, "I didn't mean to scare you."

Callie closed her eyes, waiting for her heart to return to its normal rhythm. She looked from the boat to her car cooling in the drive, windows up. No way the voice she'd heard could have belonged to Iris. "What are you doing?"

"Helping with the boat."

"Where are the guys?"

Iris held a screwdriver and pointed it toward the house. "They went in to get some water and look something up on the computer." She paused as they both heard the storm door slam. "Here they come."

Benton tossed a bottle of water to Iris. "Here you go, kiddo." He glanced at his wife. "Study ran a little late tonight."

"Just a bit," Callie agreed, looking for any sign of a practical joke on Benton's face.

"What?" Benton asked.

Callie shook her head at her husband and focused on Mitch. "Karla said to send you packing."

"On my way." He clapped Benton on the back. "A couple more days should see this done. See you Friday."Mitch drove away, leaving Benton to pack away his tools.

Callie turned her attention back to Iris. "You've got school tomorrow. You need to hit the showers. Leave those filthy coveralls on the porch, please."

Iris hopped out of the boat. "OK." She handed the tool to Benton. "I found the screwdriver you dropped, Grandpa."

"Thanks, Iris." Benton stuck the tool in his back pocket.

Callie watched silently until Iris entered the house. "Grandpa?"

"Well, she kept calling me Mr. Stillman or sir. I

couldn't talk her into Benton, so Grandpa seemed to be the next best choice." He unzipped his own grungy coveralls and hung them on a nail beside his workbench before starting toward the house.

Callie grabbed his arm. "I need to talk to you for a minute. I'd rather do it outside," she said, watching the front door.

"Something wrong?"

Callie took a deep breath, searching for the calm she'd experienced in the car a few minutes earlier. "I think we've located Steve Evans."

"Who?"

Callie nodded toward the house. "Their father."

Benton took a step back. "You did what?"

"Actually Pam found him. You know Pam and her computer. You can find almost anything in cyberspace if you know how to ask. She clearly knows how to ask."

Benton studied his feet for a few seconds. "Callie, I've had *serious* issues with this from the get go. Despite that, I agreed to help the girls, but this goes beyond that agreement. This could have repercussions for them. *Negative* repercussions. If this guy is the type of person Samantha claims, father or not, they're better off without him."

"That's why we're having a conversation about it." Callie closed her eyes. *Trust me.* "I raked Pam over the coals pretty harshly, but there might be a bigger picture we need to consider. If the man Pam spoke to turns out to be their father, it sounds like God has completely turned his life around. He's been searching for his family for a long time. If we can help bring them back together... Maybe that's what God had in mind all along."

"Sweetheart," Benton began.

"I know. Believe me, I know. But look at it this way. From the first day Iris came to my class, I've felt God tugging me toward something. Everything we've done has led us all, kicking and screaming, to this point. I can't seem to get away from it. It terrifies me to think about meeting him, talking to him, subjecting the girls to the unknown. But according to Pam, this guy has private investigators on their trail. The girls are as good as found. If we take the initiative, we'll at least be in a position to maintain some control over the situation. That's got to make you feel better."

Benton pulled Callie into a hug. "I'm concerned for the girls, but I'm more worried about you. I can't bear the thought of you putting yourself in a position to be hurt again by good intentions."

Callie leaned back, tilting her head to look up at her husband. The dim yard lights shadowed Benton's features, but she could see the serious expression on his face. "I stepped across that line several days ago. Right now, I'm just feeling my way around in the dark." She gave herself a few moments to rest in the comfort and safety of his arms. "Benton, I think I have to trust in something bigger than myself in this. When Sawyer died, it broke my heart into pieces I didn't think could ever be put back together. But this is different. I've prayed so hard for direction, for God's leadership in what He wants us to do for this family. I'd be lying if I said I wasn't scared, but this push in my spirit won't let me go." Her fingers linked behind his back and she snuggled closer. "I have to see this through."

Benton continued to hold her in silence for several heartbeats. "You're a good woman, Callie Stillman."

"It's easy to be a good woman when you have a good man behind you. I love you," she whispered.

"I love you, too." Benton bent down to meet her waiting lips with his own. She shivered when she felt him take the kiss deeper. Callie pulled herself free, trailed her hand lightly down his arm, and locked her fingers in his. "It's getting late," she whispered, her voice husky. "We need to get ready for bed."

"My thoughts exactly," Benton agreed, allowing himself to be pulled into the house.

Callie jerked awake to the sound of terrified baby cries. She squeezed her eyes shut against the noise that she knew no one else could hear. Benton's gentle snores continued uninterrupted. He turned in his sleep, wrapped an arm around her, and pulled her closer. She drew comfort from the physical contact. *Father, You told me to trust You. Please help me do that.*

CHAPTER SIXTEEN

Callie sat in her office Thursday afternoon and alternated between staring at the handsome young man pictured on her computer screen and frowning at the phone. She had to make the call but couldn't seem to bring herself to pick up the receiver.

She thought about her conversation with Benton. After two days of prayer and contemplation, he still wasn't happy with the situation, but he'd agreed they needed to arrange a meeting with Steve Evans. Curiosity had driven her to cyberspace this morning for her first look at the man who claimed to be Iris and Samantha's father. Blue eyes looked out at her from the web page. Eyes crinkled at the corners with laugh lines and fringed with dark lashes. Eyes that matched Iris and Sam's so exactly, they took her breath away. Sweat prickled Callie's brow and she fanned the air in front of her face. *Not much doubt now, huh?*

Her hand stretched across the desk. A tremor of nerves shook her, and she jerked her hand back into her lap. She smirked at herself. *Oh good grief.* He could hardly bite her through the phone. Just call him. Get a first impression. Callie leaned her head back to stare at the ceiling. Set up a meeting that would change Iris's and Sam's lives forever.

Sam and Iris. Callie shook her head. The last few days had flown by. Having Iris living in her home certainly contributed to that. Callie had forgotten what it was like to have a little girl in the house full time.

Iris seemed to be settling into her altered living arrangement. She talked to Samantha several times a day. From the bits and pieces Callie heard of those conversations, Sam seemed to be adjusting as well. Callie knew they missed seeing each other every day, but Sam's schedule made it almost impossible for mid-week visits.

Then there was Iris and Benton. They'd developed a real relationship over the last few days. At first Callie had attributed it to Iris needing a father figure and Benton being a good sport. She called him Grandpa. He called her kiddo. They picked out movies and TV shows together. They worked on the boat and played with the dogs together.

Callie had no complaint with any of that. It was Benton's protectiveness that gave her pause. If Pam's Steve Evans proved to be the girls' father...

Callie grunted. *Is there any real doubt?* If he truly wanted a chance to be a part of their lives, she didn't want her husband to see him as a deadbeat who'd taken a hike on his family but as someone who might deserve a second chance.

You can analyze it all you want, but you have to make the call. Callie snatched up the phone and punched in the number before she could think about it further.

"Hello."

"Mr. Evans?"

"Yes."

She gulped a breath. "Mr. Evans, my name is Callie Stillman. You don't know me, but I believe you've spoken to a friend of mine, Pam Lake."

"Yes of course, about my daughters. Oh, thank God! Please tell me where to find them."

Callie hesitated at what sounded like tears and relief in the masculine voice.

"Hello...Ms. Stillman...Are you still there?"

"Yes," Callie swallowed hard to steady her own voice. "I'm still here."

"My daughters?"

Now that she had him on the phone, Callie wasn't sure what to do with him. "Umm, Mr. Evans. My friend tells me you're on a book tour right now."

"Yes, that's right. But if you can give me the information I'm looking for, I'll be on a plane tonight."

"That's exactly why I've called, to arrange a face-to-face meeting. I think it's wisest to actually meet with each other before we exchange any personal information." Callie waited through a long pause on the other end of the line.

"Ms. Stillman, I really just want to know where my daughters are. If you can help me with that, you'll have my undying gratitude. There's no need for a personal meeting to stand between now and then."

Callie felt her back stiffen with determination. "On the contrary. I think a personal meeting is the next logical step."

"Please—"

"I understand your impatience, but please try to understand my position in this. I have two young girls, who may or may not be your daughters, who are trusting me to make good decisions for them. They have no idea I've initiated contact with you. Do you really think I can just hand them over to you with a phone call?" Callie heard the sound of a heavy sigh on the other end of the line.

"Where would you like to meet?"

Iris took the bottle out of Bobbie's mouth and lifted the baby to her shoulder to be burped, then patted and rubbed her niece's back until she got the desired results. She held Bobbie close for a few seconds to breathe in the smell of baby powder. "I missed you so much." She sat the baby back, smiling into her small face. "But now that it's Saturday, I get to spend two whole days with you."

Bobbie's mouth split into a wide grin.

What? Iris bent closer. "Sam, she's got a tooth."

"No way," Sam said from her place at the sink. She stacked the last clean dish in the tiny dish drainer. "All the books say babies can teethe for weeks before they actually get a tooth. Besides, she's still a little young."

"I'm telling you. My niece has a tooth."

Sam came to sit beside them. "You probably just saw the light shining on slobber or something." She reached for her daughter. "Come to Mama, sweet baby. Let's see what's got Auntie Iris so excited."

Samantha propped the baby up in her lap and ran a finger across Bobbie's bottom gums. "I don't feel anything."

"Feel the top."

"It's her bottom gums that have been so swollen."

"Top."

"I'm her mother, Iris," Sam reminded her as she felt of the baby's top gums. "If she had a tooth...she's got a tooth!"

"Ya think?" Iris laughed.

"Oh, oh..." Sam dumped the baby back into Iris's arms. "Hold her for a second. I need a picture."

"We have a camera?"

"Yep, that baby thing at Callie's church last weekend made me realize how much I've been missing. I found one on sale the other day, and I splurged with some of the money I'm saving on day care.

"Hold her up and see if you can get her to grin again," Sam instructed. She turned her attention to the baby. "Come on, Bobbie. Smile for Mama. Show us your tooth."

"Sam, you can barely feel it. It's not going to show up in a picture."

"Don't burst my bubble, Iris. This is an important day in my daughter's life, and I want pictures." Sam snapped a few more frames. "Now sit back with her and both of you look at me. I'll take some shots of you together. We'll drive over to the drugstore and get prints made. I'll buy a frame, and you can take one back to Callie's."

"Can we make two?" Iris asked. "I'll bet Grandpa and Callie would like to have one."

"I have an even better idea." Sam sat next to them, holding the camera up and away. "Smile," she told Iris. She snapped a picture. After several tries they finally got one of the three of them that was perfect.

Iris looked at the little screen and grinned. "They'll like this one."

"I think so too, but sometimes it's hard to tell until you see it on the computer screen. Let's go get them printed. We'll grab a pizza."

Iris handed Bobbie back to Sam. "Yum, one of my favorite words."

Sam headed to the bedroom. "Let me pack a bag and get her cleaned up."

Iris watched them go; then she stared at the camera in her lap. They had a camera. So many little things had changed in the last couple of weeks. She closed her eyes and reached out uncertainly. *God, are You doing all of this?*

"Iris?"

She looked up to see Sam standing over her.

"Something wrong?"

"No, not really. But do you see us?" Iris asked.

"See us?"

"Sam, you're not worn-out and stressed. I'm not tired and scared. We're going to the store and for pizza without counting our pennies first. We're laughing and having a good time." Iris shrugged with a small smile. "It's just sort of neat."

Sam sat beside her sister. "We've missed a lot of the good things, haven't we?"

"Some maybe. But we did all right, and it kept us together. That's all that matters. But it's nice to be able to relax for a change."

Samantha smiled at her little sister. "We're on cruise control now, kiddo. I know I wasn't very happy about accepting help. I can't even tell you how much I've missed you this week." She elbowed Iris in the ribs in an effort to lighten the mood. "We're almost home free. I can't think of another thing that could possibly get in our way."

Callie and Benton settled in at the table of a Tulsa restaurant. Their server brought tall glasses of iced tea and disappeared until the rest of their party arrived. Callie checked her watch every couple of minutes. "He should be here by now," she said for the third time in as many minutes.

Benton shook his head "Would you stop?"

"Sorry, I guess I'm more nervous than I thought." She took another drink and looked at the entrance again. "There he is."

"How...?"

"I looked him up on the Internet," she whispered. Callie watched as a tall man with collar-length black hair was escorted in their direction. Early forties, a finely chiseled face wearing just enough razor stubble on his cheeks to make him look both rugged and a little dangerous. Blue eyes the exact shade as Sam's locked onto her long before he reached the table.

"Here you go, sir," the hostess said. "Have a seat. I'll send your server back over to get your drink order." She retreated, but the man remained standing.

"Callie Stillman?" he asked quietly.

Callie nodded. "That's me. Have a seat, Mr. Evans. Let me introduce you to my husband."

He pulled out a chair. "Steve, please."

"Steve," she corrected and nodded to the seat beside her. "This is my husband, Benton." He nodded in acknowledgement and accepted a brief handshake.

A few seconds of uncomfortable silence settled over

the table. Callie took a drink of her tea and cleared her throat. "Steve, we're glad you could make time to visit with us this afternoon."

Steve studied the couple across the table before he answered. "Believe me, if you have the information I need, it will be more than worth it." He raked his fingers through his hair before reaching into the pocket of his jacket and pulling out a couple of well-worn photos. "I don't see any point in beating around the bush. These are pictures of my daughters. I realize the one of Iris is a baby shot and probably not of any use, but Samantha's is from the first grade. Please tell me you recognize her."

Callie took a brief look and passed the pictures to Benton.

Her husband spoke for the first time. "It's possible," he conceded. "But before we can verify anything or provide you with the information you're looking for, we need to ask you some questions...get to know you."

Steve nodded. "I've prayed so hard for God to protect them until I could find them, especially since I learned of Lee Anne's death a few weeks ago. I don't have a problem answering your questions if it leads me back to my family."

"Great," Benton said. "You can start by telling us what you've been doing for the last ten years."

"Benton—"

Benton shushed his wife. "I want to hear what he has to say for himself."

Steve drew in a ragged breath. "I can do that, but I have to be honest with you. There's not a lot I can tell you about the first five years after I walked out on my family. As long as I lived at home, I maintained a pretense that everything was all right. I continued to function, convinced I didn't have a drug problem. Once Lee Anne forced a confrontation, things went downhill pretty rapidly." He stopped to accept his tea from the waitress.

Callie gave the waitress her lunch order. She felt her cell phone vibrate in her lap and while the men ordered she took a second to check the display. One message, Pam's number. EVERYTHING OK? Callie shook her head. Their argument was over and forgiven, but Pam seemed almost as nervous about today's meeting as Callie. *Almost.* Callie typed a single word, LATER, and turned her attention back to Steve as he resumed his story.

"That whole period of time is a blur with one day bleeding into the next. I can tell you I was never in any legal trouble, never arrested. I don't know how I managed to stay out of jail." Steve leaned forward, his hands clasped in front of him. "The only explanation I have is God must have been looking out for me even then." He shrugged and took a deep drink. "I worked where and when I could. Since most of what I earned went to support my habit, I lived pretty much the same way. I'm not sure how I ended up in Chicago, but that's where God found me." Steve's voice had grown rough as he talked. He stopped for a second and chugged more tea. "Like I said, I don't remember a lot, but I do know the shape I was in when I finally came to my senses. It's not something I'm very proud of. I lived on the street, drifting from one handout to another. I landed in a homeless shelter operated by a church. Every night, after dinner, there'd be a sermon for those who stuck around. One night I stuck around." Steve smiled at the memory. "God spoke to my heart that night. I repented, and God delivered me, mind, body, and soul. I've been clean ever since."

He picked up the photos that lay next to his plate. "I look at these pictures every day. I can't believe what I allowed Satan to steal from me."

"Pam told us you've been trying to locate your family for three years. If God delivered you five years ago, why the delay in trying to find them?" Callie asked.

Steve hung his head. "I know how that must sound to you." He looked up. There was a plea in his voice when he continued. "But even if I'd known where they were, I couldn't just show up on their doorstep the next day and tell them I wanted to come home. I had nothing to offer them, no proof my life had changed. Lee Anne was a wonderful woman. But she wouldn't have accepted that from me, not after five years without a single word. I needed time to get my feet on the ground. To prove to myself I could stay clean. That I could be the kind of man my family needed, the father my daughters deserved.

"I lived in a half-way house for a year, slowly getting re-established into the world of the living. I managed to find a job and rent a small apartment. I began to feel God tugging at my heart to share my story, and others like it, with people who needed some hope."

He stopped and focused on Callie. "God has blessed that. *Back from Hell* is my second book in only four years of writing. In a world that thrives on reality shows and experiencing the problems of others from a safe distance, my first two books have been more successful than I could have dreamed. I have things to offer my family I didn't have a few years ago. I know God wants me to share my own story. I do that by visiting missions and shelters whenever I travel, but it's not enough. God wants me to write about my journey, but I need to know how it ends. I can't know that until I've had a chance to reunite with my daughters." He stopped to wipe his eyes. "So I'm begging you, if you know where they are, I need to see them."

Callie glanced to her right and received a small nod from Benton. "Steve, I can tell you right now, the girls are safe."

Steve closed his eyes at her words, his shoulders sagging in obvious relief. "Thank you, Father," he breathed aloud.

"We want to help you, and them," Callie assured him. "But you have to understand that we're going to have to take this very slowly. We've just begun to build a foundation of trust with your daughters. They've had a lot forced on them over the last year or so. Samantha's developed a very independent spirit. She's very protective where her little family is concerned."

"Can you at least tell me where they are? Who's been looking out for them since their mother died?"

"That's what we're trying to tell you, Steve," Benton answered. "Samantha has been looking out for them."

"Sam's just a baby—"

"Samantha will be eighteen in a matter of weeks," Benton corrected him. "She's spent the last year and a half focused on providing for Iris and keeping them together."

Steve buried his head in his hands, his response a two-word prayer. "Dear Jesus."

Callie continued their explanation, "This whole situation came to our attention by accident, a couple of weeks ago. Since then we've tried to work with the girls to make sure they remain together while ensuring they have everything they need. Samantha has accepted our help, but she's just waiting for one of us to fulfill her fears of betrayal. Bringing you back into their lives at this point will pretty much prove her right, at least as far as she's concerned."

"I appreciate what you've done, but—"

"We didn't say we wouldn't do it. We just have to figure out the best way to approach it," Benton assured him.

"For today," Callie said, "you're going to have to console yourself with the knowledge that you've found them, they're safe, and you'll see them soon."

Steve sat for a few seconds with his head bowed and his eyes closed. When he looked up, his expression reflected reluctant acceptance. "I've been praying for so long that God would give me a second chance with my family. I never got that opportunity with Lee Anne." He paused and swallowed hard, his voice rough with emotion. "I'll always regret that. She deserved so much better than what I gave her. If being patient for a few more days means I'll get that chance with my daughters, then I can wait. I—" He stopped to pluck his beeping cell phone from his pocket. "Sorry, I need to take this. My agent is trying to rearrange my schedule." Steve excused himself, phone to his ear, shaking his head, and gesturing broadly as he made his way to the restaurant's entry way.

Callie watched him go and turned to Benton. "Impressions?"

Benton rapped his knuckles on the edge of the table

in an impatient tattoo. "He seems sincere enough, but I'm not sure I buy into everything he's saying."

"My thoughts exactly. It's very easy to be sympathetic to what's he's been through. But how can we know for sure?"

"I'm not sure it even matters, Callie. He's their father. He has rights. Even if we walk out of here without telling him anything else about the girls, he's going to find them."

Callie nodded as Steve headed back to their table. "Yes he will. Let's put him in a position where we can keep an eye on him."

"What?"

She shook her head and squeezed his arm. "I've got an idea. Just listen."

Steve took his seat. "I apologize. I dropped today's agenda without a lot of notice. My agent and the store owners aren't very happy with me at the moment."

Callie stirred her tea. "How much longer will you be on tour?"

"Three more cities and I'm done. Why?"

She took a deep breath and began to think out loud. "I've just had a radical idea. How much trouble would it be for you relocate to Oklahoma, even short term?"

He shrugged. "I'm a writer. I can pretty much do that anywhere. This is my third trip to your state in as many weeks. Twice to Tulsa and once to a little place called Garfield last Saturday. One more won't kill me. What did you have in mind?"

Callie clutched Benton's hand under the table. "Garfield?"

Steve nodded. "A little place a couple of hours west of here. Small, independent bookstore in a busy little mall. They won a contest." Steve waved his hand in dismissal of his explanation. "That's not important. Like I said, three more stops, another five days, and I'm done. Why?"

Callie studied the restless young man seated across the table. What were the odds? Could they possibly have crossed his path last weekend? Especially Iris, who'd spent time alone in the bookstore. She shrugged it aside as unlikely. Iris had made no mention of anything unusual happening while she'd been exploring on her own.

Benton's voice jerked her back to the present. "Callie, where are you going with this?"

"I'm thinking that there's an empty apartment next door to Samantha and Iris," she told the men. "I'm thinking this could be an ideal solution." She looked at Steve. "If we can get you into that apartment, it would give you a chance to get close to the girls, without Samantha feeling like you're being forced on her.

"I'm not going to paint you any pretty pictures, Steve. You're going to have your work cut out for you. I can't think of a better answer than having you close by while maintaining separate living quarters. This way you all have a neutral corner to retreat to while you get reacquainted."

"Callie, I don't know," Benton objected.

"Hear me out," Callie insisted. "We can talk to the girls this week. Move Iris back in with Samantha, and let God do the rest." *And keep you right where we can watch you.* Callie nodded, her mind made up. "Are you up to the challenge?"

Steve's face grew animated as he considered Callie's suggestion. "I speak at missions and shelters when I'm on a tour. I ask my audience the same thing. I guess it's time to practice what I preach." He pulled out his checkbook, wrote a draft for three- thousand dollars, and slid the check across to Callie. "Take this. Use it to rent the apartment and get the utilities turned on. Whatever you have left, use it for anything the girls might need between now and then. I'll call you for the details when I'm ready to move."

Callie took the check and put it in her purse. She pulled out some pictures and handed them to Steve. "I took these with my cell phone the other day when we are at the mall. They aren't the best, but I brought them for you."

Steve took the photos, spreading them out on the table. Callie noticed no effort on his part to stem the tears coursing down his face as he got his first glimpse of the young women his daughters had become.

"Thank you," he said hoarsely, examining the pictures. "I've missed so much of their lives." He singled out one of the pictures. His brows came together in a frown. He wiped his eyes and pulled reading glasses from his jacket pocket. He looked at Callie. "You took these at the mall? Last Saturday?"

Callie saw the recognition on his face and could only nod.

"The Garfield mall. You're from Garfield?"

Callie nodded again.

"What—" Benton began to ask.

Callie silenced him with a hand on his arm and waited for Steve to continue.

"I saw her." Steve studied the picture closer. "Just for a second and I knew. Then she disappeared, and I convinced myself I was wrong like a thousand times before, but something in my heart knew." His voice broke. "I was close enough to touch her, and I let her get away."

Callie smiled through her own tears. "But not for long."

Steve didn't respond. He continued to study the pictures. "Who's this?" he asked, pointing to the baby.

Callie and Benton looked at each other and took a collective breath. Callie covered Steve's hands with one of her own and quietly delivered the second surprise of the day.

"Your granddaughter."

Saturday evening's nightmare ripped Callie from unconsciousness with a force that made returning to sleep impossible. She bolted out of the bed and hurried through the dark house. Once in the living room she collapsed into her recliner, pulled her Bible off the table, and clasped it to her chest.

"What have we done?" she whispered into the empty room. "Oh, Jesus, what have *I* done?"

Had she been taken in again by convincing words and pleading looks? Janette's face merged with the face of Steve Evans in Callie's mind. She shook her head in denial.

"Not this time," she promised herself and the child sleeping down the hall. "I will *not* go blindly into this situation a second time."

Callie considered the check sitting in her purse. Three-thousand dollars was a lot of money. The apartment and utilities wouldn't cost anywhere close to that. The money couldn't be funneled to the girls without raising questions she couldn't answer, but she could still use it to benefit them, and herself by default.

Mr. Evans would undergo a serious background check, even if she had to pay for some of it herself. Callie would know the truth of his story long before he moved to town.

CHAPTER SEVENTEEN

Callie inspected the dining room in preparation for her guests on Saturday morning. Butterflies patrolled her stomach in uneasy circles and her hands shook when she contemplated what she was about to do. *Father, if this is Your will, please bring peace to this place.* Since cooking and prayer calmed her nerves in equal amounts, she would serve fresh muffins with their conflict this morning. What a nice way to start the weekend.

The days since the initial meeting with Steve Evans had flown by in a flurry of activity. Callie ran through her mental list:

The second apartment was now leased in Steve's name. One step above shabby, it had two bedrooms, a single bath, and no furniture.

Utilities turned on.

Kitchen stocked with a few necessary groceries.

Background check complete. Pam's husband, Harrison, had located a private investigator and initiated a quiet but comprehensive investigation into the man that Steve Evans was and now claimed to be. Everything he'd told them appeared to be true. Callie shrugged off any small twinges of conscience over the expenditure, along with any invasion of his privacy.

Steve had earmarked the balance of his money for the benefit of his daughters. Things they might need before he could get here. What could possibly be better for these girls than to know their father was who and what he claimed to be? Callie still harbored doubts about the level of her involvement, but the receipt of the report, and it's validation of what she'd been told, allowed her to breathe a little easier.

And the most important piece of the puzzle: Steve was set to arrive in Garfield on Thursday. Callie felt a smile bloom in spite of the situation. Every evening this week, before she left her office, Steve had called to check on *his* girls. Even before the investigator's report had come back, Callie found herself liking this young man more and more. His last request each night? Tell me something about my girls that I don't know. She'd shared tidbits of school work and hobbies. Iris's love of books, Sam's scholarship. Steve treated each piece of information like a long lost treasure.

Sam would be here soon to pick up Iris for their weekend. It was time to break the news of their father's impending arrival. There didn't seem to be any way to avoid an emotional showdown. She only hoped it wouldn't be the next betrayal in the lives of these two innocent kids.

With nothing left to do to physically prepare for the morning Callie sat in her recliner and took a few moments to prepare emotionally.

Father, this is going to be so hard. We're going to need Your presence and direction in this place today. I have to believe You've led us to this point. Please grant us the wisdom we need to complete what we've started. Please give a calm spirit to Samantha and Iris. Help us find the words that will allow this family to begin healing... She looked up as Iris came bouncing into the room with a small suitcase.

The youngster flopped on the couch to wait for her sister. "Morning." She sniffed the air. "What smells so good?"

"Strawberry muffins."

"Yum. Can I take some to share with Sam?"

"I made plenty. Benton and I have some things to discuss with you and your sister. We'll all have some once Sam gets here."

"Have I done something wrong?"

Callie moved over to sit next to Iris. "Oh, honey, no. Why would you even think that?"

"You've been kinda quiet all week."

Callie squeezed the child's shoulders. "Nothing much gets by you, does it?"

Iris shrugged in response.

"Yes," Callie said. "We do need to talk about some things. No, you haven't done anything wrong." Barking dogs announced the arrival of a car in the driveway. She patted Iris's leg as they both stood. "Actually, I'm hoping what we have to discuss this morning turns out to be good news." *Who are you trying to convince?* Callie swung the front door open as Sam mounted the porch steps. "Morning. Come on in."

Sam shifted Bobbie from one hip to the other. "Is Iris ready to go?"

"Yes, but I've made breakfast for everyone. Benton

and I would like you girls to join us."

Samantha paused in the doorway. Her eyes searched Callie's face. "Is something wrong?"

"We just need to talk." Callie offered what she hoped was a reassuring smile and followed Sam into the house. From there she ushered the girls into her dining room.

"Let's sit in here. There's more room around the table, and I dug out Trent's playpen for Bobbie."

The table was already set with plates and cups. A basket of fragrant, pink muffins rested in its center. She settled the girls at the table and went into the kitchen to get coffee and juice. Benton crossed the room behind her.

"Are you ready for this?"

Callie stilled her nervous hands on the pot. "Not really, but we can't put it off any longer."

"It'll be fine."

Once everyone was seated, Benton asked the blessing over their breakfast. "Father, thank You for always providing for our needs. Please be with us this morning. Grant us the wisdom and direction we need to always follow Your will in our lives. Amen."

He reached for the muffins, unfolding the towel they were wrapped in. "These smell terrific." He passed the basket to Iris. "Here you go, kiddo." Benton broke the muffin open and spread butter inside.

"Thanks, Grandpa." Iris took one and passed them around to Samantha.

Sam put the muffins on the table and sat back with her arms folded across her chest. Her eyes moved from one adult face to the other. "Neither one of you could play poker and win," she told them. "You might as well get it over with."

"It?" Benton asked.

"Whatever it is that you think we're going to need *wisdom and direction* with." Sam's voice dripped with sarcasm. "The reason Callie's hands are shaking. The reason neither of you can look me in the eye this morning. I'm not blind, and I'm not stupid, so I repeat, let's have it." Her gaze settled on Callie.

Callie bore the weight of Sam's suspicious stare for several seconds, searching for an easy way to begin their conversation. She abandoned easy in favor of the truth. The news delivered in a single swift sentence.

"We've located your father."

CHAPTER EIGHTEEN

Samantha sat in stunned silence for a few seconds, allowing Callie's pronouncement to hang in the air above the table. Her mind worked to absorb the words.

"Oh, I am *so* out of here!" She pushed back her chair. "Have you two lost your minds?" Her body trembled as she stared across the table. "*Let us help you. Let me be your friend,*" she mocked. "If this is your idea of help and friendship, we were better off without them. How could you possibly think bringing a drug-addicted father back into our lives was *helping?*" She stopped and rubbed her pounding temples in frustration.

Bobbie began to cry at the sound of her mother's raised, angry voice. Callie rose to pick her up. Sam sent a single ice-blue look in her direction.

"Don't," she said, her voice sharp. "Really...just don't." Samantha picked up Bobbie from the playpen and rocked until the baby quieted. She took a few deep breaths of her own before turning to face Callie again.

"Look, I appreciate everything you've done over the last few weeks. But you had no right to do this. I understand there's probably some religious, Christian, do-gooder thing at work here, but you just stepped over a very big line." She looked at Iris. "Go get your things."

Iris kept her seat. "I don't think so."

Samantha looked at her in disbelief. "You don't think so?"

Iris shook her head. "I know you're angry, but I want to know what they found out about our father. Listening can't hurt us. If you still want to leave after we hear what they have to say, I'll go with you."

Samantha crouched next to her sister. "Sweetheart, I know it bothers you that you never got the chance to know our father. But you need to trust me. This is a very big mistake. The only thing he can bring to our lives is misery. We've had more than enough of that already."

Iris looked into Sam's eyes. "Who loves me most in the whole wide world?"

Sam closed her eyes and leaned her head against Iris's arm. "I do."

"Then do this for me, please."

Sam stood up and looked from Iris, to Benton, to Callie. Betrayal. Her life had turned into one big betrayal. Her father, Helen's husband, Louis, Callie, and now Iris. She let out a breath of surrender.

"Fine. Get it over with. At least one of us is interested." She prowled the room, baby secure in her arms, and looked for any excuse to flee.

"Sam, try to understand. This wasn't done to hurt you," Callie explained. "Pam located your father online.

Benton and I met with him last weekend. He's been looking for you girls for a long time."

"I'll just bet," Sam muttered from across the room where she continued to pace.

"Samantha, will you please sit down and listen to us for a minute?" Callie requested. "I know you have concerns, legitimate concerns, about bringing your father back into your lives. But do you really think we'd allow that to happen if we weren't convinced he'd changed? If he hadn't persuaded us that he sincerely regretted the mistakes he's made and wanted to try and make up for some of them?"

Samantha stopped pacing and glared at Callie over her daughter's head. How could these people not understand? She didn't speak as she placed a pacified Bobbie back in the playpen, positioning toys where they could be reached by her daughter's small hands. Returning to the table she took her seat and picked up her coffee with hands that shook. The liquid sloshed over the brim of her cup when she tried to drink, leaving a brown stain on Callie's tablecloth.

"You tell me," Sam began, her voice cracking, her breathing ragged, "how he can make up for *ten* lost years? You tell me how he can make up for the death of our mother?" Her eyes streamed as she faced the adults. She swiped at her face with the sleeve of her sweater. "Because I hold him personally to blame for that. If he'd loved us enough to stay, things would've been different. She'd still be here." *We'd still be a family.* "So you tell me what he could have possibly said, or done, to convince you that this was a good idea."

"Sam, no one can change the past, but he wants to be a part of your future," Callie said. "Trust me when I tell you that I didn't believe him at first. His story has not been taken at face value. Steps have been taken to verify everything he told us—"

"I don't care what he wants or what he said." Sam's voice was harsh when she interrupted.

Iris laid a hand on her sister's arm and rubbed gently. "So, where's he been for my whole life?"

Callie faced the youngster. "Well, he spent a lot of time living on the street and in shelters. But he accepted Christ a few years ago. Once he'd proven to himself that he'd beaten his addictions, he started searching for you guys. He's a writer now."

Samantha shook her head. *Oh yeah, he's a changed man.* "Now it all makes sense. You guys heard the word 'Christian' come out of his mouth, and you bought this fairytale, hook, line, and sinker, didn't you? You guys pretty much have Christian stamped on your foreheads. Don't you think he could see that and know what you needed to hear?"

"Samantha," Callie began.

"I'm not saying it's a bad thing. It works for you guys, but it doesn't work for everyone." Sam put her head in her hand. "Talk about naïve."

"Sam," Callie tried again.

Sam looked up as Benton scooted his chair away from the table and left the dining room.

"Sam," Callie continued, "if you could just give him a chance."

Benton came back into the room with a shopping bag in his hands. "They say a picture is worth a thousand words, so I bought some of each at the bookstore yesterday." Benton placed a book in front of each of the sisters. "Here you go, girls." He turned each volume over so the author's picture on the back cover faced up. "Words and pictures. Any questions?"

Sam couldn't stop herself. Her fingers brushed across the glossy picture of the father she'd almost forgotten. He looked the same. She opened the book and read the flyleaf then flipped to the first page and read the dedication.

To my family, may the Lord keep you until we are reunited.

Each word ripped a new hole in her heart. Stubbornness settled around her shoulders like a protective cloak as she placed the book next to her plate and looked at Callie. "This doesn't say a thing about the person he is."

Iris finished her own study of the books. "Sam, they're telling the truth. I recognize him."

Sam snorted, dismissing Iris's statement as wishful thinking. "Sweetheart, you couldn't possibly. You were just a baby..."

"No, Sam. I saw him two weeks ago."

Sam stared at her sister. "Where? When?"

"At the mall, the day we went to have Easter pictures made. Do you remember when I went to the bookstore?"

Sam nodded.

"There was, like a ton of people there. They were all crowded around a table stacked with books." She tapped the book. "He was signing them for people. He smiled at me."

Sam sent an accusing glare in Callie's direction.

Callie shook her head. "I swear to you. I didn't have a clue."

"I don't believe this, or you—"

Callie opened her mouth to speak, but Benton beat

her to it. "Stop right there."

He got to his feet and leaned across the table on fisted knuckles.

"Let me share some things with you that Callie neglected to mention. You're found, end of story. It has nothing to do with Callie, me, what you want, or what you don't." Benton lowered himself back into his seat. "You two have been hiding, for months, from foster parents and officials that weren't even looking for you."

"You just said—" Sam's voice was barely there.

"I'm not done. That all changed six weeks ago when your father found out about your mother's accident. He's had private investigators on your trail ever since. You've managed so far, but how long do you think you can hide from determined professionals?"

Sam shrugged in response, striving for an outward show of disregard, but her insides shook at Benton's news. *Private investigators?*

"If Callie and I hadn't gotten to him before they got to you, you'd be smooth out of options."

The outward show lost ground. Sam began to cry, her shoulders lifting with each silent sob. She sniffed. "Yeah, like I have so many right now."

"More than you would have if we hadn't intervened. Think about it. You're kids. You're father has a home in Chicago. He would have been within his rights to swoop down on you two with no warning and sweep you both back to Illinois."

"Good luck with that," Sam shot back, her face hard with determination.

Benton nodded. "You're right. You're almost eighteen. You could have fought that action and

241

probably won. You and Bobbie, snug in your own stubborn little world, but you wouldn't have Iris."

Sam looked at her sister. He wouldn't dare. *Would he?* Sam felt her shoulders droop in the face of that uncertainty. *Ten years and he's still messing up my life.* "What happens now?" she asked.

"He's coming to see you," Callie told them. "Actually, he's moving here so he can be close to you."

Sam was on her feet again, voice calm but determined. "I am *not* living with this guy. Iris can do what she wants, but I have a perfectly good home. I'm staying in it."

"That's the plan," Callie assured her. "He's rented an apartment in your building. Your father knows he has a lot of ground to make up. He agrees that everyone maintaining their own space, especially at first, is the best possible arrangement. And the best part of the whole thing," she provided with a smile, "is Iris can move back to your apartment. With your dad next door, you are no longer *unsupervised* minors. There's no need for her to stay here."

"Yes!" Iris exclaimed, fist pumping once in the air. "I mean, thanks Miss Callie, but..."

"You don't have to explain or apologize, Iris. I understand.

"We've loved having you here, but we'll pack up your stuff and get you back home this afternoon."

"You guys have this all worked out for us, don't you?" Sam asked in resignation.

"Not really," Benton answered. "I know you feel like we're pulling all the strings right now, but we aren't. All we can do is give you guys the chance God wants you to have. What you do with it is up to you."

CHAPTER NINETEEN

Sam watched from the bedroom door as Iris tucked Bobbie into the crib for the evening.

"I can't believe I'm home to stay," Iris whispered as she rubbed the baby's back.

Sam moved to the crib and stooped to kiss her daughter good night. She brushed a hand over Bobbie's dark curls then draped an arm around Iris's shoulders, guiding her out of the bedroom. "Well, you won't see much of us, at least not until schools out," Sam reminded her.

"I know, but it's still great to be home." Iris opened the refrigerator and peered inside. "You want a glass of tea?" When Sam shrugged in response, Iris abandoned the tea pitcher and came to sit next to her sister. "Sam, talk to me. Tell me about our father. Maybe if you share some memories with me, you won't be so afraid."

"Iris, I'm not afraid, at least, not the way you mean." Samantha stared into her past, her voice quiet when she finally continued. "He was a good dad. My earliest memory is of him, not Mom. I remember sitting on his shoulders and looking down at Mom while she laughed up at us. I don't know where we were, but I don't think I was very old. I'm not surprised that he's a writer now. His degree is in journalism. Before he got messed up with drugs, he wrote articles for a magazine. He traveled a lot, but he never came home without something special hidden in his suitcase for me. I can remember standing at the door, waiting for his car to turn into the drive, or getting up early when he got home past my bedtime. I'd go bouncing into bed with Dad and Mom and kiss him awake to get my gift."

Samantha's smile was sad as she continued. "The week you were born was the best week of my life."

"Aw."

Sam's lips twitched up. "Not because of you, Dilbert. I had Dad all to myself for a few days. He took me to the store and bought me a new baby doll. He told me since Mom had a new baby to take care of, I needed one, too."

"Sam, those are great stories. Can't you look forward to this, even a little?"

Sam closed her eyes. "What if I let myself love him again...and he doesn't stay?"

"Why would he come back if he didn't plan to stay? It's gonna be all right." Iris studied her sister. "You're not still mad at Callie and Grandpa, are you?"

Sam leaned her head against the back of the sofa. "I'm not sure mad was ever the right word. Confused, hurt. He can do us so much more harm than good if they're wrong about him. I know we've never really talked about it, but I just assumed, after all of this time, that he was dead, too. To find out he isn't...to see how easily they found him. Maybe I should have tried to track him down when Mom died. Our lives might have been a lot easier."

"Sam, I thought the same things as you. He was either dead or a druggie. Why would we look for him?" Iris was silent for a second. "Can I ask you a question?"

"Yeah."

"Do you believe in God?"

"Me? I thought this was an *us* question."

Iris shook her head. "Not so much anymore. I think I know about me. Now I just need to know about you."

"Iris—"

"No, Sam, I'm serious. Grandpa said God wanted us to have this chance." Her eyes were intent. "I think I believe them. There's just too much stuff that's happened in the last few weeks. Things we just knew were going to tear us apart. We're still here. We're still together. Now our father's coming back."

Samantha closed her eyes. Doubt warring with an internal hunger she'd fought to ignore for weeks. What would happen if she stopped fighting and yielded to it? Maybe all of these new people in her life—and Iris— were on to something she needed for herself.

"Why don't you call April before it gets any later? Let her know you don't need a ride to church tomorrow."

"But I want to go," Iris began.

"Calm down, goofy. We'll go together."

Later that evening Sam sat alone in the living area of their apartment. Midnight had come and gone. Iris and Bobbie were both sound asleep.

The day had left her physically exhausted and

mentally drained, but sleep wouldn't come. *Why does my heart feel so empty?* Have things changed that much in the last few weeks? What am I missing?

Sam continued to read by the light of a small lamp. There was so much here she didn't understand, but the ache in her heart had grown calmer with each word.

When she couldn't hold her eyes open any longer, she closed Iris's Bible and got ready for bed.

The next morning, Callie watched with tears running down her cheeks as, hand in hand, Iris and Samantha walked to the front of the church and accepted Christ into their hearts.

CHAPTER TWENTY

Steve wove his way through a maze of stacked boxes to answer the door of his new apartment. He zigged when he should have zagged, and banged his shin on an untethered coffee table that had mysteriously maneuvered into his path. *I can't even turn around in this place.* The bell sounded a second time while he took a moment to rub his bruised leg. "Hang on just a second," he called out in mild annoyance. He shoved the table and a couple of heavy cartons aside and threw the door open. His impatient scowl changed to a welcoming smile.

"Callie, come in if you can get in."

She took a step into chaos. "Good gracious, did you bring all of Chicago with you?"

Steve made a face at the boxes. "I didn't have a lot of time to sort stuff out. Since I didn't know what the situation would be, or how long I'd need to stay here, I just threw stuff into boxes and called for a truck. I figured I could sort it all out once I got settled." He looked around. "I'm pretty sure I brought too much. I—" A second knock on the door interrupted his explanation.

Callie held up her hand. "That'll be Benton. I told him to meet me here." She opened the door, shifting to allow Benton to enter. Almost immediately her cell phone rang. She looked at the small screen. "It's Iris. I told her to call me when they were both home for the day."

"So, are you ready to meet your family?" Benton asked.

"I thought so until I heard Callie's phone ring."

Benton clapped him on the shoulder. "It'll be fine. They're good girls." He looked Steve in the eye. "The news of your return was hard on them. Can I be straight with you?"

"Of course," Steve replied.

"We've grown very fond of your daughters. They've shown a lot of spunk, and they've survived some pretty tough times." The older man studied Steve with a stern expression. "They deserve some stability in their lives." He stopped, eyes locked on Steve's face. "You're going to want to be real careful not to hurt them again."

"I appreciate what you're saying and everything you've done for my family." Steve replied, his gaze unflinching. "You don't need to worry. This is going to be a new beginning for all of us."

Benton nodded and Steve felt some of the tension in the air recede. "Good. Then we can move on. I just wanted you to understand where we stood."

Callie closed the phone and rejoined the men. "Ready to walk next door?"

Steve took a deep breath. "Wow...OK... I'm ready, I

think." He reached for the doorknob. "Oh, wait. Presents. I'll be right back."

Steve returned, carrying a small shopping bag and an enormous stuffed panda.

Callie covered her mouth. "Oh my."

"I'm meeting my granddaughter for the first time," he said defensively. "I couldn't show up empty handed. I wanted to bring a puppy. I settled for this."

"Good choice," Callie assured him.

"Arnie...I named him Arnold. I couldn't keep saying 'hey you' for the entire trip. Anyway, Arnie kept me company on the drive," Steve continued. "I belted him into the passenger seat, and he made the perfect travel companion. Not a lot of chatter or backseat driving." He buried his face in the bear's fur. "I can't believe I'm stalling. I don't think I've ever been this nervous in my life." He sucked in a couple of deep breaths. "Let's do this."

Steve's feelings, mood, and expectations changed fifty times in the short walk from one apartment to the other. Thoughts raced through his mind at warp speed. How will they act? What will they say? He'd heard movement through the thin walls earlier and assumed Samantha and the baby were at home. Everything in him had wanted to run over there right then. But he'd waited, sticking with the pre-arranged plan. Now the wait was almost over. *Thank you, Father, for answering this prayer.*

They paused at the door. Steve returned Callie's questioning glance and answered her unspoken question with a short nod. She knocked twice before throwing open the door that would either answer his prayers or destroy his dreams.

His writer's brain noted details he filed away for later use. The worn furniture, the cramped space, the neat room. *Is that lavender in the air?* Steve blinked at the aroma. For a second he found himself transported back to the home he'd made with Lee Anne and their daughters. Lavender had been her favorite scent. The homey smell sent a shiver along his spine. The shiver snapped him back to the present.

Iris and Samantha stood in the small living area. He recognized them only by the pictures Callie had provided a few days earlier. A baby sat in a playpen next to the couch. No one said a word. Father and daughters looked at each other over a mountain of black and white fur. Steve's eyes blurred with unshed tears. *My babies.*

Dropping the bear and the small bag on the floor, he took a couple of hesitant steps forward. He started to speak but had to stop and clear some of the emotion from his throat. "I've lectured myself for days about the need to move slowly. I know I need to give us all some time to get reacquainted. I will," he promised. "But I simply have to hold onto you both for a second. If I don't, I'll never convince myself this moment is real."

The hand he placed on Iris's shoulder shook. "Iris, I feel like I'm seeing you..." His throat clogged with tears. "I feel like I'm seeing you for the very first time." He pulled the child into his arms, receiving a slightly reserved embrace in return. Leaning close, Steve stroked her hair and whispered in her ear. "Hi, baby. Can I call you baby?" Iris pulled back to look into his eyes and nodded in response. He brushed her forehead with a hesitant kiss and turned to Sam.

"Sam—"

"Samantha," she corrected. Icicles hung from the single word response.

Oh, sweetheart, you'll always be Sam in my heart. He continued without missing a beat. "Samantha, you've grown into a beautiful young woman." He held out his arms in open invitation, allowing her the option to refuse. After a brief hesitation, she stepped close but stood rigid in his embrace. His eyes closed, and he breathed a silent prayer. *Father, I've hurt her so badly.*

"We're going to make it through this," he promised, rubbing her stiff arms. Samantha took a silent step backward, and Steve's gaze dropped to the baby.

He squatted down and met the curious blue stare of his granddaughter. "You must be Bobbie." Steve held out a hand. Bobbie grabbed his fingers with a bright smile and pulled them straight to her mouth. Masculine laughter filled the room as he diverted his hand to her cheek and looked up at his eldest daughter. "May I hold her?"

Samantha's glance went to the ceiling, her only answer a wordless shrug.

Steve stood with the baby, holding her close. Bobbie strained her head back to get a better look at the stranger. Then with the easy acceptance of the very young, she nestled against his shoulder. He breathed deeply of talcum powder and baby lotion, rubbing her back. "I'm your Grandpa. We're going to be good friends."

Samantha took a step forward, her arms outstretched, her tone bitter. "I'll take her now."

"Sam," Iris hissed, her hand on her sister's arm in apparent restraint. "He's not going to hurt her."

Steve heard a muffled groan from Samantha as she turned her back, shrugged away from Iris, and crumpled into Callie's outstretched arms. The sound of her tears almost broke his heart.

He buried his face in the baby's neck. *What now, God?* Steve raised his head and spoke to his daughters. "I know it's probably another violation of my take-it-slow plan, but I brought gifts."

With a kiss to her cheek, he returned Bobbie to her playpen and retrieved the panda. His eyes shifted from the baby to the bear that was ten times her size and much too big for the playpen. "You'll have to grow into yours," he said with a laugh and placed it on the floor. Steve sat down on the couch. "Samantha, Iris, please come sit with me." He waited until his daughters took places on either side of him. Iris faced him with open curiosity. Samantha sat as far away as possible, her face streaked with recent tears, her eyes locked straight ahead.

"I wanted everyone to have something special to mark this day. I looked at rings, but since I didn't know your sizes, I decided on these instead." He opened the small bag and retrieved two long, narrow, jewelry cases. Iris accepted hers. Sam refused to move, so Steve opened her case and laid it in her lap. Gold ID bracelets nestled inside each box. Each bracelet glittered with four small stones next to their names.

"I have one, too." He moved the cuff of his shirt aside to reveal a heavier version of the dainty bracelets he'd just given his daughters. "I had today's date engraved on the backs. They each have our birthstones on the front." He lifted Iris's from the box. "A ruby for yours, Sam, peridot for Iris, topaz for me, and a diamond," his voice caught at the words, "for your mother. I'll understand if you aren't comfortable wearing them right now. I'll be praying for your feelings to change."

Benton cleared his throat. "We're gonna head back to the house."

Steve looked up and stood. "Let me walk you out. I'll be right back," he told his daughters. He followed Callie and Benton out and pulled the door shut. With his eyes closed, he leaned back against the peeling paint. "Thank you seems so inadequate for what you've given me."

Callie nodded toward the apartment. "Don't thank us yet. You've got a big job in there."

"I don't have anyone to blame for that but me. With God's help, we'll make this work."

"I know you will. God's already working on it. I wanted to tell you in person. Both of the girls accepted Christ into their lives on Sunday."

"Thank you, Jesus," Steve whispered.

Callie laid a hand on his arm. "That isn't a cure-all, but it's a step in the right direction. Iris already seems pretty easy with the situation. I'm sure Sam will come around in time. She's had to be mother, father, and provider for her little family. She isn't going to surrender any of those responsibilities without a fight."

"Samantha was always too independent for her own good, even as a toddler."

"Benton and I have run up against her independence on a number of occasions lately. I don't envy you at all. You're on the right track, and we're praying for you." Callie reached for Benton's hand. "Come on. You're taking me out to dinner."

Steve watched them climb into their individual vehicles. "Dinner." His memory bombarded him with images of long-ago meals. Lee Anne seated at the table across from him, a six-year-old Sam on one side, and a blue-eyed baby in a high chair on the other. He fixed his jaw in determination. "I think it's time to be a family," he whispered, opening the door to the apartment. "Girls, get your bags. Dinner's on me."

Steve carried Bobbie out of the restaurant two hours later and considered the mall that loomed across the parking lot aglow in a sea of spotlights.

"We've got a little time before the stores close. How 'bout we walk around the mall?"

"Cool," Iris agreed.

"No thanks," Samantha insisted. "We both have class tomorrow."

Steve looked down at his granddaughter. "We have a yes and a no. What's your vote?" He leaned his head down to the baby and listened intently. With a shrug of apology he looked at Samantha. "Bobbie votes yes. I guess we're going to the mall."

Samantha rolled her eyes. "Told you that, did she? I am amazed."

Iris grabbed her sister's hand. "Come on, Sam. Don't be a spoil sport."

"Yeah. Don't be a spoil sport." Steve smiled.

They drove the short distance to the entrance, searching briefly for a parking spot. Steve rubbed his hands together as they entered the mall. "All right, where to first?"

When Samantha refused to answer, Steve reached over and took the baby again. "Come here, sweetheart.

Mama's in a snit." With Bobbie in one arm, he hung his other across Iris's shoulder. "Looks like the choice is all yours."

"Can we go to the arcade?"

"You got any money?"

Iris giggled, "No."

"Hmm." Steve pulled out his wallet. "Good thing I do. Lead on." They wove through the crowded aisles, leaving Samantha little choice but to follow behind them. He pulled bills from his wallet and pressed them into Iris's hand. "Go for it, baby."

"Wow, thanks," Iris said before melting into the bells and whistles of the resident video games.

Samantha stood, her arms crossed, eyes glued to Iris, watching her move from game to game. "This isn't going to work, you know."

"What?" he asked.

"This golden goose thing you've got going on. You can't just breeze back into our lives and buy your way in. Jewelry, dinner, a wallet full of cash..." Sam shook her head. "You might earn a few short-term brownie points, but I'm not impressed, and Iris is smarter than that."

"Samantha, that's not what any of this is about." He raised his hand to silence her objections. "I accept that you have issues with me. I understand you have doubts and questions we're going to need to deal with. But you need to get used to the idea that I'm back to stay." Steve reached over to lay a hand on her shoulder. When she took a quick step away, he shook his head sadly. "I didn't expect you to accept me back into the role of father in a day, but can you try and give me a chance to prove myself?"

"I'm here. That's about all the chance I can offer you. It's certainly more than you've given us in the past," Samantha answered. Molten lava had replaced the icicles in her voice. "I can promise you I won't pack up and take off in the middle of the night. We're through running. What we've built in Garfield is worth protecting. We'll still be here when you're long gone. I've picked up after you once. I can do it again." Her eyes dropped to Bobbie, sound asleep in his arms. "I just hope you get it out of your system before Iris and Bobbie get too attached."

Steve refused to rise to her bait. "Can we talk about establishing some sort of daily routine?" he asked her instead. "Even though we're in separate apartments, I'd like to have family dinners in the evenings before you go to work. I'd also love to watch Bobbie while you're at work."

"You want kitchen duty." Samantha stopped him. "It's all yours. I enjoy cooking, but with my schedule, any meal I don't have to fix is a good one. I'm sure Iris will feel the same, but Bobbie is mine. We're both happy with our current arrangement."

"I can accept those terms, for the time being. But I want you to know I'm going to do everything in my power to bring us all together, under one roof, just as soon as possible."

Sam stood straighter as Iris started toward them, the spoils of her arcade session clutched in her arms. "Good luck with that."

CHAPTER TWENTY-ONE

Callie grinned when Sam fell in next to her after church on Sunday morning. "Hey there."

"Hey back. I have a gigantic, *huge* favor to ask," Sam said, juggling Bobbie from shoulder to hip.

"OK."

"I spoke to Pastor Gordon this morning about doing that baby presentation thing."

"Dedication," Callie supplied.

"That's the word. Anyway, we're going to do it next Sunday."

"Sam, what a wonderful idea."

"You don't think I'm rushing things a little?"

"Absolutely not. You've made a commitment to God. You want to include your daughter in that. I can't think of anything more appropriate. What's the favor?"

Samantha pulled Callie out of the throng of people and out onto the sidewalk before she answered. "Do you think Terri would be willing to be Bobbie's godmother?"

Callie cocked her head. "Terri? Really?"

Sam nodded. "I know it seems sort of sudden. But I can already see how much they love each other. Do you think she'll think I'm weird?"

"I'm sure she'd be honored. I'll ask her for you if that's what you want."

"No, I can ask her. I just wanted to see what you thought about the idea. But that's just a small part of the gigantic favor." Sam paused, and looked at the ground, her voice a shy whisper when she continued. "Would you guys do it with us?"

"Hmm?"

Sam sighed. "You and Benton. I want you and Benton to be Bobbie's honorary grandparents."

Callie felt tears and a smile fighting for control of her expression. "Honey, I don't even have to ask Benton to know the answer to that question. We'd both be very honored." Callie took the baby out of Sam's arms. "Come to Grandma, precious. Is your father excited? It was so good to see all of you sitting together in service this morning."

"This has nothing to do with him."

"What?"

"This has nothing to do with him," Sam repeated. "This is for Bobbie. I want you to be there for her because you've already been there for us. I'm so grateful to you."

"Sam, we didn't do it for gratitude. Leaving your father out of something like this—"

"I'm not *leaving him out.* At least not in the way you mean. I...I don't even know how to say it. I'm not leaving him out to be mean or vindictive. But I can't include him just because people think it's the right thing to do either." Frustration laced her explanation. "How can I make everyone understand?"

She took a few fretful steps away before turning back to face Callie. "I don't know him, all right? I know that probably sounds stupid, but it's the only way I can explain it. He's my father, but he's not my *dad*. Right now, he's just a guy I used to know. Until, or *if*, that changes, it would be worse to include him than to just let him watch from his seat." Sam raised her hands in a gesture of defeat. "I know you hoped we could all fall back into being a big happy family. I don't know if that's ever going to happen."

Callie watched the seventeen-year-old stare across the parking lot to where Steve and Benton were engrossed in an animated discussion. Iris joined the men, seeming perfectly comfortable with the way Steve draped an arm around her shoulders while continuing his conversation.

"It seems so much easier for Iris. I'm happy for her, but..." Sam's voice and thoughts trailed off.

"I understand what you're trying to say," Callie assured her. "You have to do what's right for you. But," she angled Sam's face so that they were eye to eye, "we're all praying about the situation. Are you?"

"Every day," Sam whispered. "I'm trying, but I won't make Bobbie's day a lie. You guys are the best thing that ever happened to her. That's what I want people to see next Sunday."

Callie jumped when a car horn sounded from behind her. Benton stood next to his truck making chatterbox motions with his hand. When she looked his way his motions changed to spooning imaginary food into his mouth.

She nodded at him, waved, and turned back to Sam. "Are you coming to service tonight?"

"Should be. Steve's cooking for us, again. We've had dinner over there every night. If nothing else, I've been reprieved from kitchen duty."

"All right." Callie kissed the baby before starting across the street to join her husband. "We'll see you later." She crossed over to Benton. "What were you two guys talking about so seriously?"

"Just keeping tabs on the situation. He's trying to get a better feel for the town, wanted to know about Garfield's schools, banks, and local realtors. It sounds like he's thinking about settling here. I gave him directions out to the house and told him to come see me when he was ready to get serious." He turned Callie toward their vehicle. "What's for lunch?"

"I have a steak marinating in the fridge. If you can hold on to your hunger pangs for a few more seconds, I have important news."

"What could be more important than red meat on hot coals?"

"Sweetheart, I just found out this morning we're going to be grandparents again."

CHAPTER TWENTY-TWO

Sam rubbed her fingers over the diaper tabs Monday afternoon to make sure they were stuck properly. Her fingers brushed Bobbie's tummy and the baby gurgled up at her. Sam grinned. "Ticklish are you?" She bent down to nuzzle the plump belly, turning it into a game, relishing these moments alone with her daughter. Yesterday, today, and tomorrow. Three days off in a row was a rarity. "And we're going to enjoy every single minute, aren't we, sugarplum?" The baby jabbered her response as Sam scooped her up and carried her into the living room.

When Iris came through their front door, Sam glanced at the clock in confusion. It was just after two in the afternoon. "What are you doing home from school?"

Iris closed the door and backed up against it.

Sam frowned at the guilty look on her sister's face. "Iris?"

"I had Dad check me out of school early."

"You did what?"

"I had Dad check me out," she repeated. "I wanted to talk to you."

"Iris, you see me every day. We share an apartment. Why would you need to skip school to talk?"

"That's sort of what I wanted to talk about."

"You're not making any sense."

Iris moved to the table and began to set out chocolate cookies and glasses of milk. "Come sit down, Sam."

Sam put Bobbie in her playpen and moved to stand by the table. "Iris, you need to answer my question."

Iris motioned to the snack.

"Not this time," Sam said. "I need to know what's going on."

Iris dropped her eyes to the floor. Sam had to strain to hear her answer. "I'm moving in with Dad."

"Excuse me?"

Iris looked up and sucked in a deep breath. "I said I'm going to move into the spare bedroom in Dad's apartment."

Sam took a step back. Her sister's words hit her with the suddenness of a slap to the face. Without a word to Iris, she turned and marched out of the apartment straight to her father's door. She didn't knock, she simply threw the door open hard enough that it bounced against the wall behind it.

Her father sat on his sofa, hands clasped between his knees, his head bowed. *You better be praying.*

He stood to face her wrath. "Sam, you need to calm down."

"Calm down?" Samantha faced him, anger making her face feel feverish. She fisted her hands and rested them on her hips. "Calm down? I don't know what harebrained idea you've put in Iris's head, but I forbid it."

"Samantha, it's not your choice."

"Who are you to say that to me? Who's been taking care of her for the last year and a half? Heck, for the last ten years? It hasn't been you. So if it's not my choice, and it certainly isn't yours, whose is it?"

"Samantha, if you'll calm down and listen, I'll tell you." He rested his hands on her shoulders. "Iris came to me with this. As much as I want us to be a family, I would not have made this suggestion so soon."

Sam shook off his hands. "You're a liar!"

"He's not lying, Sam."

Samantha turned to the door to find her little sister standing on the threshold holding Bobbie.

Iris walked into the room and placed Bobbie on the sofa. She took the time to arrange pillows around her niece. That done, she faced her sister. "Do you remember when we were at Callie's house...the day they told us about finding Dad?"

Sam nodded mutely.

"You told them I could do what I wanted. Did you mean that?"

Sam nodded again. "Yes, but I didn't think..."

Iris shook her head and crossed the room to stand in front of her sister. "I didn't know I'd feel like this. I know this makes you angry, but please don't hate me."

Sam closed her eyes against the pleading she saw on Iris's face. "I could never hate you, sweetheart." As her tears slipped free, Sam pulled Iris into a hug. "Do me a favor?"

Iris nodded.

"Watch Bobbie for me for a little while. I need to take a walk."

Samantha didn't know where she was headed. She just walked. Tears streaked her face. She wiped them away absently.

Tears of betrayal. What could Iris be thinking? They'd been a team. They'd made the impossible work for them. Did that mean so little to her?

Tears of revenge. She'd leave it to them. Garfield wasn't the only place she could live. *Except it is.* She didn't have the money to take off again. The money left in the bank account technically belonged to Iris. She liked her job. Graduation was just days away. Sam sighed. For the first time in a long time, she had people she could call her friends.

Tears of indignation. Who did he think he was? He could say all day that this was Iris's idea. Sam couldn't accept that. Somewhere along the line, he'd planted the thought in Iris's head.

Tears of self-pity. Sam had sacrificed her whole life for Iris, and all it took was *four days* of something better than what she could provide for her sister to make it all pointless.

Tears of resignation. There wasn't a thing she could do to change the situation.

Finally, tears of resolve. She'd show them both. She'd be the bigger person. Iris would only be next door. When Steve got tired of this new game he was playing, Iris would need her to pick up the pieces, again. Once he went away, things would go back to normal.

Normal. All the heartache, all the struggle, the living

from day to day. Was that the normal she missed and wanted? With that thought she looked up and realized where her path had taken her. Right to the door of Valley View Church. Had she really walked five miles? She didn't see any cars in the lot, but decided to try the door anyway. It swung open under her hand.

Samantha knew she should go home, but she needed to sit for a few minutes. She walked into the darkened sanctuary and sat in the back row of pews. Peace settled around her and she took a deep breath. Even empty, this place vibrated with life. New tears flooded her eyes. Her whispered plea seemed loud in the cavernous room. "Oh, Jesus. I don't know what to do."

Sam lost track of the time as she poured her heart out to her heavenly Father. Someone coughed behind her, and she scrambled to her feet. "I'm sorry. I know I probably shouldn't be in here, but the door was unlocked. I just wanted to sit for awhile."

The overhead lights snapped to life. Sam blinked, finally able to focus on Dave Sisko. He motioned for her to sit back down.

"You're fine. Sam, right?"

Samantha nodded. "I was taking a walk and ended up here." She looked around the empty room. "It's so peaceful."

Valley View's youth pastor nodded in response. He sat down in the pew in front of her and turned around so they could talk. "It's an anointed place, even when there's no one here. A good place to come when you're confused or hurting."

Sam bowed her head at his statement.

"What's wrong, Sam?"

"Nothing...everything." She shrugged. "Just stuff."

"You want to talk about it?"

She shook her head. "It wouldn't do any good. I just needed...something."

"Did you find any answers?"

"I don't think there *are* any answers." She stood to go. "I'll be fine."

Sisko took a card and a pen out of his pocket. He scribbled on the back and handed it to her. "Read this later, it's one of my favorite verses. It might help."

Sam took the card. "I don't have a Bible yet. Iris..." She swallowed and didn't finish.

"That's OK. I can tell you what it says. Psalms 91:14-15. *Because he hath set his love upon me, therefore will I deliver*—or rescue—*him: I will set him on high, because he hath known my name. He shall call upon me, and I will answer him: I will be with him in trouble; I will deliver him, and honour him.* You're not alone, Sam." He held out his hand. "Come on. I'll drive you home."

Bible study wrapped up early Monday night. The ladies sat around the table in Callie's dining room. No cheesecake remained. For that, Callie was extremely grateful.

Her idea of a top-your-own cheesecake party had been a success. She'd provided a plain cheesecake and a chocolate one along with numerous toppings on the side then encouraged everyone to create their own personal favorite. Much sharing and comparing ensued, each lady in attendance convinced hers was the *perfect* cheesecake creation.

"That was fun," Karla said. "What gave you the idea?"

"Something I read in a holiday planner somewhere. An idea for when you had several tastes to please."

"I loved the one Sophie did with the chocolate and caramel drizzled over it and chopped pecans sprinkled on top," Terri told them. "I bet it would have tasted even better with the chocolate cheese cake."

"You have to stop." Pam leaned back to unsnap her jeans. "You're killing me. Save your ideas to try on Gary."

"Not going to happen," Terri answered with a sad smile.

Pam's eyes narrowed. "Oh honey—"

"Now you stop," Terri told her friend. "Gary called last night. His company is sending him straight to Houston when he finishes in Atlanta. He's going to be gone for at least another two months."

"And when he comes back?" Callie asked.

"They're moving him to their home office in New York, permanently."

"He had the nerve to break it off with you over the phone?" Pam asked indignantly. "That...that..."

"Would you stop?" Terri laughed. "It wasn't like that. Yes, we ended it over the phone, but only because he didn't want to make it worse on either of us by waiting until he got home. We had a long conversation. Neither of us is ready to surrender our careers. We've both prayed about our relationship. We agreed this is a good indication that God has other plans for our lives. We're going to have dinner a final time when he comes home to pack up his apartment. We'll go our separate ways as friends."

Callie reached across the table and squeezed Terri's hand.

"I'm good with this, guys," Terri assured her friends. "I know God has someone out there for me. I want a home and babies, but it needs to have the right husband and father first. I'm willing to wait until he comes along."

Silence settled over the table for a few seconds. Callie moved on to a happier topic. "Sam came to me after church yesterday. Bobbie is going to be dedicated next Sunday. She wants Benton and me to stand as honorary grandparents—"

"Ohhh." Terri interrupted. "That's so sweet. I knew about the dedication. She asked me to stand as godmother. She didn't mention the grandparent thing."

"So," Karla wondered, "is her father going to be invited to this little party?"

Callie shook her head. "Probably not. When we were talking about it, I tried nudging her in that direction. I don't think she's ready to take that road. Iris, on the other hand, is happier than I've ever seen her, talkative and outgoing. She was glowing in class yesterday morning."

Pam shook her head. "It's a shame. I had some initial doubts about Steve, but he seems so sincere in his desire to mend his family. It was great to see them all at church together Sunday."

"You were there for their initial meeting, Callie. How'd it go?" Karla asked.

Callie laughed, standing to retrieve her purse. She took out a handful of photos and passed them around the table. "I knew you'd ask, so I snapped a few shots with my phone. Benton met me over there and they got their *man* moments out of the way. Just a few gently delivered words of warning to let Steve know we'd all be keeping an eye on the situation."

"He didn't—" Terri laughed.

"Good for him." Pam applauded.

"Well, I was on the phone, so I don't think Benton meant for me to hear what he said, but I think it cleared the air between them. I saw them talking after church yesterday. Steve was looking for information on the town. Benton seems to think he's serious about relocating for good. He certainly brought everything he owns with him. You couldn't even turn around in his apartment on Thursday afternoon."

"Details, Callie," Pam prodded. "How did the girls react when they saw him?"

"Cold reservation from Sam, a slightly warmer reception from Iris. Like I said, Iris is not even the same child. If yesterday was any indication, there hasn't been a lot of thawing out on Sam's part."

"We need to be patient. The whole thing is going to take some time," Terri agreed. "I see Sam every day. I know they're having dinner with Steve in the evenings, but she hasn't shared any details with me."

Karla spread the photos out on the table and tapped one. "These are just about the worst pictures I've ever seen." She squinted. "What is this big black and white blob?"

"Well, I couldn't very well ask them to pose for me." Callie answered in her own defense. "That 'blob' is simply the biggest stuffed panda in the world. Steve's present for his granddaughter."

"She'll be six before she can even get her arms around it," Karla joked.

"Yeah, it was pretty funny to see it propped up next to her like a big black mountain. He had gifts for the girls, too. Gold ID bracelets with Thursday's date engraved on the back and matching birthstones next to their names on the front. I saw Iris wearing hers yesterday. I'd bet money Sam's is still in the box."

"Like I said, I see Sam every morning, and I've not seen it on her. I'd have remembered something as unique as that," Terri told them. "She'll warm up. What girl can resist jewelry and attention from a handsome man? Well..." Terri fumbled. "I mean, not that Sam views him that way of course...but—"

Karla pounced on the adjective. "Handsome?"

"I'm a single woman with eyes in my head. I'd say handsome applies."

Karla studied Terri with pursed lips. "You know, there's only eight or nine years difference in your ages..."

"Don't even go there," Terri warned.

"What?" Karla asked, innocently.

"And don't give me that innocent act either. There will be *no* matchmaking attempts from you three. God and I can find my own man, thank you very much. He's the only matchmaker I'm interested in."

CHAPTER TWENTY-THREE

Tuesday afternoon found Callie focused on her computer screen, all of her attention dedicated to the changes she needed to make to her spreadsheet. She settled her reading glasses more firmly in place. "I will find the problem in this formula," she muttered aloud. That had become her mantra an hour ago. So far, it had failed to produce the necessary results. The phone rang and she snatched it up. A dial tone greeted her. An irritated glance at the flashing buttons on the phone revealed the light blinking on her private line. Her finger jabbed it impatiently.

"This is Callie. How may I help you?"

"You busy?"

Callie smiled at Terri's question and turned away from the computer. "Just updating our inventory spreadsheet. I can't get the thing to come out even. My eyes are almost crossed, and my next step will be banging my head on the keyboard. You are a welcome distraction. What's up?"

"I think we might have a red-alert situation over at the apartments."

Callie leaned back in her chair, giving her full attention to her friend. "How so?"

"I was busy when Sam brought the baby in this morning. I didn't get a chance to talk to her, but she was by herself."

"So..."

"Iris always comes in with her."

"Maybe Iris had to be at school early."

"That's what I thought, too, but when Sam picked up Bobbie at lunch, I mentioned it and she almost took my head off."

"Uh-oh."

"She told me to mind my own business, and I quote, 'if that's possible.'"

"That doesn't sound like Samantha."

Terri huffed into the phone. "I know. She apologized, but there were tears in her eyes when she left. Something is definitely up. Everything was fine on Sunday. You said so yourself. So what happened between then and this morning?"

Worry sizzled along Callie's nerves. "We knew it would be an adjustment for her."

Terri interrupted. "Adjustment, yes. But, Callie, she was crying."

Callie pushed her readers up and pinched the bridge of her nose. Her first inclination was to brush this off as empathy on Terri's part. But what if something was really wrong? Now that Terri had voiced her fears, Callie's own insecurities wouldn't rest until she checked it out for herself.

"OK, I'll stop by there after work. It'll make us both

feel better."

Steve paced his apartment, waiting impatiently for Iris to get home from school. He could hardly wait to see the look on her face when she saw the results of his day's labor.

The small room that passed for a second bedroom had received a thorough cleaning before he went to bed last night. Steve had spent the morning prowling department and furniture stores.

The nondescript beige carpet was now covered with a pale pink shag area rug. The single window bore ruffled curtains in a mixture of pink, purple, and yellow. But the final touch, the prize of his shopping excursion, was the white oak canopy bed delivered two hours ago.

Steve stopped in the doorway and surveyed his handy work. It had taken him an hour to get the pieces maneuvered into the cramped room and assembled. The full-sized bed barely left room to open and close the door. The accompanying nightstand and three-drawer chest completed the look but left little space in the room for anything but sleeping. He was glad he'd resisted the urge to buy the matching dresser and desk. They would have ended up in the hallway.

Steve ran his hand over the comforter that matched the canopy and the curtains. The transformation of the room was perfect. He hoped Iris thought so. His smile turned to a frown. If only Samantha would make an effort at accepting him. Her words from their first night at the mall haunted him. *"We'll still be here when you're long gone."*

She didn't expect him to stay. He really couldn't

blame her for those doubts, but he longed for the chance to prove her wrong. There had to be a way to make her see that he wasn't going anywhere. Nothing would make him happier than to decorate rooms for Samantha and Bobbie. Not that there were rooms here to decorate. His apartment in Chicago had been twice this size and he'd considered it small. They'd need more space if they ever managed to be a family again.

He sat on the edge of the bed and bowed his head into his hands. "God, please make us a family again. I know I messed up, but we're all back in one place, sort of. Please give me the wisdom I need to complete what we've started."

The front door slammed. "Dad?"

Steve jumped up, smoothed the spread, and hurried out to the front room.

"Hey, baby. Welcome home."

Iris stepped into the circle of his arms with a deep sigh.

"What?"

"Home. I like the sound of that." She pushed back. "Let's get started moving my stuff. I got it all boxed up last night."

Steve looked down into the eyes of his daughter, fighting the lump forming in his throat. "I have a surprise for you first."

Iris's eyebrows climbed beneath her bangs. She looked around the room. "Where?"

Steve chuckled at the anticipation glowing in her blue eyes. "Close your eyes."

"Da-ad."

"Close them." He moved behind her, placed his hands on her shoulders, and turned her down the hall.

After checking to make sure her eyes were closed, he nudged her forward. "No peeking."

Iris answered with a giggle. Steve placed a hand over her eyes to insure her compliance to his request. He positioned her in front of the door and took a single step back. "OK, take a look."

Iris took a couple of steps into the room and turned in a circle to take everything in. "Oh, Daddy." She sat on the bed and bounced experimentally.

"Daddy." Steve's smile spread across his face. "I like the sound of *that*." He moved to sit beside her. "Do you really like it? It's not too pink?"

Iris folded herself into his arms. "It's perfect. You're perfect. The world is perfect. Thank you."

"Oh, Iris, I have so much lost time to make up for—"

"No," Iris interrupted. "Not, thank *you*. Thank *God*. I just wish Sam—"

Steve tilted her head up and laid a finger across her lips. "No bad thoughts today. Just keep praying. Your sister will come around to things when the time is right. I have a few ideas about that, too. Now, let's go get those boxes."

Moving Iris didn't take long. A couple of trips apiece and her stuff was transferred.

Sam sat on the sofa in the smaller apartment, arms crossed, watching their every move with tear-brightened eyes, making no offer to help. Steve and Iris let her brood. An hour later, Iris had everything put away in drawers and the room's tiny closet.

Iris followed Steve to the kitchen. "Moving is hungry work. What's for dinner?"

"Meatloaf, my own secret recipe." Steve pulled a

bowl from the fridge.

Iris peered into the bowl. "You have a secret meatloaf recipe?"

"Yep."

She boosted herself up onto the counter. "What makes it secret?"

"Oh, this and that," he answered, patting the mixture into a loaf pan, "hamburger, a little sausage, some cheese...fried ants."

"Yuck!"

"Don't knock it 'til you try it, baby." Steve laughed, sliding the pan into the oven. With the timer set, he turned and pulled Iris from the counter and into a hug. "No ants," he said, laying his head on top of hers. They stood in each other's arms for several seconds. Finally he took a deep breath and released Iris with a quick swat to her backside. "Do you have homework?"

"Just a little. There are only a couple of school days left," she reminded him. "I'll do it after dinner."

"Homework first. Gotta keep those grades up."

Iris faced him, hands fisted on her hips. "You've turned into such a...a *father*," she said in playful exasperation. "I like it."

"You can butter me up all you want. The homework still gets done before dinner. Open the front door please. The oven will make it too stuffy in here."

Iris turned toward the living area with a small smile for herself

and an exaggerated groan for her father. She opened the heavy wooden door and raised the glass on the storm door before sitting on the floor in front of her father's coffee table. She pulled her math book out of her backpack.

Life just didn't get much better than this. The worries of a few weeks ago were things of the past. The relationship with her father had grown into something very special in just a few days. Iris rested her chin on her fist and stared into space.

How had that happened? She missed her mother. There was still a great big sore spot in her heart that hurt when she picked at it, so she, mostly, left it alone. Having her father back didn't make that hurt any less, but it gave her something new to focus her attention on. *Why has it been so easy for me and so tough for Sam?*

When Sam came back from her walk yesterday, she'd picked up Bobbie and disappeared without saying a word. Iris wouldn't be surprised if her sister skipped family dinner again tonight. Sam was hurting, and Iris blamed herself for part of it.

"Twenty-nine."

Her attention snapped back to the present. "What?"

"You were concentrating so hard, you had smoke coming out of your ears. I thought I better give you an answer before you went up in flames."

She closed her notebook with a chuckle. "Not even close."

Her father frowned at the closed textbook.

"I'm done."

"Just math?"

"Well, I had me some English, but I done did it all ready."

Steve grabbed her by the collar, pulling her to him, nose to nose. "You're a brat with a fresh mouth."

His facial expression was tight, but Iris saw his lips twitching to keep from smiling.

She batted at his hands and struggled not to giggle.

Callie parked her car in front of Steve's apartment. She straightened her shirt as she got out, reaching back into the car for the cake she'd bought on the way. Her excuse for being here. Furnishing dessert for their dinner made her look like a friend bearing gifts instead of a nosy busybody. *I hope.*

She stepped to the storm door and froze, her forward motion arrested by the sight of Iris's shirt collar clenched in Steve's fist, the sneer on his face, and Iris's futile efforts to break free.

Callie yanked the door open even as she breathed a prayer. "Oh Jesus, not again. Let her go!"

Steve jerked back. "What?"

"I said let her go. What do you think...?" Callie closed her eyes. The roaring in her ears became the cries of a battered little boy. She raised her hands to her face, the cake landing at her feet. "Not again." Her heart pounded. She couldn't breathe. The world faded to black around her.

CHAPTER TWENTY-FOUR

Steve caught her before she hit the floor. He scooped her up and carried her to the couch. "Iris, go get a cold washcloth."

He patted Callie's cheeks. "Callie, come on. Wake up."

Iris handed him the cloth. "What did she say?"

"'Not again.' Not again what?"

Iris watched with round eyes. "We should call Grandpa."

"Let's give it a second." Steve placed the cloth on Callie's forehead and chaffed her hands. "Come on, Callie. Open your eyes."

Callie's eyes fluttered open. She jerked away from Steve, hands flailing wildly. "Get away from me."

Steve sat back on his heels, doing his best to stay out of her reach. "Hold up, Callie. What's gotten into you?"

She sat up and pulled Iris to her side. "You had your hands around her throat."

Steve and Iris looked at each other. Iris pulled away.

"Oh, Miss Callie, no..."

Steve motioned her quiet. He looked at Callie with all the sincerity he could summon. "Callie, we were playing with each other. I would *never* lay a hand on one of my children in anger."

Callie stared into his eyes for several moments before shifting her gaze to Iris. "Playing?"

Iris nodded.

Callie closed her eyes, her shoulders slumping back into the couch. "I'm such an idiot." She pushed herself up. "I need to go." A mound of destroyed chocolate cake blocked her path. "Iris, can you get the broom for me?"

"I'll take care of it," Steve said. "Are you going to be all right?"

Callie looked at the ceiling and shook her head with a grim chuckle. "I wish I had the answer to that question." With her hand on the doorknob and silent tears tracking down her face, she turned back to look at father and daughter. "I'm sorry." She hurried through the door, brushed past Samantha without a word, and rushed to her car.

"What did you do to her?" Samantha demanded.

Steve looked up from the mess he was cleaning. "Excuse me?"

"Callie just left your apartment in tears. What did you do to her?"

"Sam."

"I won't allow it. You broke my mother's heart, you've stolen my sister, and now you make Callie cry. If you're trying to alienate me from my friends in the hopes of making me run to you, it won't work."

"Sam, I—"

She turned her back on him and looked at Iris. "I came over to make sure your homework didn't get lost in the joy of your new living arrangement."

Iris took Sam by the hand. "Come look at my room. Dad—"

Sam jerked her hand away. "Not interested. Homework?"

Steve dumped the dustpan. "Calm down. We took care of her homework. Where is Bobbie?"

"Asleep. Don't tell me what to do. I don't answer to you. I'm only going to ask you one more time. What did you do or say to make Callie cry?"

Steve scrubbed his face with his hands and made a command decision. Samantha was just going to have to learn to deal. He grabbed his keys from the table before facing his eldest daughter. A finger stabbed in Sam's direction. "You are acting like a two-year-old. I'll be back, with answers to your questions, in a bit. Finish dinner while I'm gone. That's an order, *not* a request."

He walked out the door leaving Samantha sputtering in his wake.

Steve hurried up the steps and knocked on Callie's front door. He stepped inside when Benton pulled it open. "Is Callie all right?"

The older man shrugged. "She's resting on the couch. She was pretty upset when she got home, but she's calming down now."

"May I talk with her?"

Benton stroked a hand down his beard. "Maybe tomorrow. I think she needs—"

"Benton, who is it?" Callie's voice filtered up the hallway.

He shrugged again and motioned for Steve to precede him down the hall.

Callie swung her feet to the floor when she saw him. Steve shook his head. "Stay put." He took a seat beside her while Benton settled in his recliner. "Are you all right?"

Callie nodded. "Steve, I'm so sorry. When I saw what I thought I was seeing, I lost it. I jumped to the wrong conclusion, and I made a fool out of myself. Please forgive me."

He waved her explanation away. "Apology accepted if it makes you feel better. But why would you think...I mean...how could you possibly...?" His voice dried up when he noticed fresh tears on her face. "Aw, gee. Never mind. I didn't mean to make you cry again. Sam will have my scalp."

Callie hiccupped a laugh. "Gave you a bad time, did she?"

"Raked me over the coals pretty good," he admitted. "She's convinced I'm to blame for whatever caused you pain. Judge, jury, and executioner. She'll get over it."

Callie took a deep breath and looked at Benton.

Benton shrugged. "It's your story."

"Don't—" Steve began.

"No." Callie interrupted him. "I owe you an explanation." She took a deep breath and closed her eyes. "I work at an OB/GYN clinic. It's a busy practice, but in spite of that, sometimes you just get caught up in the lives of your patients.

"A few months ago we had a patient who was separated from her husband. They had a daughter and a newborn baby boy. Somewhere along the way, the authorities became concerned about child abuse and put the children into protective custody until they could complete their investigation.

"Mom was one of those patients I mentioned. Friendly, outgoing, always so loving and patient with her kids. I knew she wasn't guilty, and when she asked me to testify on her behalf, I said yes. I didn't think much about it, and I didn't pray about it at all. I just sat up there on that stand and swore to tell the truth." Callie's voice broke. "We buried Sawyer six months ago. I was right about Mom and a hundred-percent wrong about Dad. He beat that child to death."

"Callie..."

"I promised myself, and God, that I would never put myself in that position again. When I walked into your apartment tonight and saw...well, *thought* I saw, your hands on Iris, all I could think was *not again*. That I'd made the same mistake twice and put three more children in danger. I couldn't deal with it. I handled it badly. I'm sorry."

Oh, you poor, broken angel. Steve glanced across the room at Benton then faced Callie again. "I have two things to say. First, from the outside looking in, I think you're putting a lot of blame on your shoulders that doesn't belong there. Second, thanks."

Callie tilted her head. "For?"

"For having the courage to put yourself in that position again. For being a wonderful, selfless, thoughtful Christian woman. Your willingness to follow God's direction, in spite of the pain it caused you, has put my family in a position to heal. I can't imagine what you must have gone through, especially today. So thank you."

Steve took Callie's hand. "Will you be

uncomfortable if I share this with the girls? If I don't come back with an answer, Sam will be on your doorstep before morning."

"It's never been a secret. Tell them whatever you think they need to know."

He released her hand and held his arms out in invitation, smiling when Callie leaned in to accept the hug. He squeezed and whispered in her ear. "You're like our own personal angel."

Steve allowed Benton to lead the way out to the driveway. Benton boosted himself onto the open tailgate of his truck. Steve leaned against the nose of his vehicle, facing the older man. "Is she going to be all right?"

Benton shrugged and looked back at the house shadowed by trees and twilight. "I don't know. She was crying when she got home. That turned into quiet introspection before you got here. Now she seems more embarrassed than anything else." He crossed his arms over his chest. "It's been an up-and-down few weeks."

Steve studied his feet. "I'm sorry."

"Not your fault," Benton interrupted him. "What happened today was no more your fault than what happened to Sawyer was Callie's. Circumstances. Bad timing. Cosmic joke. Only God knows for sure. When that little boy died, I thought I was going to lose Callie to her own grief. She didn't leave our bedroom for most of the week, wouldn't eat, didn't get dressed. She cried, and prayed, and read her Bible, looking for answers I'm sure she would have found if she could have seen them through her self-imposed guilt. For months, I've watched her function around, through, and in spite of the hurt, refusing to confront it. As much as it pains me to see her upset, if helping you guys finally makes her deal with things, maybe that's part of what God's trying to do." Benton finished with a deep breath. "What did you want to talk to me about?"

"I've decided to stay in Garfield. I need to start looking for a permanent place to live. I figured you could point me in the right direction."

"Did you call any of the realtors I mentioned to you the other day?"

"I will," Steve said, "but I've always favored older homes. They have more personality than new ones. I thought, given your line of work, you might have a recommendation for me."

Benton pursed his lips. "What are you looking for?"

"Big, roomy, nice yard, more than one living area would be ideal, but if it has plenty of bedrooms, then a single living area would work."

Benton tapped his lips with steepled fingers. "You know, I just might know a place. We did a complete remodel on a house last year. Huge thing. They had it on the market for awhile, but with the housing slump, things that size just weren't moving. I think the owner took it off the listings until things improved a bit."

"Sounds great."

"It's pretty pricy."

"I'm pretty blessed."

Benton chuckled and pushed himself off the tailgate. He offered his hand to Steve. "I'll check on it and give you a call tomorrow."

"Well?"

Samantha's question stopped Steve in the doorway. The single word hung in the air between them like a small storm cloud. The atmosphere in the apartment crackled with the electricity of her anger.

Steve ignored her and crossed into the kitchen. A shiny new microwave sat on a small cart, both prizes from his shopping trip earlier in the day. Deliberately taking his time, he removed food from the refrigerator and fixed a plate and a glass of iced tea. He programmed the timer and stared out the small kitchen window while the oven did its job.

"I asked you a question."

*One...two...three...*He removed his dinner with a potholder, sat down at the table, and blessed it before forking up the first bite. His mental count to ten reached eight before Sam spoke again.

"Are you deaf?"

Steve continued to chew. *Twelve...thirteen...*He decided to extend his count to twenty.

Samantha moved to stand across the table from him. "Don't you dare ignore me. I want to know what you did to Callie to make her cry, and I want to know what you did to fix it. *Now.*"

Steve laid the fork aside and took a swallow of his drink. "I'm not ignoring you, Samantha. I am trying to eat my dinner. While I eat, I'm trying to remember all the reasons why I shouldn't turn you over my knee and treat you like the spoiled child you're acting like. Somehow I don't think a spanking would go very far in rebuilding our relationship." He scrubbed his face. "I'm going to finish my dinner, and then I have some things I need to share with you and your sister, but I'm only going to tell the story once, so you'll have to wait until I get ready to tell it."

Samantha yanked out one of the chairs as he took another bite. She sat heavily and glared at him while he ate.

Steve made an effort to diffuse Samantha's temper with neutral conversation.

"How was school today?"

Sam crossed her arms in silence.

"Where's Iris?"

Sam jerked her head. "She took Bobbie next door to change her."

"Did you eat?"

Sam narrowed her eyes.

Steve shrugged, focusing his attention on his dinner, taking the time to enjoy every bite. The plate full of food satisfied his stomach, but he decided to treat himself to a second piece of meatloaf. It was petty of him, but somewhere that afternoon he'd made the decision to take control of the situation. He was the parent after all.

He rinsed his plate and laid it in the sink before motioning to the sofa. "Go get your sister and we'll talk."

Steve settled into the single easy chair while Iris returned from laying Bobbie down in his room. She took a seat next to Sam.

"Are you done with your little show of power?" Sam asked.

"I don't know, Sam. Are you done with your temper tantrum?"

Iris interrupted their sparring match. "Guys, please."

She looked at her father. "Did you talk to Callie?"

Steve took a deep breath and faced his younger daughter. "Yes, sweetheart. She'll be fine."

"But, what—"

"She thought I was going to hurt you."

Iris cocked her head in question. "Why?"

"A few months ago, Callie had a friend, a patient at the clinic where she works. There was some suspected abuse, and the state took this woman's children into protective custody while they investigated. The kids were small. A little girl and a newborn baby boy, both delivered through the clinic. Callie felt like she knew the people and the situation well enough to testify on the mother's behalf when the case went before the judge.

"Callie didn't go into a lot of detail tonight, but long story short, she served as a character witness for her friend. The court released the children back to the mother and the little boy was beaten to death by his father six months later."

Samantha gasped.

"Oh, Daddy," Iris breathed.

Steve nodded. "Callie blames herself for the death of that little boy. She feels like she interfered in something she should have left alone. She promised herself, and God, that she would never get involved in anyone's business ever again."

Sam broke her silence. "That's crazy. The courts wouldn't have released those children on Callie's testimony alone."

"I agree with you, Sam. But Callie doesn't see it that way. She's been blaming herself for all these months. When she came over today and saw Iris and me wrestling around, she thought I was really angry with Iris and about to hurt her. She doesn't know me well. All she saw was another child she tried to help in the hands of an abusive adult. It freaked her out."

"She's better now?" Iris asked.

Steve shrugged. "Callie still has ghosts to deal with, but I think watching our situation will help her. I would never abuse either of you. As we work toward a resolution to our problems, she'll see that and understand her part in bringing us back together. Benton thinks, and I agree with him, that's been part of God's plan all along. Not just getting us back together as a family but helping Callie forgive herself for something she needs to put behind her. Callie laid a lot on the line when she decided to help you girls. She put her own peace of mind and her heart at risk by reaching out to you and finally to me. I don't intend to let her down."

Samantha pushed herself up from the sofa. "And I am. Is that it?"

Steve frowned. "What do you mean?" He wasn't following Samantha's logic.

"You two aren't going to let Callie down, but I am by refusing to accept you back with open arms." Sam snorted. "That's pretty low, and it won't work. You can't guilt me into doing what you want."

Steve studied his eldest daughter. He responded to her with a mirthless chuckle. "Guilt was never my intention. I only stated the facts. But let me share something with you. Guilt is an ineffective weapon if the person it's aimed at has nothing to feel guilty about. Feeling guilty, Samantha?"

"You wish." Samantha went back to Steve's room

and retrieved her sleeping daughter. For the second time in as many days she stormed out the door.

Steve watched in silence as Iris hurried after her sister. He let her go. He needed a few minutes to himself. Alone in his apartment, he bowed his head in prayer. "Father, thank You. Thank You for bringing us back together. Thank You for giving Callie the courage to follow your direction. Give her rest and healing tonight. Please guide me now. I'm moving forward. I really meant to go slow, but I can't. Iris needs some stability, and even if Sam won't admit it, so does she. Grant me wisdom."

Iris followed her sister, slamming the door of the smaller apartment behind her. She leaned against it and waited for Sam to put the baby in the crib in the next room. Sam joined her in the living room a moment later. "What?"

"You're wrecking everything!"

"Go home," Sam said.

"No."

Sam picked up her car keys. "Then I'm leaving. Watch the baby."

Iris shook her head. "You'll have to move me first, and I'm not going anywhere."

Sam sank to the couch, head down, voice soft. "Iris, I don't want to fight with you."

"Then stop acting like a spoiled brat." Iris moved away from the door and paced the small space in front of her sister.

"Sam, I love you. I probably owe my life to you, but you're wrong. You won't listen to Callie. You won't listen to Dad. Maybe you'll listen to me." She threaded her fingers through her long brown hair, pulling it back from her face. "I thought we were Christians now."

Samantha frowned in response.

"How can we be Christians if we don't do what God wants us to do?"

"What are you talking about?"

"Miss Callie talked about forgiving people in class this week. The Bible says—"

"Iris, you don't understand."

"I understand plenty. I understand we're here because this is where God wanted us. How else could two kids, and a baby, make it on our own like we did? Grandpa said this was God's plan for us, and I still agree with him. We have a chance to have a family again, and you're messing it up."

Sam's reply was a whisper. "I can't."

"Well, I can. I can't explain how or why. I just know he's our father, and I love him." Iris wiped tears from her face. "But I love you, too. You're making me choose between you, and it's not fair. I thought you loved me."

Sam sat back as though slapped, her own tears slipping down her cheeks. "You know I do. But I can't do this, Iris, not even for you."

Iris closed her eyes against a pain she didn't know how to deal with and turned to leave. "You know where to find us if you change your mind." She closed the door softly behind her.

CHAPTER TWENTY-FIVE

Samantha decided to wave the flag of truce on Saturday afternoon. She let herself into her father's apartment and stood in the doorway of her sister's new room. A very nice room, she admitted to herself. Iris lay on the bed, facing the far wall, obviously engrossed in the book she was reading.

Sam took a step inside. "Nice digs."

"Hey," Iris closed the book and reached for the baby she hadn't seen in three days. "Thought you weren't interested."

Sam shrugged and sat on the bed. "I missed you. Bobbie missed you. Can we please not fight anymore?"

Iris bounced the baby. "I'm all for that. I missed you too."

The girls sat in silence for a few moments. Sam picked up the book Iris had discarded. She released a soft huff of breath. It was one of their father's. "Is he any good?"

Iris nodded as she glanced at her watch. "Sam,

please give him a chance. It's time to finish dinner. Will you stay? Dad would like that."

"Where is he?"

"He had an errand to run this afternoon. He should be home any minute. Come on. Let's get everything on the table before he gets back."

The two girls worked in companionable silence as they put a light Saturday evening meal on the table. Sam popped garlic bread into the oven while Iris grated cheese over the salad. Homemade vegetable stew simmered in a slow cooker.

Steve walked through the door just as the timer for the bread sounded. Sam noticed his raised brows when he saw her in his kitchen, and was thankful when he held his peace. He picked up Bobbie from the playpen and held her close for a few seconds.

"Dinner smells great. Thanks for finishing it up." He pulled out a chair and settled Bobbie in his lap.

"She can play while you eat," Sam said.

Steve shook his head. "She's fine. I missed her. I'm glad you decided to join us tonight, Sam. I have a surprise for everyone later."

Sam smiled stiffly at her father. "I was going to let you sit with Bobbie while I spent some time with Iris. But if you have plans, Bobbie and I can just go home after dinner. I've had a long day."

"Sam," Iris began.

"I know you've worked hard today, Samantha, but I need you to come with us for an hour or so. I promise we'll be back early. What I want to show you requires both of you."

Sam sighed heavily. *Why can't he ever take no for an answer?* "Fine, but I'll drive my own car."

"We can stop wherever you need," Steve offered.

"I'll drive my own car." Samantha pushed her half-empty bowl away.

"Sam, you're acting like a baby, again," Iris said.

"Iris, apologize to your sister." Steve's demand was soft but firm.

"But...she's—"

"Samantha needs to come to terms with everything in her own way."

Iris spooned up a bite of stew. "Since when does that include rudeness?" she muttered, just loud enough to be heard.

Sam sat at the table in silent confusion as her father took her side. *Why is he taking up for me? I don't need his help.* She wasn't sure what she needed anymore.

"Iris is right," she whispered. "I was rude, and I apologize." Sam's appetite vanished. She pushed her chair way from the table and reached for her daughter. "Let me take her home for a little while. I need to get her fed before we go."

Steve watched them leave before he retreated to his room. He sat on the side of his bed and bowed his head. "Father, You've answered my prayers by bringing us back together. I'm more grateful than I can say, but I need Your help to reach Sam. I know it's just been a handful of days. Could You please soften her heart? Please help her accept what I want to do for all of us. I'm trying to be patient, Lord, but I need some direction."

A little later Steve stopped his car in front of a vacant house on the outskirts of town. The two-story house sported fresh blue paint with white trim. A comfortable porch wrapped around three sides. An old-fashioned porch swing hung by the front door and rocked slowly in the evening breeze.

"Is this the surprise?" Iris asked from the passenger seat. "A house?"

"A home, I hope. Can you do me a favor?"

"I'll try."

"Just look and listen for now. I promise I'll answer your questions, but let me try to sell this idea to your sister first."

They climbed out of Steve's car while Sam unbuckled the baby.

"OK, we're here," she said. "What's the big surprise?"

Steve dug a key out of his pocket, crooking a finger for his daughters to follow him up the walk. He unlocked the door and ushered them into a spacious living room with shining hardwood floors and a high-beamed ceiling. He studied Sam for a few seconds. "I have some things to say and some things to show you. I'm not going to ask you to agree with anything, but I am going to ask for your promise to hear me out."

Samantha looked at her father through narrowed eyes. She nodded her head.

"I bought this house today." At Sam's sharp intake of breath, Steve looked at her and held up a finger. "You promised," he reminded her.

"I wanted to make a statement about permanence. I felt that buying this house made the statement better than simply talking about it. You girls have put down some roots in Garfield. I've checked out the school system and other aspects of the town. I like what I see. It's obvious we're all comfortable worshiping at Valley

View. I think we could be happy here if we gave ourselves half a chance."

Steve motioned for the girls to follow him, leading them into a spacious kitchen with stainless steel appliances. "The house just underwent an extensive renovation. Everything here is brand new, just what I thought we needed. An old house with a solid foundation dressed up and ready for a new beginning." He opened a door, switched on a light, and started down a sturdy flight of stairs.

"There's a full basement with its own kitchenette. The space has been divided into a living area and two bedrooms with a full bath in the middle. It's the perfect place for someone who wants to be part of a family but still feels the need for her own space on occasion."

"Wow..." Iris couldn't hold back any longer. "Sam, you and Bobbie could live down here forever."

Sam shook her head, turned, and marched back up the stairs.

"Sorry," Iris whispered.

Steve laid a hand on his younger daughter's shoulder and nudged her back up the stairs. "Not to worry," he whispered as his eye's followed Sam up the steps. "I'm hoping we have someone more stubborn than Samantha on our side." He led them back to the living room. He took Bobbie from Sam and continued the tour.

"In addition to the living area and the kitchen, the main floor has two bedrooms and a bath. Those will be for Iris, and a play room for my granddaughter." The next door he opened revealed a room with soft yellow walls and white trim. He turned Bobbie so she could see the space intended for her. "Whatcha think, sweetheart? You and the panda could be real happy here, huh?" Just as he had a few nights ago, he bent his head and pretended to listen to her response. "A puppy? We'll talk."

"Oh, get serious," Sam muttered.

Steve ignored her. "Finally, the upstairs has three more bedrooms and two baths. Two of those bedrooms will be mine. One for sleeping and one for office space. The other will be a guest room."

"Are you done?" Sam asked.

"Nope, follow me. I have two more things to show you." He led them back to the kitchen, through a separate laundry room, and out the back door. They stepped into a large fenced backyard complete with a swing set and a doghouse.

"This is community property. A place for relaxing and playing and entertaining those new friends I'm sure we'll all have. Our first party could be a combination housewarming and graduation celebration." Steve carried Bobbie over to the doghouse. Stooping down, he snapped his fingers, and whistled softly. A sleepy blond Labrador puppy, complete with a red bow around its neck, toddled out to sniff at him and the baby.

Iris rushed over for a better look.

"This is Angel," he said, "official guard dog." The puppy flopped down on her belly and closed her eyes. "I guess we'll have to work on the 'guard dog' portion of her duties."

Iris sat down and pulled the puppy into her lap. "Sam, we have a puppy!"

Steve raised a hand before Samantha could speak. "That concludes the showing portion of my surprise, now for the telling." He sat the baby in Iris's lap so they could both get acquainted with Angel and then turned his full attention on his eldest daughter.

"Samantha, there's no way I can make up for the time we've lost. I know you blame me for most of the hardships you and your sister endured. That's OK, because I blame me, too. I look at you and I see a more mature person at seventeen than I've been for the majority of my adult life. I want to get to know you. I want a chance to see the excited little girl who used to meet me at the front door reflected in your adult eyes." He stretched an arm around her shoulders and for once, she didn't flinch away from him.

"I want this for us. I want you and Bobbie to have the security of a home, forever, if you need it. Callie told me you have a scholarship. I want you to take advantage of that. Buying this house seemed like the best way to show you how serious I am when I say I'm not going anywhere."

He pulled her into a full hug. "That's all I wanted to say."

Sam pushed herself away from her father without a word, went back into the house, and slammed out the front door.

Iris scrambled to follow her sister. Steve held her back.

"Let her go, baby. She's got a lot to think about."

"But..."

Steve shook his head. "Samantha's got to work through this on her own. Bobbie's here. She won't go far, and she won't be gone long." He sat on one of the swings and motioned Iris into the one next to him. "Let's pray for her. God's the only one who can help her right now."

Iris nodded and turned the swing toward her father as he prayed.

"Jesus, I know You've brought us back together for everyone's good. Please comfort Sam's heart. Help her understand that she can trust me. She's hurting, and it's not her fault. Keep her safe."

Callie pulled the clip out of her hair, staring at her reflection in the bathroom mirror. They'd taken their long awaited trip to the lake today. Most of the day had been spent zipping around the water. The guys had been eager to experiment with what their handiwork had accomplished. By lunchtime, they were satisfied that their boat was seaworthy and sure to be the envy of the fishing trip just a few days away.

She grinned at the memory. The late May sun had been hot and the water cold. Her arms and face were sunburned. The wind had whipped Callie's hair into a bird's nest of tangles. The pale blue T-shirt she'd worn with her denim shorts would never be the same and brushing these tangles out of her hair would be a lengthy and painful operation. Callie was ready to do it all over again. *We need to take April and Randy out there this summer.* Braced for the unpleasant task ahead, she picked up the hairbrush.

A frantic pounding on the front door interrupted her pleasant thoughts of summer fun. Callie hurried down the hallway and pulled the door open. The rebuke forming in her mind died on her lips. Sam, eyes red and swollen from crying, stumbled into her arms, fresh tears coming between ragged breaths.

Callie's heart went to her throat. "Sam, what's

wrong? Has something happened to Bobbie?"

Sam clung to her like a lifeline. "No."

With a sigh of relief, Callie led the sobbing teenager into the living room and pulled her down to the couch. She held her for a few minutes until the sobs became hiccups and finally dried up completely. "Are you going to tell me what's wrong?"

"He bought a puppy!"

"You don't like dogs?" At Sam's stricken look, Callie rushed to reassure her. "No, sweetheart, I'm not trying to be funny, I can see how upset you are, but...'he bought a puppy'?"

Sam got up to pace the floor in front of Callie's couch. She opened her mouth to speak a couple of times and stopped in favor of more pacing.

Callie sat back, willing to give the youngster the time she needed.

"He bought a house," Sam finally said. "A big house, with a huge yard, and this wonderful old porch swing. The house came furnished with a pretty little puppy in a perfect little dog house."

"Oh my."

"Yeah. His idea of a surprise. No warning. Just...look what I did. A done deal complete with a bow around the puppy's neck." Sam's pacing resumed. "The house is great," she conceded scornfully. "Big three-level monstrosity. The basement's all done up as separate living quarters. There's plenty of room for everyone to have their own space. Iris is in love with the puppy. She drooled over the house while he showed it to us. I'll bet they're off buying furniture and curtains as we speak."

"And you're feeling betrayed."

"Ya think?"

Callie patted the seat beside her. "Come sit down. Your pacing is giving me a headache."

Samantha flopped onto the couch, crossing her arms with a militant expression. "Who does he think he is? You should have heard him at dinner. I got a little snippy, and Iris called me down. He rushed to my defense, told her I needed time to adjust to things in my own way. Now this. He lied. He's pushing me, and I'm not ready. I told him, I told you all, not to push. He's throwing money and gifts around. He's completely lured Iris over to his side."

"Sweetheart, this isn't about taking sides."

"Of course it is," Sam objected. "Did you know Iris moved in with him a couple of days ago? They're over there all happy and cozy and she has no clue. He hasn't been here. There's no guarantee he'll be here tomorrow. And when he's gone I'll be left to clean up after him, again."

"Buying a house is a pretty big statement on stability."

Sam waved that away. "He gave up a house and a family before. Who's to say he won't walk away again once the new wears off?"

"Did you come here to blow off steam or get some advice?"

Sam rubbed her eyes, looking at the floor. "I don't know. Neither...both."

Jesus, give me the words she needs to hear. Callie took Sam's hand. "Sweetheart, I'll admit your father has rushed into all of this a little quicker than he probably should have. I know you're overwhelmed. But he's just trying to make up for lost time."

"He can't."

"He knows that, but it's human nature to try. You're never going to be eight or nine years old again, Sam. Iris is long past the baby she was when he left. He can never get those years back, but I truly believe he loves you. He's trying to make the present and the future a better place for all of you."

"He wants me to use my scholarship."

"And you should," Callie said. "You have Bobbie's future to think of. If you can't get around this any other way, be selfish for a few minutes. What gives Bobbie a better life down the road? A smart mother with a high school diploma, waiting tables in a restaurant, or a smart mother with a college degree and a career in...I don't know...rocket science?"

Sam took a shaky breath. "That's taking advantage of him for all the wrong reasons. He wants forgiveness and love. I won't use him like that."

"You know what? I'd be willing to bet, if you asked him, he'd take being used for now because he knows it's just a means to an end." Callie was quiet for a few seconds, allowing that to soak in. "Sam, did you ask Jesus to forgive you a couple of weeks ago?"

Samantha nodded.

"What if He'd said to you, 'Maybe I will, but you've rejected me in the past. Before I forgive you, you're going to have to prove to me that you mean it this time.'?"

When Sam remained silent, Callie continued. "He didn't say that. He didn't ask you for anything. He just offered to love you." She tilted Sam's face up. "You told me once you didn't know if you could ever believe in a God who'd taken so much away from you. I understood that. But, honey, He's trying to give some of it back to you, and you're fighting Him. I don't understand that. You said when you and Iris first came to Garfield, it just felt right. I believe in divine intervention in our lives. You accepted salvation for your soul. He's trying to deliver you from some of the other troubles as well."

Fresh tears trailed down Sam's face. *Delivered...rescued* "I'm being rescued."

"What?"

Sam shook her head. "Something Sisko told me a few days ago."

Callie nodded her understanding. "Sometimes, the person God has to rescue us from is ourselves." Callie stumbled over her own words. *God, are you trying to rescue me, too?* She swallowed around a lump in her throat as those words struck home and sank into her own heart.

"He's your father, Sam. He's made some serious mistakes, but he's asking you, in every way he can think of, to forgive him. You're going to have to do that eventually. Not for him, not for Iris or Bobbie, but for you. Wouldn't it just be easier to get it over with? Accept the security he's offering."

"I'm scared."

"Trust me. I know the feeling," Callie assured her. "I can promise you it'll get better, but you're going to have to put some effort into it."

Sam took another deep breath, steadier this time. "Will you pray with me?"

"Oh absolutely." Callie gathered Sam back into her arms. They both bowed their heads.

Callie closed her songbook as the praise team took

their seats. Pastor Gordon walked to the pulpit, laid his Bible aside, and looked out over the crowd.

"We have another special treat for you this morning. I hope most of you have had an opportunity to meet Samantha Evans and her sister Iris. Both of these girls accepted Christ into their hearts a couple of weeks ago. Samantha wants to extend that commitment to her daughter, Bobbie, by dedicating her to the Lord today.

"Girls, come on up here. I understand we have some honorary grandparents and a godmother that'll be joining them." A slide show of recent pictures paraded across the giant screen at the back of the platform as everyone took their places. The pastor laughed as they sorted themselves out in front of the stage.

"Let's see if I have this straight. Callie and Benton, you guys are brand new grandparents, and Terri, you're the godmother." He looked down at Iris. "You're the aunt?"

"Yes sir."

"That's an awful big job for such a little girl. Are you sure you're up to it?"

"Yes sir," Iris repeated with a giggle.

"Good deal," he said with a wink. He looked at Sam, "Will she let me hold her?"

"I think so," Sam said, handing Bobbie to the preacher.

The pastor took the two steps up to the platform and held Bobbie up for everyone to see. "I know you're seeing pictures, but look at this little doll. Isn't she adorable?"

Murmured oohs, and aahs echoed through the auditorium in response.

Rejoining everyone at the bottom of the stage, the

pastor handed Sam a white New Testament with Bobbie's name engraved on the front. "This is for Bobbie, and we'll have a certificate for her as well. Let's pray."

Sam took a sudden step forward, laying a hand on Pastor Gordon's arm before he could go any further. Callie's heart lifted when she caught the gleam of gold on Samantha's wrist.

Pastor Gordon listened quietly then whispered a few words to Sam. He waited for her nod before stepping back up on the stage to look out over the congregation. "I've just learned that we're missing an important member of Bobbie's family. Steve Evans, this is your granddaughter we're about to dedicate. We can't do this without you."

Callie sat on the couch Sunday night after service listening to the sound of thunder rumbling in the distance. She shook her head. Spring in Oklahoma was always an adventure. Her eyes went back to the open Bible in her lap. "This has to be it," she whispered. Psalm 91:14 and 15. "Because he hath set his love upon me, therefore will I deliver him: I will set him on high, because he hath known my name. He shall call upon me, and I will answer him: I will be with him in trouble; I will deliver him, and honor him." Delivered, rescued, same thing. Sam and Iris were *rescued*. Was she?

Callie closed her eyes and searched her heart for the remnants of guilt and the terrified cries of a lost little boy. They were gone. Callie took a deep cleansing breath. She'd slept uninterrupted last night. And while one night didn't mean every night, it was a step in the right direction. Her heart was finally at peace, and like

Lazarus newly raised from the dead, she had no intention of looking beneath the grave clothes to see if it was for real. She knew in her heart it was.

When she looked back on the spring of her fifty-fourth year, would Iris and Samantha be the defining chapter in her life, or would it be something else? Would it be the hugs and words of forgiveness between Samantha and Steve that she remembered, or the freedom of guilt lifting from her own shoulders that brought joy to her heart? Callie shrugged. "Probably some of both," she whispered.

"What?"

She smiled up at her husband, took the bowl of ice cream he handed her, and made room for him on the sofa. "Thanks," she said around her first bite. "You make the best chocolate sundaes ever."

"You've got chocolate syrup," Benton leaned over and kissed the corner of her mouth, "right—"

Thunder cracked overhead. The lights flickered and went out. Benton groaned against her mouth. "So much for our movie date."

Callie took his bowl and put them both on the end table. "We have work tomorrow. We should probably just go to bed."

"I'm not sleepy."

She met his objections with a kiss. "Isn't that handy? Neither am I."

ABOUT THE AUTHOR

Sharon Srock went from science fiction to Christian fiction at slightly less than warp speed. Twenty five years ago, she cut her writer's teeth on Star Trek fiction. Today, she writes inspirational stories that focus on ordinary women and their extraordinary faith. Sharon lives in the middle of nowhere Oklahoma with her husband and three very large dogs. When she isn't writing you can find her cuddled up with a good book, baking something interesting in the kitchen, or exploring a beach on vacation. She hasn't quite figured out how to do all three at the same time.

Connect with her here:

Blog: http://www.sharonsrock.com

Facebook: http://www.facebook.com/SharonSrock#!/SharonSrock

Goodreads: http://www.goodreads.com/author/show/6448789.Sharon_Srock

Sign up for her quarterly newsletter from the blog or Facebook page.

Made in the USA
Lexington, KY
25 November 2015